Please return / renew this item by the last date shown above
Dychwelwch / Adnewyddwch erbyn y dyddiad olaf y nodir yma

**ISBN
978-0-9575730-0-0**

Novel Publishing
www.novelpublishing.com

Printed and Bound in Great Britain

Cover photography by Dani Dunca

Novels by Jean Mead

The Other Famous Five
A novel for children

The Widow Makers
Historical Fiction

The Widow Makers: Strife
Historical Fiction

Freya 800 AD
Viking era fiction

Dedicated

To my sister, Maureen Anne Kill

Chapter 1

It was the last day of Kate's happiness. Unaware that disaster drew near, thirty-eight-year-old Kate sat in the front passenger seat of the car, sleepily hypnotised by the sunlight flickering on the windscreen. Adam, her husband, was driving. Their three young daughters were on the back seat, engrossed in magazines and comics.

The family had been travelling for more than three hours with only a brief stop at a motorway service station. There were only a few miles to go before they reached their destination, Shore Cottage at Breckon Bay. Seeing the signpost for Breckon Templar, Adam pulled off the by-pass.

The change of direction brought Kate fully awake. Although she glanced at the three girls she didn't speak; such peace was rare.

Instead she looked to Adam, driving competently with an easy self-assurance that came so naturally to him. The long spell of summer sunshine had burnished his skin, and streaked his short blond hair with glints of gold. She was never indifferent to his attractiveness and there were times, like now, when it caused her to feel a piercing anxiety imagining another woman taking an interest in him.

Sensing her scrutiny Adam looked towards her fleetingly. There was a hint of a smile on his mouth and like a soothing balm it eased the agony of her jealousy.

Content for the moment, she folded her hands on her lap, turning her gold wedding band between her thumb and forefinger.

She glanced at him again, but Adam didn't shift his concentration from the road ahead and the caravan being towed.

Closing her eyes, blanking out his detachment, she tried to focus on arriving at Shore Cottage. For two blissful weeks Adam would be beside her and she could be certain that he wasn't with another woman. There would be no late meetings, long lunches, and pretty women at the office to tempt him.

Shore Cottage was special to her. It had been their holiday destination since the girls were small. The stone house was positioned perfectly, overlooking the wide sandy beach and far enough away from the village to give a sense of being marooned in a kids' paradise.

'We're almost there,' Adam said cheerfully. 'Collect your things together, girls. We'll be arriving in a jiffy.'

His words brought an immediate frenzy of activity on the back seat. Eight-year-old Beth wailed as the contents of her pencil case spilled onto the floor. Carla snapped at Annie accusing her of tearing a celebrity magazine. Within seconds a squabble erupted.

Adam looked at Kate, his pale blue eyes glinting with amusement. 'I thought the peace was too good to last.'

Kate turned toward the children. 'Annie, give Carla the magazine. Beth, pick up those crayons,' she snapped briskly.

A mutinous glance passed between the two older girls. Annie flung the magazine at Carla. Ignoring the fallen crayons, Beth, folding her small arms defiantly, flopped back in the seat.

Mentally distancing herself from the row, Kate glanced through the window looking between the trunks of the pine trees to the sea beyond.

It's the magnificent scenery that makes us return time after time, she thought. The glorious sandy beach is perfect when the weather is as good as it is today. Her gaze was held by the violet line where the sea met the horizon. She wondered if the darkness held a brewing storm. She loved the night storms, silver lightening splitting the indigo sky, the raging sea beating onto the shore, and the gale-force wind rattling the windowpanes of the old cottage.

Adam broke into her reverie. 'We're here,' he said turning onto the lane leading to the cottage.

It was more of a track than a lane. There was a thin strip of short grass growing down the middle and small boulders poking out of the sandy verges, some dangerously hidden by wiry tufts of grass. Driving slowly, the overgrown pink and white valerian and long sea grass brushing against the tyres, Adam navigated cautiously.

Shore Cottage lay at the end of the track. It was the only residence. The seclusion was part of the charm.

Getting the first glimpse of the stone cottage through the overhanging trees, Kate's insecurities disappeared. In the lovely surroundings, with the promise of a heavenly holiday with her family, it was impossible to believe that Adam was deceiving her and having an affair.

Driving between two stone posts, ancient megaliths stolen from a nearby field more than a century before, Adam pulled the car up on the sparse gravel driveway.

With a whoop of joy, eleven-year-old Carla opened the door instantly the car came to a standstill. Scrambling out, she made a dash across the neglected lawn, her blue cotton skirt billowing behind her. With an ungainly leap she landed on the top of the wall separating the garden from the beach, scuffing the toes of her white sandals in the process. Silhouetted by the sun, she looked out over the sea, shielding her eyes from the silver glare on the water.

Annie emerged with an air of languid boredom, a customary mood since passing her fifteenth birthday. Adam spoke from within the car. Ignoring him, Annie adjusted the band holding her chestnut pony tail.

Closing her mind to her parents' conversation, she gazed blank-eyed at the sun-dappled sea. She was wearing a white tee-shirt and short blue skirt. The backs of her slender thighs were creased with red lines from the upholstery. The thin ankle straps on her sandals had slipped down and she stood heron like, sliding first one and then the other back behind her heels. Closing the car door, she ambled across the weedy grass to join Carla.

Blonde-headed Beth, the baby of the family, succeeding in unfastening her seat belt, clambered out quickly, slamming the car door behind her. Yelling boisterously she ran towards her two sisters.

The banging of the door irritated Adam. 'How many times have I told you not to slam it?' he shouted bad-temperedly.

Sighing, he climbed out and stood stretching his arms and yawning loudly.

The cottage has hardly changed, Kate thought, satisfied that everything was as she imagined it would be. Someone, Mrs Hanson probably, had planted red geraniums in the two stone troughs beneath the front windows. The scarlet blooms were bright against the grey stone of the house. The paintwork looked fresh, the gloss startlingly white with the full sun on it.

Adam, retrieving the front door key hidden beneath a flowerpot, said 'It's a miracle Mrs Hanson doesn't get squatters in.'

'Hurry up darling. I'm bursting for a pee,' Kate said jiggling on the doorstep.

The front door opened onto a square hall. The kitchen and living room doors were closed, the air motionless and warm, smelling slightly of old damp and musty curtains.

Wrinkling his nose, Adam went to the backdoor and threw it open. A slight current of air blew through the hall.

Dashing up the stairs, Kate made for the bathroom.

When she came down Adam was outside, looking out across the untended garden to the impossibly blue sea beyond. The sky was cloudless but for wisps of whiteness on the horizon, marring the china blue.

Coming up behind him, she held his arm possessively. 'I do so love coming to Shore Cottage. It's a bit like coming home after a long absence.'

Absentmindedly, he kissed her cheek, his glance barely leaving the far-end of the beach. Daydreaming he was wondering why the holidaymakers and day trippers preferred to stay down there. Perhaps the string of beach shops and the three cafes are the draw, he thought. If so it was fortunate that the beach near Shore Cottage had no such amenities. Beyond the cottage, great boulders as big and grey as elephants cut off access to the cliffs of the headland. Perhaps as they were difficult to climb they were seen as disadvantages and not objects of natural beauty.

The girls were paddling at the water's edge. Carla tucking her blue print skirt into her knickers waded into deeper water until the rippling waves lapped at her knees. Laughing, she flung an arc of spray at Beth, the droplets flashing a liquid rainbow which melted into the sea. Squealing with delight, Beth kicked water at Carla.

Hearing their laughter, Adam withdrew from Kate. Feeling put-upon and irritated, he said 'You'd think they'd give a hand unpacking the car before going off like that?'

'I don't expect it even occurred to them.' Kate said waspishly.

Marching to the end of the garden, he yelled loudly, 'What

about giving a hand?'

Quietening, the girls looked from one to another. Then without saying a word they began to trudge up the beach, sulkily kicking warm sand with their wet toes.

Adam was lifting the last bag from the car as the girls arrived.

Hardly bothering to acknowledge him, the three grabbed their possessions from the pile he'd heaped near the car and lugged it indoors. Clattering noisily up the stairs, banging the old banister with their cargo, they chucked everything onto the beds.

In the kitchen, stocking the fridge from supermarket bags, Kate heard the girls rattling back down. Glancing through the open door she saw the tail-end of a shrimp net as it was carried through the front door.

Adam's laughter came to her through the open window.

Two blissful weeks together, she thought. If this beautiful weather keeps up, it'll be fantastic.

Beth came running into the kitchen. 'Daddy said we're going to light a bonfire on the beach and have a barbeque. And stay up late.'

Kate rumpled the child's blonde hair. 'Sounds like fun.'

'It'll be sthuper,' Beth lisped, grinning.

Shooting a sticky hand into a bag of groceries, she yelled 'Have you found my chocolate drops?'

Kate grabbed a box of eggs before it was knocked carelessly aside. Lifting Beth's dirty hand out of the bag, she said 'No, I haven't. Now leave this stuff alone. Go and help gather wood for the fire.'

Scampering to the door, Beth shouted over her shoulder, 'If you find them, don't let Carla eat any.'

'I won't. Now get from under my feet, Beth, or we'll never

get things sorted out.'

'Okay,' she shouted from half-way down the hallway.

***

The weather had been glorious during June and the first two weeks of July so it was disappointing to see mist lying over the sea, and the weedy lawn drenched with rain on the first morning of the holiday.

Standing at the kitchen window looking out, Beth was churlish. 'It's not supposed to rain on holiday.'

Kate was sympathetic. 'I think it'll brighten up, sweetheart.'

Putting another slice of toast with the stack she had already made, Kate brought it to the table.

Adam's face was buried in yesterday's newspaper.

Glancing at him, Kate asked 'Do you think it will brighten up?'

Lowering the paper, he looked over the top. 'The forecast is good. Give it an hour and it'll be warm enough to go to the beach.'

Beth came to the table. 'Bet it doesn't. It'll rain all day and we'll have nothing to do.'

'Stop being such a misery guts,' Kate said amused.

Annie reached for the marmalade jar from the centre of the table just as Carla grabbed it.

'Oi! I was just getting that,' Annie snapped.

'Just stop that, you two,' Kate said firmly.

Putting aside the paper, Adam sighed. 'Behave, both of you. And you too, Beth.'

Beth whined, 'Why is it always my fault?' Folding her small arms she looked mutinously towards Carla.

Carla grinned mischievously.

Giving a vicious kick beneath the table, Beth caught Carla's shin with the toe of her trainers.

Carla screamed, 'Ouch! You little pig.'

'If you two don't behave…' Adam was interrupted by the ringing of his cell phone.

Sighing he rose from the table, and picked the phone up off the worktop.

Kate's eyes were on him as he spoke. His voice was too serious for the call to be from a friend or relative. After a brief conversation he pocketed the phone, and it wasn't lost on Kate that his hand trembled.

'There's a major problem at the bank.' His worried eyes met Kate's. 'Tony Everett wants me there immediately.'

'Now?' Kate shouted angrily. 'We only got here yesterday. How can they call you back at a moment's notice?'

He stood rock still, his face grave.

Kate's voice rose hysterically, 'What can possibly be so important that it's worth ruining our family holiday for?'

Silent, he turned to go upstairs.

In two fast strides she crossed the kitchen and ran after him. Her heart was racing, the beat thumping in her ears. She didn't believe a word he said. The bank would never expect an employee to give up a holiday. It had to be a woman that had called him. The whole thing had been stage managed between them. Adam had purposely got her here with the children, only to dash back to his fancy-woman. Furious, she almost lost her footing on the top stair; grabbing the banister to save herself, she snapped a nail painfully.

Adam was searching in the wardrobe as she came into the bedroom.

Brushing him aside, Kate pulled an ivory shirt off a wire hanger and threw it at him.

He was standing quite still, shielding himself from her anger. 'Will you pass me another one?'

'You only need one,' she snapped. 'There are plenty of ironed shirts at home. If you're going there, as you say you are, why do you need another one from here?'

Exasperated, he shouted 'Of course I'm going home. Where do you think I'm going?'

Throwing the shirt onto the bed, he gave a long-drawn-out sigh. 'Don't be like this, Kate. You know I wouldn't go, if I didn't have to.'

Turning on her heel, angry tears in her eyes, she clattered down the stairs.

For a moment he stared unseeing at the shirt lying crumpled on the bedcover. Grabbing it, he stuffed it carelessly into the bag. With a sinking feeling in the pit of his stomach, he came down, his footsteps heavy on the stair-treads.

Taut with anger, her mouth resentfully sullen, Kate remained at the kitchen window, staring out and seeing nothing.

Silent, their eyes avoiding their mother's stiff back, Carla and Annie cleared the kitchen table.

Beth sat sulkily, her lips drawn back a little, her breath hissing faintly through her small white teeth.

From the doorway, Adam said in a monotone 'I'll see you tomorrow evening.'

Turning quickly, Kate glared. 'Oh, you are coming back. I thought you'd stay and see more of your lady friend.'

A muscle in his cheek twitched. 'How many times do I have to tell you, Kate? There is no other woman.'

With a twisted laugh, she said 'You expect me to believe that lie?'

Exasperated he glanced at Annie and then his eyes came back to Kate. 'Why don't you send me off with a chaperone?'

The idea hadn't occurred to her, but it was perfect. 'Go with your father, Annie. Make sure he doesn't get up to any mischief.'

Annie's eyes opened wide in surprise and outrage. 'But I've only just got here. Why me? Why not Carla or Beth?'

Kate snapped, 'Don't be so ridiculous. They're too young.'

Annie saw that remaining at the cottage would be far from pleasant. Her mother in this mood would be a nightmare. It was better to go back home, sleep over at Millie's, and spend tomorrow strolling around the shops.

'I'll just get a few things together. I will only be a moment,' she said in a monotone.

In silence they listened to her hurrying footfalls on the stairs.

Angry, Adam shouted 'Happy now, Kate? You've browbeaten everyone into submission and got your own way once again.'

With an exaggerated shrug, Kate turned to look out of the window.

Near tears, Beth glowered. 'The holiday is ruined.'

Stooping to her, Adam held her close. Kissing her damp cheek he tasted the strawberry jam she had wiped from her mouth.

'We'll be back tomorrow. I promise.'

Wriggling out of his arms, Beth stormed out into the wet garden.

Annie rattled down the stairs, her bag banging on the banister. Irate, she made straight for the car.

Slipping passed her mother, Carla followed Annie.

Kate was in two minds whether to bother to see the pair off, but hearing the car doors open, she went out and stood on the porch. Beth and Carla eyed her suspiciously from the nearby withered hydrangea bush.

Glancing grimly in her direction, Adam tossed his bag and laptop onto the back seat.

From the front passenger seat, Annie gave a half-hearted wave to Carla and Beth. Both girls were breaking brown twigs off the dying bush.

Without a farewell, Adam slammed the car door closed. The engine kicked into life. A sense of abandonment washed over Kate. In a few short minutes everything had changed.

'*Sod it!*' she muttered under her breath.

As the car disappeared, a light drizzle began to fall.

Forced indoors, Beth sulkily kicked the board at the bottom of the white melamine kitchen unit with the toe of her trainer.

Turning her petulant face to Kate, she snapped, 'Why are you always so horrid to everyone?'

Exasperated, Kate sighed. 'I didn't make them go. Your dad's boss telephoned and asked him to go back to the office.'

Beth's bottom lip jutted. 'Well, it seems funny to me.'

Kate slapped down the tea-towel she was folding. 'Seems pretty odd to me too, but I'm not going to sulk about it, although I do feel like doing so.'

Carla remained silent. Kate sensed the child's sidelong glances.

For the first time in their lives, Kate felt like slapping the pair of them. Instead, she filled the kettle. Sitting at the kitchen table, she waited for it to come to the boil. It wasn't that she wanted a cup of tea. It was just something to do until her world came back to some sort of normality.

Chapter 2

Sleepless, Kate lay staring at the clock on the bedside table flashing the passing minutes in a ruby glow. She wished she could rest, fall into sleep, but it was impossible to turn her mind away from the row with Adam. The hour changed and the cycle began again. She sighed tiredly as 01 appeared.

Turning onto her back she looked at the dark ceiling. For hours her mind had gone round in circles, riding a mental treadmill of guilt and shame.

The sound of the sea came to her, accentuated in the darkness, the incoming tide rushing to the shore, the surf beating onto the sand.

Annie should be here, she thought, diving into the water before breakfast and beginning the second day of her holiday. Thinking of Annie brought her close to tears. Sending the child home to act as her father's chaperone was the most shameful thing she had ever done as a mother.

A longing to caress her eldest child, to feel the warm silkiness of her hair was almost more than she could bear. Lying with her arm over her eyes, swallowing tears, she tried to think of tomorrow. Annie and Adam *would* return and they would all get on with the holiday.

Her hand touched the sheet where he should be sleeping. She imagined him beneath the familiar duvet on their bed at home. He would be lying on his side, his face to the window, breathing the air coming through the open casement.

An image of a woman lying beside him came into her mind. Kate's breath caught and she gave a cry of misery. The woman laughed and Adam kissed her bare shoulder.

Feet pattered across the small landing. The bedroom door creaked open and Beth, in pink pyjamas, stood in the opening, the landing light behind her.

'Mummy,' she murmured 'I can hear the sea. I think it's coming into the garden.'

Kate rose tiredly. 'The sea can't do that.' The woman and Adam were still in her mind and her voice was edgy, sharp as broken glass.

Expecting to be sent back to bed, Beth whined plaintively, 'I can hear it, Mummy.'

Kate tapped the duvet, 'Come into bed with me. We can listen to it together,' she said softly, burying the sigh on her lips.

Pattering quickly across the cold floor, giving a little giggle, Beth snuggled under the bedcover.

Kissing her forehead, Kate said 'Go to sleep.'

Raising her small head off the pillow, her dark green eyes glinting in the light from the landing, Beth whined 'I will, if you go down and see if the waves are in the garden.'

Kate smiled. 'I'll go and look, if you promise to go to sleep?'

'Promise, on my honour,' Beth said with a grin.

Throwing the duvet off, Kate got out of the warm bed and padded barefoot across the lino to the bedroom door.

The landing was gloomy, the overhead light so feeble it barely lit the top of the stairs. Looking down into the darkness, a frisson of fear stippled her skin with gooseflesh as ancient ghosts and demons of her imagination stirred in the blunt blackness below.

Clutching the banister, she came down slowly, groping for the next tread with her bare toes like an old blind woman.

Stepping cautiously off the last step, the coconut matting at the front door prickling the soles of her feet, she fumbled for the light switch. It didn't come to hand immediately and panic caused her heart to beat in fast hard thumps. Finding the small brass dome, she flicked the switch on. The light bulb wasn't much brighter than the landing light, but in the glow Kate's nerves ceased to jangle.

As Beth was sure to be waiting, ears cocked for the creaking of the old hinges, Kate opened the front door.

The scent of wet sand, seaweed and long dead shells was on the light breeze blowing off the sea. Breathing in the fragrant night, Kate turned her eyes to the infinite blackness of the sky devoid of star or moonshine. She had forgotten how intensely black a coastal night could be. Even the far-off headland jutting into the sea fused into the darkness.

A night bird called from the stand of pine trees beyond the dunes. She was aware of the incoming tide beating repeatedly on the sand.

The night was perfect, soft with the warmth of the past day. Reluctant to close the door, she stood, her feet growing cold on the stone step. The traumas of the day seemed less significant - viewing the magnificence of the night.

***

Kate came awake to silence, and the grey morning light showing at the chink between the curtains. The tail of an awful nightmare was still with her. She had dreamt that Adam had left her, taking Annie with him.

Adam's angry words came back, the echo of them as potent as when they were spoken.

She felt like crying.

Turning onto her back, she lay staring at the plaster rose in the centre of the ceiling, trying to decide what she should do. Neither Adam nor Annie had answered the voicemails or texts she'd sent, although she had tried to make contact more than a dozen times. It was torment not knowing how she stood with Adam.

At the sound of light footsteps on the stairs, Kate rose onto her elbow.

Carla came into the bedroom carrying a mug of tea. At the window she pulled one of the blue curtains aside.

'Beth wants to go to the beach, but I've told her to wait until you are up.' Careful not to spill a drop of tea, she put the mug onto the bedside table.

Kate's eyes screwed against the light. 'Thanks, Carla. You're a good girl.'

Sitting up, lifting the pillow from behind her lower back, Kate placed it against the headboard, leaning into it wearily.

Carla remained at the bedside, her knees pressed against the mattress, staring at the pattern on the duvet cover.

Kate hadn't the patience or energy to chatter. Her thoughts were entirely bound up with Adam. 'Go down and tell Beth to wait until I come downstairs before she goes anywhere,' she said, almost as a dismissal.

With a twinge of guilt, she listened to the child's hurrying footsteps on the stairs.

In the kitchen Beth's response to being told to stay indoors was predictable, a shout of irritation and the slamming of a door.

Sighing, Kate reached for her mobile phone and read in the tiny window, Message Box Empty; she stared at the words in silent despair. Tears brimming in her eyes, she flung the phone down on the duvet and reached for the mug of tea.

It's fruitless to keep on trying, she thought. Adam has decided not to talk to me. Annie's silence is hardly surprising, being sent home on the first day of her holiday was sure to

19

make her cross. Annie is like Adam, both are stubborn.

The cell phone drew her eyes and she willed it to ring. But the silence went unbroken but for the clicking of her fingernails on the china mug.

It was impossible to resist trying one more time. Placing the mug on the table, she picked up the phone and pressed 1 to connect her to Adam. It rang out but there was no answer. She nearly threw the thing to the wall. Scrolling to Annie's number, she let it ring several times before disconnecting.

Downstairs an argument broke out between Beth and Carla. A piece of crockery smashed.

Closing her mind to the racket, Kate dialled the home telephone and imagined it pealing in the empty house. After ten rings she gave up.

Climbing out of bed, she flung on a robe and went to the antiquated bathroom. Ten minutes later, dressed in a green print skirt, white top and sandals, she went downstairs clutching the phone. Trying Annie's number again, and failing to get a reply, she wondered how long they intended to ignore her.

Carla was placing small plates on the table as Kate came into the kitchen. 'What time is dad getting back?'

'Yeah, what time?' Beth said without ceasing to kick a tennis ball against the kitchen unit.

'I don't expect they'll be very late,' Kate answered, trying to sound cheerful.

'What time?' Beth kicked the ball viciously.

'Stop that, Beth. How many times do I have to tell you not to play with a ball in the house?' Kate snapped.

A look of defiance flashed on Beth's face. 'Are you going to be horrid to us again?'

Tight lipped, just holding onto her temper, Kate said 'I'll

have less of your rudeness, young lady. One more word and you'll go straight back upstairs. There'll be no beach for you at all today.'

Throwing the ball into the hall, Beth stormed out.

'Take no notice of her, Mummy. She's just in a bad mood because the sun isn't shining,' Carla said wanly.

Kate ruffled the child's hair. 'You're a good girl, Carla, the least trouble of the lot.'

Though the day was grey, threatening rain, Kate made an effort to get the girls onto the deserted beach.

Equipped with shrimp nets, a faded canvas windbreak, a small yellow bucket, red ball, an ancient basket containing bottles and sandwiches and an old tartan blanket, they crossed the sand Indian fashion, making for the fringe of green seaweed left by the ebbing tide.

Choosing the best place to erect the windbreak, Kate poked the bleached poles into the sand. Fairly confident it would stay put, she spread the blanket in its lea, anchoring it with the basket and beach paraphernalia. Sitting crossed legged in the centre she kept her eyes on the girls.

They were running along the water's edge. Carla's bright yellow jumper and green shorts brilliant against the grey sea. Cart-wheeling, Beth flashed like a beacon in her red and orange outfit.

Jumping, Carla crested a small wave, the soles of her feet sinking into the slippery sand as she landed.

Laughing, Beth dashed passed her, running into deeper water. In seconds they both came out, shrieking with laughter and shouting 'Its freezing cold.'

Kate waved to them. 'Come and dry off.'

Later, all three lobbed a ball back and forth and fished in the rock pools with shrimp nets, even finding a few tiny crabs to put in the yellow bucket.

Kate's mind was never far away from Adam and Annie and her eyes went constantly to Shore Cottage.

In the late afternoon a mist came in on the tide, a grey-white vapour deadening the sound of the waves. The gulls were silent, flying further inland. Quite quickly the temperature dropped. The veiled sea and the slowly rolling mist were eerily hushed.

Kate started to collect the scattered belongings together, calling to the girls playing in the dunes. Beth eventually appeared, Carla following a moment later.

With the load of paraphernalia it was difficult to hurry across the sand. Shore Cottage seemed far away; before they drew near the mist was at their heels.

Near tears, insisting that the fog was following them, Beth clutched her mother's skirt. Carla, hampered by the shrimp nets, blanket and the bucket, trotted to keep pace with her mother.

Reaching the garden gate, Kate dumped the windbreak. Taking the blanket from Carla's arms, she said 'Just leave everything in the porch. I'll get it later.'

'This'll make Daddy late,' Carla said glancing at the greyish mist now shrouding the garden wall.

'I don't think it will go very much further than the beach; that's why it's called sea mist,' Kate said unlocking the back door.

Running in, Beth made a dash for the stairs. 'Need a pee,' she said still running.

Watching her mother unpack the basket, Carla said 'I wish my daddy was here. It's a bit scary.'

Kate turned from the fridge. 'There's nothing to worry about. It's only a bit of fog.'

'Phone him, Mum. See how long he's going to be.'

'I will in a moment.'

Kate stalled for several minutes before picking up her cell phone and scrolling to Adam's number. She stood in paralysed dismay listening to it ringing out.

Gazing at her, Carla waited in anticipation. As the moments drew out, her eyes were questioning, her small elfin face pinched with worry.

Kate retried the number hoping that the ringing phone might prick Adam's conscience. Or that Annie tiring of listening to the incessant sound would pick it up.

'Maybe they're out of range,' Kate lied, aware that Carla would guess that something was seriously wrong.

Beth came into the room, wiping her wet hands down her shorts. 'What did he say? What time will they be here?'

'We don't know. He's not answering his phone,' Carla said, directing a slightly mutinous glance at her mother.

'Why?' Beth pouted.

'Ask Mum.'

Kate didn't wait for the question. 'I'll try his office.'

Dialling, she wished she had put aside her reservations about calling him at work and telephoned earlier. Checking her wristwatch she saw that it was already 5.45, fifteen minutes after the reception closed for the day.

'I'm sorry. It's too late to get him there. Maybe they're on the way,' she said pocketing the phone.

'Seems funny to me,' Beth said.

'Everything seems funny to you,' Carla shouted bad-temperedly.

'Girls, this isn't the time to start arguing.'

They threw murderous looks at one another.

Needing something to restore her nerves, Kate took a bottle

23

of Beaujolais off the top of the fridge and opened it. Pouring the red wine into a cheap glass, she thought how Adam would hate her drinking alone and so early.

Where was he? Where was Annie? Why were they not answering? They were both behaving selfishly and without a thought to the possibility of an emergency. One of the children might be trying to reach him.

'Bugger it.'

Beth turned in her chair. 'Did you say something, Mum?'

'No sweetheart,' Kate muttered, realising that she must have cursed aloud.

'Shall we play monopoly?' Carla said glancing up from a magazine.

'Good idea, but after supper,' Kate suggested switching on the oven.

Pizza and salad were eaten in virtual silence.

Kate wasn't sure if the girls were listening for the car or too disappointed by its non-arrival to bother to argue.

Before nine o'clock the mist thinned, the trees beyond the dunes materialising out of the gloom.

With the fog virtually gone, Carla was sure that her father and Annie would soon arrive and everything would get back to normal.

Going upstairs on the pretext of going to the bathroom, Kate tried Adam's phone again but without success.

At ten o'clock the girls went up to bed.

Kate sat by the light of a candle, her legs up on the old couch, sipping the last of the wine. The house was silent but for the vague resonance of the sea. At two o'clock she made her way up the staircase, avoiding the treads which creaked.

Eventually she fell into a comatose slumber. Waking early, the same sinking feeling that had come to her yesterday came to her again on seeing the other side of the bed empty.

Automatically her hand went to the phone and she dialled Adam's number. Getting no reply she tried Annie but with no result.

In the kitchen she searched the drawers for a telephone directory, and dialled the number of a car hire company.

When the two girls came into the kitchen, Kate was putting food from the fridge into plastic shopping bags.

'What are you doing?' Beth shouted seeing suitcases stacked at the door.

'I'm very sorry, Beth. But we must go back home. I have to talk to your father.'

'Why, when he will come here today?' She was near tears, her bottom lip trembling.

Carla bounced in. Seeing plastic bags on the table and the empty fridge door open, she stopped in her tracks. 'What's going on?'

Unable to hold back tears, Beth cried. 'Mum is being horrid again. She's making us go back home. She's ruining the holiday.'

Car tyres crunched on the short drive.

With a whelp of glee, the two children dashed to the back door, flinging it open they charged out, only to halt abruptly on seeing a navy blue car parked near the dying hydrangea bush.

The driver, a young man, climbed out and smiled at them.

With a shout of alarm the two girls came running in.

'There's a man outside…' Carla shouted.

Sounding tired and depressed, Kate explained 'He's delivering the hire car.'

Outside, Kate signed the paperwork, the girls watching from the porch.

A green car drove between the granite gate posts, and the

delivery man got in. Smiling he gave a friendly wave from the passenger seat. The driver tapped the horn before driving off, heading for the nearest town.

The girls remained on the porch, silent, sulky, hardly able to comprehend that the holiday was over after just two days.

Fifteen minutes later, Kate drove away from Shore Cottage. The girls sitting on the back seat close to tears.

It was impossible not to look twice at every silver saloon she drove passed, searching for Adam's BMW. Checking the number plate, becoming horribly familiar with the pang of disappointment on seeing it wasn't his.

On the motorway she concentrated on getting home. The girls sat silently, a picture of miserable disappointment.

With no one speaking to her, Kate turned on the radio. Listening to the news she heard the newsreader give an update on the multiple vehicle accident that had occurred on the motorway the day before yesterday. The death toll had risen to seven overnight.

She stared at the radio, her skin pricking with gooseflesh. For one horrific moment she thought she was going to faint, her skin was clammy, the palms of her hands sticky on the steering wheel.

A gigantic juggernaut rumbled passed the car on the inside lane. Terrified, Kate swerved away from the enormous tyres. A horn blared and then a car accelerated passed her, going so fast it appeared as a red flash in the side window. She gave a startled cry. She and the girls were in deadly danger; frightened, she focused her entire attention on keeping the car in the centre of the lane. A motorway services was ahead. Indicating, she slowed, tucking the car in behind a white van travelling on the inside lane.

Driving up the slip-road she felt weak with relief to be away from the speeding traffic. Parking in a wide parking bay, she didn't trust her trembling hands to steer into a narrow space; she turned off the ignition. Opening the door, she climbed out. Clinging to the edge of the roof, she took several deep breaths of the damp air tainted with exhaust fumes.

Wide-eyed with fright, the girls stared at their mother.

'Sit there for just a minute. I'll be right back,' Kate said with a tremor in her voice.

The girls' eyes followed her as she dashed between parked cars heading for the services block.

Inside the glass and steel building, Kate went straight to the newsagent's. Near the doorway there was a stack of today's papers, grabbing one off the top, she opened it searching for a report on the accident. Horrific photographs were spread across the centre pages; there wasn't a car that was recognisable. It was no use staring at the gruesome pictures looking for Adam's, every vehicle was just a mangled wreck. Closing the paper she hurried towards the till, fumbling in her bag for change.

Deciding that all she could do was get home quickly and phone the local police, she went back to the car.

The journey was a nightmare not knowing if Adam and Annie were involved in the accident. It made sense that they were; otherwise why wouldn't one or the other have answered her numerous calls? They hadn't phoned because both were unable to do so. Why had it not occurred to her that they may have had an accident? Stupidly she had focussed on Adam being unfaithful and not considered his safety and that of her beautiful daughter.

Two and a half hours later junction 26 was ahead, her exit. Easing off the accelerator, indicating, she steered into the slow lane. The roundabout was busy. Her turn came to join the traffic from the right. Glancing in the rear view mirror she caught the look of fear on little Beth's face. Neither child had spoken since they left the motorway services.

Fifteen minutes later she drove into the small cul-de-sac of newly built detached houses. Adam's car wasn't on the drive. The curtains in her and Adam's bedroom were pulled across the window. She was positive that they hadn't been left that way when they departed for Shore cottage. A sense of relief swept over her and she came close to stopping the car in the middle of the road to weep.

In the back, the girls started to unfasten their seat belts.

Shaky, tears blurring her vision, Kate parked on the red-brick drive, the bumper touching the white doors of the integral garage.

The front door opened and Annie stood there.

Shocked and relieved, Kate shouted, 'Annie.'

Annie looked deadpan. 'You're back! I was going to call you tonight.'

Kate looked into her daughter's eyes. 'Are you all right, Annie?'

'Of course I am. Why shouldn't I be?' Turning, she went back into the hall.

Following her, Kate said 'Where's your father?'

Annie stopped in the kitchen doorway. 'I don't know. I haven't seen him since we got back.'

'What do you mean?'

Annie shrugged her shoulders. 'As soon as we arrived, he left for the office. I haven't seen him since. Last night, I stayed over at Millie's. I got back this afternoon.'

An awful premonition hit Kate. Before Annie had finished explaining, she ran upstairs. Coming into the bedroom, she saw a few of Adam's discarded personal belongings littering the double bed. Sick with dread, trembling, she opened the wardrobe door. Several clothes hangers had fallen to the floor and lay scattered over her shoes and handbags.

The hanging rail was empty.

Adam had gone.

She was seized by panic so intense for an instant she thought of killing herself. She took two backward steps, the back of her knees met with the bed and she slumped down, the air driven out of her lungs. Unblinking, her eyes stayed on the empty space, vast and bleak without Adam's clothes.

'Adam,' she sobbed.

Downstairs the girls were squabbling, Beth's angry voice rising hysterically. Kate thought to go to the doorway and call for quiet but she hadn't the energy to move.

Putting her head in her hands, she rocked back and forth, an aching desolation and hopelessness crushing her entirely.

Annie stood in the bedroom doorway. 'Mum,' she said softly.

Sobbing, Kate buried her head still further, her dark brown hair falling over her face.

Crossing to the bed, Annie sat beside her, putting her arm around Kate's narrow shoulders, her eyes on the empty space in the wardrobe.

Annie drew her mother towards her. 'Don't cry, Mum,' she said her own voice breaking.

Kate sobbed 'He's gone, Annie. Your father has left me.'

Silent, Annie stared at the empty rail, her arm tightening around the slim form of her mother.

Minutes later, Annie rose. Without a word she left the bedroom and went downstairs. Kate was only slightly aware that Beth and Carla fell silent.

Reappearing a moment later, Annie brought brandy in a

kitchen tumbler. 'Drink this, Mum. It'll make you feel better.'

'I think I'm going to be sick, Annie.'

Annie was forceful. 'No you're not. You're going to drink this down and then we must tell Beth and Carla what has happened.'

Kate's face contorted as she began to cry again. 'Poor Beth and Carla, they'll be devastated. How will we manage, Annie?'

'We will,' Annie said placing the tumbler in Kate's cold fingers. 'Take a sip.'

Kate shuddered as the fiery liquid hit her throat and empty belly.

The television went on downstairs, the volume raised too high. Annie went to the top of the stairs. 'Turn that down. I told you, Mum isn't feeling very well,' she called down waspishly.

Beth shouted something back but her words were indistinct.

Putting the glass to her mouth, Kate swallowed two mouthfuls of the brandy in quick succession.

Coming back into the room, Annie said 'Are you ready to talk to them?'

Kate brushed her dishevelled hair off her forehead. 'I suppose I have to tell them something,' she said tearfully.

'Tell them the truth, Mum. Otherwise there'll be endless questions. Beth will drive us crazy asking when he's coming back.'

Kate frowned. 'He might come home, Annie. This could be his way of punishing me for sending you home with him.'

'Let's go down, Mum. The sooner it's over the better.'

Kate tipped the glass to her lips, swallowing the remainder of the brandy.

With Annie supporting her, she stood and crossed to the bedroom door.

Beth was sitting on the floor in front of the television. Carla perched cross-legged on the tan settee. Both girls turned towards Annie and Kate as they came into the sitting room.

Wordlessly, Annie slumped down on the arm of the settee, leaving Kate standing alone.

'Are you crying, Mummy?' Carla asked unwinding her legs and putting her feet on the floor.

'Yes, I am afraid so,' Kate said her eyes filling.

'Why?' Carla's voice was full of fear.

Annie retrieved the television remote from the low table and switched off the set.

'Oi! I was watching that,' Beth wailed.

Trying to speak calmly, Kate said 'You can put it back on in a minute, Beth. But first I have to tell you something very important.'

Her eyes bleak with foreboding, Carla said 'Has something horrible happened to daddy?'

Kate touched her daughter's shoulder. 'It's nothing like that, darling. But something has happened. Daddy has gone away for a while.'

Carla dark eyes flooded with tears. 'How long will he be away?'

Floundering, Kate looked to Annie.

'He's taken all his clothes and gone away,' Annie said forthrightly.

Standing quickly, Beth ran to her mother and punched Kate on the thighs with her balled fist. 'It's your fault. He wouldn't have left us if you hadn't been so horrid. I hate you,' she shouted running from the room. Dashing upstairs she slammed her bedroom door shut.

Kate crumpled onto the settee. Covering her face, she sobbed.

Putting her head onto her mother's shoulder, Carla cried

quietly.

Crossing the room, Annie went through the open patio doors into the garden. Sitting on the swing, her feet on the ground, she rocked gently.

The evening was a disaster. Beth refusing to come out of her room sat watching television with the volume turned up. Ashen, Carla curled up in her father's favourite chair, a small tight bundle of despair. In the kitchen Annie drank Coca-Cola, stealing tots from the vodka bottle. For several hours, Kate stayed close to the window overlooking the driveway, lifting her head to look out at the sound of every car engine.

Hours later the summer half-darkness descended.

The girls, exhausted by the emotions of the long day, vanished silently to their bedrooms.

Kate remained at the window, too overcome by misery to move. Eventually, in the early hours she made her way upstairs. Undressing, carelessly dropping her clothes to the floor, she folded back the duvet and climbed into bed.

Turning off the bedside light she looked up into the darkness, drowning in loneliness and despair.

The light fragrance of Adam's hair was on the pillow. Her eyes brimmed and she cried bitter tears into the linen where his head should be.

Chapter 3

Next morning, Kate was the first to rise. She was sitting at the kitchen table with a mug of tea when Annie walked in.

'I didn't expect you to be up,' Annie said scuffing the soles of her flip-flops over the floor tiles as she made her way towards the kettle.

'I hardly slept,' Kate said without explaining that she had spent more than an hour searching for a farewell note from Adam.

Annie turned on the recently boiled kettle. 'Do you want another cuppa?'

Kate slid her mug across the table. 'Yes, I'll have another one. It's all I've done this morning, drink tea.' She glanced at her wristwatch.

'Are you going out?' Annie said.

'No. Why?'

'No reason.' Too tired to explain that it was the third time her mother had glanced at the watch face, Annie yawned.

The kettle boiled and Annie poured steaming water over the tea bags in the two mugs.

Outdoors a car engine revved to life. Standing quickly, the chair legs scraping on the floor, Kate looked out of the open window. The neighbours' car was pulling away from the adjacent house. She stood watching for a moment until the red saloon turned right at the junction, vanishing behind the privet hedge bordering the main road.

Turning back to the table she sat despondently. 'I will ring your father's office at nine o'clock. If he's there, I will apologise for what's happened and ask him to come home.'

She gave a wan smile. 'This nightmare may be over before the end of the day.'

Annie put a steaming mug in front of her mother. Softly she said 'Don't get your hopes up, Mum.'

Kate looked up sharply. 'Why do you say that?'

Annie remained silent for a moment and then she sighed. 'Oh I don't know. It's just that he's been acting a bit peculiar lately.'

'That's nonsense,' Kate said in Adam's defence. 'He has been perfectly normal. It's just your over-active imagination. What is happening between your father and me is just a misunderstanding that will be ironed out the moment I talk to him.'

Before Annie could make a reply, Kate rose quickly. Crossing to the sink she threw away the remainder of the tea and began rinsing the mug under hot running water.

Annie sidled out of the room, escaping to her bedroom.

Hardly aware of her daughter's departure, Kate went to the open window. Arms folded protectively across her midriff she stood staring out, the reflection looking back a white haunted mask.

Three doors away, a new navy blue Mercedes, Peter Chandler at the wheel, reversed out of the double garage. Mrs Chandler in a pale pink dressing gown was at the front door, waving as he pulled off the driveway and onto the road.

Consumed with envy for their marital normality, Kate gnawed at her lower lip, her fingers picking at the soft flesh of her upper arms. She wondered how long it would be before everyone in the cul-de-sac was aware of her broken marriage. The humiliation of being a betrayed and deserted wife would be hard to bear.

In her mind's eye she saw a removal van parked on the drive, what was left of the furniture after Adam had taken his share, being loaded onto it. The new owners of the house, a young couple, were waiting for her to hand over the house keys.

Turning from the window she checked her wristwatch. There were only ten minutes to fill before she could call Adam's office. To waste time, she switched on the kettle and stood listening to the water heat up. Her hand absentmindedly spread across the plastic lid. Coming to the boil the steam touched her thumb; flinching, she moved her hand quickly.

Forgetting the tea she walked into the living room and sat on the settee, her eyes on the telephone. On the dot of nine o'clock she dialled, her fingers trembling so badly it was difficult to press the buttons accurately.

The phone at the bank rang three times before being answered by a brisk young woman. Kate managed to get Adam's name out, repeating herself twice. There was a brief pause and then the clipped voice of Tony Everett, the chief accountant, came down the line.

'Mrs Fontaine.'

Hasty, falling over her words, Kate began apologising. 'Mr Everett, I'm sorry to disturb you. The girl must have misunderstood me. I want to speak to my husband, Adam.'

Tony Everett coughed before saying 'Mrs Fontaine your husband is not here. He was asked to come to the office a couple of days ago but he did not show up. We have not heard from him.'

Panic swept through Kate, leaving her unable to reply.

'Do you have a number where we might contact him?' Mr Everett asked brusquely.

Trembling, Kate replaced the receiver and then sat staring at the grey telephone for long minutes.

So it's true, she thought. Adam has left me. He's left the office. Left the children. Left everything that once mattered to him. He loves me no longer. I will never see Adam again. Never touch him. Feel his skin beneath my hand. Hear his voice. His arms will never encircle me. He will not call my name nor say that he loves me. Tonight will come and I will not have seen him. Rocking, she keened like a widow at a graveside.

Carla and Beth were coming down the stairs, their chatter bordering on a disagreement. Fortunately the pair went through the side door and out into the garden.

Rising, Kate began to pace, because it was impossible to remain still.

The sound of a car engine stopped her in her tracks. Hurrying to the window she saw a silver coloured BMW come to a standstill at the curb.

Dashing into the hall, she called out, 'Adam.'

Opening the front door, she looked into Tony Everett's aggrieved face. The disappointment was crushing.

They had met on several social occasions related to the bank. He was a balding, burly man with a penchant for pinstriped suits and those he wore had been purchased before he had run to fat.

With his usual bullishness, he said 'I need to talk to you.'

The last thing she needed was this odious man in the house but seeing no way out of it she stepped aside to let him enter.

'You know why I'm here,' he said, walking into the sitting room.

Kate felt as though she knew nothing, least of all why Tony Everett, chief accountant at Brand's Commercial Bank had deigned to call.

Without being invited, he perched on the very edge of the settee, legs apart, his paunch and bulging crotch indecently on show.

Fixing her with a penetrating stare, he spoke sharply, 'Do you have any idea where Adam is?'

Like a sore invalid, Kate lowered herself into the chair opposite.

She was holding a tissue in her clenched hand, 'I thought he was at work. That's why I telephoned.' She blew her nose gently. 'I haven't seen Adam since he left the holiday cottage where we were staying. He came back here because you asked him to. He has since disappeared. I have no idea where he is.

'Have you called the police?' he asked brusquely.

Kate hunched into herself. 'I don't think they will be able to help. Adam has left me. He's taken his things and gone.' Tears brimmed in her eyes and she sniffed into the tissue. 'I have no idea where he might be, that's why I called the bank. I hoped I would find him there…'

Rudely he cut her explanation short. 'I have to tell you something very unpleasant, Mrs Fontaine. Your husband has embezzled money from the bank.'

Kate's head jerked back in surprise. 'Adam would never do such a thing,' she said hotly.

The thought flashed into her mind that Adam was being set-up by Tony Everett. For some reason the odious man wanted rid of Adam. Perhaps it was because Adam knew him for what he was, inept, a financial dinosaur, and a bully.

Haughty in Adam's defence, she said sharply, 'Adam would never steal. It's ludicrous to suggest it.'

She caught the malicious glint in his eyes and she dreaded what he might say next.

'Well, Adam has,' he said drawing the words out slowly 'and to the tune of several hundred thousand pounds.'

She blinked back tears. 'It's impossible.'

He gave a supercilious laugh. 'Impossible! Why? He didn't

find deserting you and the children impossible. I believe you have three girls.'

Kate gave no reply. Sitting rock still, she stared at a red cotton thread lying on the carpet near her left foot.

Drawing his cumbersome body up off the settee, he crossed the room. Glancing out of the window, he said 'Has he taken his passport?'

Last night and again this morning I scoured this house for a letter from Adam. Why didn't it occur to me to look for his passport? How stupid I have become. I have allowed Adam to be my brains, she thought with self-disgust.

Tony Everett half-turned towards her. 'Well. Have you searched for it?'

Numb with self-pity, Kate's 'No' was hardly perceptible.

Coming back to the settee, he plumped down, the leather creaking with his weight. Addressing her as he would a financially errant client, he said 'The bank will want the money back.'

Lifting her head, Kate said in disbelief, 'You think I have it?'

His eyes scanned the room. 'You have this house. It'll have to be sold and the equity given to the bank.'

Kate showed a flash of spirit. 'This is the children's home.'

Pulling himself up, he gave a short grunt. 'You will hear from the bank's solicitors, Mrs Fontaine. They will organise an estate agent to begin proceeding.'

Kate didn't speak until she got to the front door. With her hand on the door catch, she met his eyes. 'Have you involved the police?'

He didn't reply immediately. Then drawing out his words, he said 'The bank would prefer that our clients and shareholders are not made aware of the deficit. We will look to you to make up as much of the missing money as you can. If you should hear from your husband it would be wise to call us immediately.'

In a moment he was gone.

Standing with her back to the door, too shocked to move, she heard the car fire into life. Then the road fell silent but for a small dog yapping nearby.

Long moments later, gathering what strength she had, Kate moved to the living room and sat in the armchair, staring at the place where Tony Everett had perched.

A ghost of his presence was in still in the room, repeating the terrible words that had been spoken. However many times she heard that Adam was a thief, she would not believe it.

She thought again of her suspicions regarding Tony Everett. She knew instinctively that he was involved and blaming Adam. What mental torture, bullying, Adam must have endured to make him want to disappear. But running, capitulation of any sort wasn't really in Adam's character. So why had he not stood his ground? Fought back? Why desert her and the children? He had packed practically all his personal belongings, so he didn't anticipate coming home in a hurry.

Fresh tears blinded her. I will not see him tonight or hear his cheerful call as he comes through the front door.

'Adam, I can't cope without you,' she sobbed into her hands. 'I love you so very much.'

Giving herself up to grief, she cried inconsolably.

The living room door opened and Liz, Kate's close and long term friend, hurried to her side. Near tears herself she knelt beside Kate, circling her with her arms.

Burying her face in Liz's blue tee-shirt, Kate wept.

Annie stood at the open door. She looked lost and far younger than her fifteen-years.

Seeing her hovering there, Liz said softly 'Annie, fetch a brandy for your mother.'

Annie was glad to do something. Her mother's uncontrollable sobbing had frightened her so much she had telephoned Liz. Thankfully Liz appeared a few minutes later.

Pouring the brandy into an ordinary glass, Annie took a mouthful, swallowing it quickly, coughing as it hit her throat. Wiping her lips with the back of her hand, she tipped another measure into the glass.

Coming back into the living room, hoping that Liz wouldn't smell the spirit on her breath, she handed her the glass. The sight of her mother was awful, too awful to stay in the same room and Annie retreated quickly. The near full brandy bottle, too big a temptation to ignore.

Liz opened Kate's hand and put the glass between her cold fingers. 'Now Kate, listen to me,' she said gently. 'You're going to drink this. When you are calmer, we will talk this through and see what can be done to put it right.'

Snuffling, wiping her nose with the tissue she was still clutching, Kate nodded jerkily. In a small voice, she said 'Liz, he's left me.'

Liz's voice was soft with concern. 'Annie's told me a bit about what happened.'

Kate sniffed. 'The drive home was awful, Liz. I thought Adam and Annie had been caught up in the motorway accident. When we got here, he had gone. The wardrobe and drawers all empty. There's hardly anything of his in the house.' Her mouth trembled. 'I don't know where he is. I can't even talk to him.'

Fresh tears glittered on her dark lashes. 'If I could just speak to him, perhaps I could get him to come back to me.'

'Has he taken his passport?' Liz said.

'That's what Tony Everett asked.'

Startled, Liz's head jerked back. 'When did you talk to him?'

'He came here this morning.' A shadow came to Kate's eyes. 'He came here. This is all so terrible, Liz. Tony Everett said that Adam has embezzled hundreds of thousands of pounds from the bank.'

Too stunned to speak, Liz stared open-mouthed.

'I don't believe him. Adam would never do it,' Kate said wiping her red eyes.

Liz's thoughts raced. If Adam is innocent, why has he fled? With that amount of money at his disposal he could be anywhere. Poor Kate and the girls are on their own. And Kate, God love her, is going to be hard pressed to survive in the big bad world without Adam fighting her corner.

'You don't believe he'd do such a thing, do you, Liz?'

Doubting his innocence, Liz found it almost impossible to meet Kate's eyes.

'Oh, Liz you do,' Kate wailed.

She took Kate's hands in hers. 'At this precise moment it doesn't matter if he did or didn't take it. All that matters is getting you and the girls organised. You must think coherently, Kate. This isn't the time to fall apart. You have the girls to consider. So let's be practical. First we find out if his passport is missing. Next we check your finances and see what is available to meet immediate bills.'

She tried to smile, 'Okay. Are you with me on this?'

Kate sighed tiredly. 'Yes, you're right. What would I do without you?'

Standing, Liz brushed creases from the knees of her trousers. 'Where does he normally keep his personal papers, passport included?'

Following Kate upstairs, hearing Carla and Annie talking in

the kitchen, Liz doubted that they would find Adam's passport or anything else relevant to the new life he had chosen for himself.

In the bedroom, Kate opened the top drawer of the mahogany tallboy. Taking out a box file, she handed it to Liz. It was practically empty just as Liz expected it to be, his passport, driving licence, car and insurance documents were all missing. Several cheque book stubs lay with Kate's and the children's passports. Liz glanced at a recent stub.

With a sickening feeling that things were going to get worse, she said 'Kate, do you and Adam have a joint account?'

'No. I have an account for my personal stuff.'

'And is there any money in there to tide you over?' Liz said with foreboding.

'Not much. I bought the kids some new clothes just before the holiday and a couple of things for me. Why? What are you getting at Liz?'

Liz's face was serious, her hazel eyes shadowed with concern. 'It will not be possible to access the money in Adam's account. What's in yours is all you have until we can sort out social security.'

Shaking her head furiously, Kate rose off the bed. 'I'm not going down that route. It's not as though we're on the breadline. Adam earns a very good salary.'

'I don't doubt it, Kate. But you can't get his money out of his account without his permission and you don't have that.'

It was inconceivable that Adam would let her and the girls down. In his defence, Kate said 'He'll get money to us. He knows I have virtually nothing. He will not let us starve. Adam's not like that. He's never been mean to us.'

Not until now, he hasn't, Liz thought.

Liz had believed Adam was a man of integrity. But minute

42

by minute the foundation of her trust was crumbling. His selfish departure had left Kate and the kids in a terribly precarious position. Kate, adoring him as she did, would find it impossible to accept that he had abandoned them to their fate. Accepting would mean that she had lost faith in Adam, and Adam was her raison d'être. Without Adam beside her, Kate was likely to go to pieces. That would leave the children in desperate peril.

Trying to sound up-beat and positive, she said 'Let's have some lunch. I'm famished. Perhaps the girls are too.'

Later, checking Kate's bank account, Liz reckoned she had just enough money for a weekend shop at the supermarket.

Although she pleaded with Kate, she could not persuade her to seek help at the social security office. 'She preferred to trust in Adam,' she said rather loftily after a large glass of wine with lunch.

Liz thought differently. Adam had gone, and all the wishing in the world wasn't going to make the bastard return.

At four-thirty Liz left to get ready for the evening at her bistro, promising to return when the restaurant closed if Kate was still awake.

As the door closed behind her friend, Kate went back into the safe haven of the sitting room. Standing at the window, she watched the neighbouring houses, dreading the return of husbands in the early evening.

In the back garden, Carla and Annie talked quietly. Annie sipping Coca-Cola laced with vodka. Beth was playing on a trampoline at a friend's house, her shrieks of laughter coming to them from two doors away. Morose, Carla was envious of Beth's ability to forget that their daddy had gone. Annie, tapping her fingernail on the side of the glass, wondered if she would ever laugh again.

Chapter 4

The house seemed to quiver with tension on the first Saturday without Adam. The girls were aimless, padding about barefoot, bickering one moment, pensive and silent the next. When a door opened, from habit they looked up expecting their father's shadow to fall across the floor and his absence reawakened the grief and shock of his leaving. In every room and along the upstairs and downstairs hallway his masculine presence, the faint fragrance of aftershave, was a renewed reminder that he was no longer here.

Neither Kate nor the girls had made plans for the day. Adam usually made the suggestions and it was his routine that they all worked to. It was as though this first weekend without him was a blank canvas that chance and time would eventually fill.

No one was yet used to not having a car. Catching a train or a bus to go anywhere was too much trouble on such a miserable day.

Outdoors the air was humid, the sky blanketed with grey flat cloud. There wasn't a breath of air coming in through the open windows.

It had rained heavily during the night, the lawn was soaked. During the downpour the dark soil in the flowerbeds leached small stones and muddy water onto the grass, which was in need of mowing. The plants were heavy with water, the flower-heads drooping and splattered with mud.

Her flip flops clicking on the stair-treads, Kate came down carrying a pile of washing. There were hollows under her eyes and two fine lines ran from the corner of her down-turned mouth.

'What's for lunch?' Beth asked, looking up from crayoning a

picture at the kitchen table, as her mother appeared

'Oh, I don't know. Ask Annie,' Kate said stuffing a sheet and duvet off her bed into the washer.

Annoyed that she was to do another meal, Annie clicked her tongue. 'Pizza I guess,' she said churlishly.

Beth's face screwed in complaint. 'We had that yesterday,' she said, vigorously colouring in a snowman with a blue crayon.

'Well, you're having it again today,' Annie yelled.

Beth whined, 'Mummy. We had pizza yesterday.'

At the end of her tether, Kate's voice rose in temper. 'Yes and if you're not quiet about it, you'll have it again tomorrow.'

Beth gave a plaintive, 'Why?'

Speaking for the first time in an hour, Carla yelled 'It is because we're very poor, you idiot.'

With a small frown on her face, Beth threw down the fistful of sticky crayon she was holding.

'Does that mean we'll starve and have no clothes to wear? Will I have to stop going to my school? I never really liked it there anyway. So it'll be okay being poor. I can go to Osborne's Junior instead. Most of the kids there are poor.'

Frightened by the image, Carla shouted 'Beth, you are so, so, stupid.' Bursting into tears she fled from the kitchen, dashing upstairs, her bare heels thumping on the treads.

'Now look what you've done, you little pig,' Annie screamed at Beth.

Kate hadn't the energy to bring order. Standing beside the washing machine, she put her hands to her forehead.

The back door opened and Liz came in. 'Oh my! Are you rehearsing a murderous drama? Can anyone join in?'

Red faced with anger, Annie stomped from the room.

Rumpling Beth's hair, Liz said 'Are you the troublemaker

here, you little vixen?'

Beth grinned. 'Auntie Liz, do you know, we're very poor. We can only eat pizza from now on. I have to leave my school and go to Osborne's Junior. The kids there swear all the time.

'Sounds like fun,' Liz smiled.

'Ignore her, Liz,' Kate said, filling the coffee percolator.

'Go and torment someone else, Beth. I want to talk to Auntie Liz.'

'Okay,' the youngster said getting down and running out of the open kitchen door to the wet garden.

As soon as they were both seated at the kitchen table, holding steaming mugs of coffee, Kate said seriously, 'I have decided that I must go and see Adam's parents. My own too. It's important to explain what's happened before the girls let something out of the bag.'

'Do you think Adam may have contacted his mother and father?' Liz asked tucking a lock of dark blond hair behind her ear.

Kate paused before answering, 'I don't think so but then you can never tell. Everything he's done in the past week has surprised me.' Her face clouded. 'I am desperate to talk to him. I'll do anything, see anybody, and go anywhere, to find him.'

A car pulled up close by and Kate tensed, her hearing honed to the sound of the front door opening. After a moment silence fell, the chance that Adam might walk in passed. The moment of hope vanished and a debilitating sense of, let down, becoming horribly familiar, washed over her.

Liz moved, crossing her legs at the knees.

Kate had lost the thread of the conversation. A picture of Adam's parents' house came into her mind and she said, 'I'll find out the departure times of the early trains to Bristol. Annie can mind Carla and Beth.'

Mentally, Liz rearranged her day off. She would change the blue sweater at Debenhams another time, and get her hair cut the following week. 'I'll drive you there on Monday if that suits you. You can't do this on your own,' she said.

The journey time was an opportunity to talk seriously to Kate about social services and the urgent need to get her finances sorted out.

'You're doing too much for us, Liz. I can't keep relying on you. You've hardly had a break from us since…'

Liz touched Kate's cold hand. 'Actually, I want to help. What are friends for if not to be there in times of trouble?' Smiling wanly, she went on 'You will get through this. It might not feel like it now, but you will.'

I'll never get through this, Kate thought, never in a million years.

***

As arranged, Liz arrived at Kate's early on Monday morning. She already thought of the Fontaine family house as Kate's; she had no illusions that Adam Fontaine would return to it. The bugger was most probably sunning himself in some warm clime, exempt from extradition, without a thought to how his family back home were faring.

She did not share Kate's belief that he would send money. Kate was in the mire as were the girls. Somehow or other she had to convince her to face up to reality and sort out her finances.

Locking the car, Liz walked towards the back door.

Emptying the dishwasher, Kate's thoughts were with Adam's elderly parents. Adam was born to them when they were middle-aged. Albert and Daphne Fontaine were fiercely proud of their graduate son and his degree, a maths first. The news she would bring today would be devastating to them.

Since leaving home for university, Adam had made few trips back to see them. No doubt some of the blame for this lay with her. She should have arranged visits but there was always so much else to do. Most weekends the girls had activities, drama lessons, swimming, riding. Adam had his rugby and golf.

The last few days had made her think more clearly about the way she had behaved towards him. Jealousy had made her try to keep him to herself. Not only had she vetoed attending social occasions organised by the bank, but also those events at the golf and rugby club. It saddened her to think that her possessiveness had prevented visits to his parents. It was pure selfishness on her part not to want to share him with the elderly couple. The soul searching, self-flagellation, ceased as the back door opened and Liz walked in.

'Gosh, everything's very tidy in here,' she said cheerfully.

Kate smiled weakly. 'It's the insomnia. I get up at all hours and clean the house.'

'Go to the doctor's and get something. You've got to sleep, Kate.'

Kate sighed. 'Perhaps things will be better after today. As soon as I've faced his mum and dad, perhaps things will look different.'

'It's not for you to face up to anything, Kate. You have done nothing wrong. This is Adam's problem. He's the one that should be apologising and sorting thing out.'

'Ah, but he's not here, is he?' Kate answered sadly.

Liz thought that given the chance she could positively strangle Adam for what he was doing to Kate. In just a few days she had withdrawn into herself, lost her spark and what little self-confidence she possessed. Every conversation was now a struggle. The Kate she knew had withdrawn to somewhere else but not far enough away to escape the problems gathering to besiege her.

Falsely cheerful, Liz said 'Are you ready to go? Or is there something else you have to do first?'

'I'm ready. The girls are organised. They are going to Millie's for breakfast and then to the cinema this afternoon.'

Glancing around the kitchen, Kate checked that everything was in order. Taking her black leather bag off the table, she slung it over her shoulder.

Outside, she followed Liz down the red brick path at the side of the house to the blue mini parked on the drive.

The air was fresh with past rain. With hardly a cloud in the pale blue sky it promised to be a glorious day. Kate felt guilty dragging Liz to Bristol, when she should be enjoying a day in her pretty garden.

Liz's home was a lock cottage on the nearby canal. Years ago, when renovation of the canal was under consideration, Liz bought two derelict cottages near the lock, cheaply. The smaller one became her home, the other the bistro *The Cut Above*. It had proved to be a worthwhile enterprise. Eventually the renovation scheme began and the canal was made navigable. Almost overnight narrow boat hire companies moved into the canal basins. The following summer, holidaymakers and private owners were passing through the lock frequently.

Thinking of Liz's fragrant garden brought Kate's mind to the times when she and Adam had been visitors, long summer evenings sitting outdoors drinking wine by lamplight, enjoying the tranquillity of the water when the lock was still, and then walking home, Adam's arm around her shoulder.

Those strolls were so different from the walks they took

when they first knew each other. In their late teens they had both professed to be fiercely political; her father accused them of ersatz Leninism. It had amused her but not Adam. At the time he had been a strong supporter of the cause. Wherever Adam marched, she went with him, sleeping rough in Manchester, London, and Brighton.

'Penny for them,' Liz said changing gear, slowing down to join the traffic on the by-pass.

Kate smiled. 'They're worth a fortune.'

'That's inflation for you,' Liz said, putting her foot down on the accelerator.

Arriving at Adam's childhood home, 4 King George's Avenue, a grey post-war semi-detached council house, Kate saw that it had deteriorated a lot since she was last here. The window frames and guttering which were once dark blue, almost indigo, were faded, the paint flaking. The front door had a whitish bloom like a November sloe. The garden was overgrown, thistles and dandelions flourishing in the small patch of long grass. It passed through her mind that perhaps Albert Fontaine, Adam's aged father, was ill and unable to handle repairs.

Making no comment, Liz climbed out of the car.

Together she and Kate went through the weathered picket gate and up the cracked and uneven path to the front door.

Lifting the fake chrome doorknocker, Kate wondered why she was putting herself through this ordeal, when she could have telephoned.

Albert Fontaine, a shrivelled man with hunched shoulders, looked blankly through the thick lenses of his spectacles at the two women standing on the doorsteps. It took him a moment to identify his daughter-in-law.

'Kate, I'll be damned. You're about the last person I

expected to open the door to.' Smiling, revealing the plastic gums of his false teeth, he pulled her close planting a kiss between her ear and mouth.

The kitchen door opened and Daphne Fontaine came into the hall, wiping her hands on a floral pinafore.

'Kate! What a lovely surprise.' Her round face creasing in a smile, she looked expectantly beyond the open door. 'Where's the family?'

Kate's eyes threatened to brim with tears. 'I'm afraid they're at home. It's just me and my friend Liz.'

Daphne's face fell. 'Oh, we would have loved to see them.' Making an effort to hide her disappointment, she hadn't had sight of Adam for many months, she looked cheerfully towards Liz. 'Come inside. I'll make a brew.'

Sensing trouble, a steely look came into Albert's rheumy eyes.

Ushering the two women into the living room, Daphne indicated towards a decrepit settee. 'Make yourselves at home.'

The threadbare seat of the old fashioned cottage suite sank into the loose springs as Liz and Kate sat down.

Slumping into an elderly armchair, Albert fixed his gaze on Kate. 'So where is our Adam?'

Looking at the carpet, Kate said softly 'Adam has left me. I do not know where he is.'

Stiff with rheumatism, Albert rose slowly out of the chair, and took his pipe off the beige tiled mantel piece.

Daphne began to cry quietly, dabbing her eyes on the hem of her pinafore.

'When did he go?' Albert said harshly.

His tone startled her and for a moment Kate was at a loss to remember what day Adam had left.

Seeing that Kate was close to falling apart, Liz stepped in to

52

answer Albert, explaining calmly 'The family were on holiday last week. Adam was recalled to the office for an important meeting. He left the holiday cottage and drove back. Two days later, unable to contact him, Kate hired a car and travelled back home. When she got there, she found that Adam had packed his stuff and left.'

Kate was crying quietly, touching her nose with a tissue.

Albert believed he was only hearing the tip of the story. 'What, there was no big row? Adam just upped and went without a word?' His eyes went to Kate for confirmation.

Liz answered for her. 'There was no row. Adam said he had an urgent meeting. He never went to the office. There was no note, no explanation, nothing.'

Glancing from beneath hooded eyelids to his wife, crying quietly into her pinafore, he said impatiently, 'Don't fuss, Daphne. He'll turn up.'

'Perhaps he won't,' she said, her voice breaking.

Ignoring her, Albert turned to Kate. 'Is there nothing else you can tell us?'

It was obvious that he blamed her for Adam going away, Kate thought truculently. He supposed she had done something to turn Adam against her and he had fled. Adam was the victim, not herself and the three girls back home.

The unspoken accusation rankled and she was tempted to tell him about the visit from Tony Everett and his allegation that Adam had embezzled hundreds of thousands of pounds from the bank. It was on the tip of her tongue to say it but she held back. She would never accuse Adam when she believed him innocent.

Daphne slowly rose from the chair. 'I'll make a cuppa,' she said to no one in particular.

For the next hour there was a stream of speculation from

53

Albert and Daphne about Adam's possible whereabouts.

Sitting perched on the edge of the settee, empty cup and saucer in her hand, Kate listened to the flow, her head aching.

Seeing they were getting nowhere, Liz quietly suggested they get back to the girls. Relieved to have an excuse to leave, Kate stood immediately.

In the hall, she kissed Daphne on the cheek. 'The girls will phone you at the weekend.'

Daphne blinked away tears. 'You will let us know if you hear anything, anything at all?'

'I'll call immediately.' Kate promised.

'Take care, Kate. I'm sorry for your trouble,' Daphne spoke through tears she could no longer hold back.

Albert said nothing but goodbye.

Climbing into the car, closing the door, Kate glanced through the passenger window to the unhappy couple standing at their front door, the old lady holding onto her husband for support.

Starting the engine, Liz drove from the kerb. They travelled in silence for the first few miles. The grey streets of suburban Bristol falling away, the landscape changing gradually until they were motoring through rural territory, dotted with large houses, the gardens the size of small parks.

Glancing at the minor mansions, Kate tried to imagine the families living behind the stone walls. Unashamedly envious of the wealth and security they must surely enjoy.

Ahead, three men in grimy uniforms of a utility company were tearing up the tarmac.

Braking for the road-works red traffic light, Liz glanced at Kate's pale profile. 'Shall we stop at the next pub for a glass of wine?'

Drawing her eyes away from a spectacular house, Kate said

'Let's do that.'

Driving for another three miles they came to the Fox and Hound, a small free-house. It looked appealing with scarlet geraniums cascading from cast iron window boxes and huge sunshades almost an exact red on the outdoor terrace.

Kate perked up the moment she was out of the car. She had dreaded visiting Adam's parents. It had been much worse than she had imagined it would be. She had found Albert Fontaine intimidating, not by what he had said, but the way his piercing grey eyes had looked from beneath hooded lids. As though he didn't trust what she said to be the truth. Now it was over, she was beginning to relax. The knots in her stomach unravelling.

Waiting for Liz to get her bag off the back seat and lock the car, Kate glanced to the spiraea japonica hedge growing on three sides of the car park; the glossy green leaves were scattered with blossoms reminding her of pink candyfloss, miniature spears sticking out of foliage.

Locking the car, Liz slung the strap of her bag onto her shoulder, and fell into step with Kate. Underfoot the cracked cement was gritty, tiny particles getting into their sandals.

Going into the bar, Liz led the way. They came out a moment later holding glasses of white wine.

Sitting at a table, a huge red parasol protecting them from the afternoon sun, they both agreed that the pub was a real find.

The view was wonderful; it was a pleasure just to sit and look over the fields. A heat haze shimmering over the golden crops of corn and barley. Way beyond the agricultural acres, green folding hills crested with lavender fused into the pale transparent sky.

How Adam would love this, Kate thought with a raw agony of yearning. A lump came to her throat and she tried to swallow tears. Her eyes brimmed and the heat haze took on watery aspect, like torrential rain flowing down a windowpane.

Travelling towards home, Kate's finances were the main topic of conversation, Liz taking the opportunity to discuss how the family were to stay afloat financially.

Dealing with finances was alien to Kate and she found it difficult to concentrate on Liz's questions. In recent days her mind was like a cerebral wheel, spinning around and around. The same questions circling with monotonous regularity. Where was Adam? Was he safe? Would he contact her soon? Would she ever see him again?

'I suppose the girls' school fees for the winter term were paid before the start of the summer holidays,' Liz said changing gear prior to turning onto the main road.

That this hadn't occurred to her, made Kate feel doubly inadequate. Her reply was monosyllabic, 'I guess so.'

The turn negotiated, Liz changed up a gear, accelerating smoothly.

'So at least they can stay at their respective schools until the spring term. It'll give you time to find a comprehensive for Carla and Annie and a junior for Beth.' She smiled. 'Though she does seem to have her heart set on going to Osborne's Junior, if only to take part in the bad manners and swearing,' she said light-heartedly.

'Moving will be bad for each of them,' Kate said seriously. 'Annie's just beginning her GCSE's. It is Carla's first term in seniors. And Beth...'

Overtaking an old Volvo, her eyes darting to the rear view mirror, Liz said 'I wouldn't worry too much about Beth. The little scamp will turn everything to her own advantage.'

The road ahead was empty and Liz increased speed. 'I had a thought whilst you were talking to Daphne. If Adam hasn't closed his bank account, which we have yet to find out, the mortgage on the house will be paid until the money in the current account runs dry. It'll be the same with all the direct debits.'

The first ray of hope, however insubstantial, made Kate alert. 'I guess you're right. Adam is unlikely to have cancelled the direct debits and cleared out his account.'

She looked towards Liz for confirmation that Adam wasn't the sort of man to allow his family to end on their uppers.

'I may have a few weeks to sort everything out. Perhaps we are not in such a black hole after all.'

As another idea came to her, Kate's face clouded. 'If I ring the bank manager, he might put a stop on the account. Then I'll be in real trouble.'

Liz's eyes were on the traffic ahead. 'What about internet banking. Can you check his account through the computer? Do you know the password he uses?'

Kate slumped back in the seat. 'I'm afraid not.'

'It can't be too difficult to guess what he may use. It could be his mother's maiden name or one of the kids' birthdays. It'll be something he's unlikely to forget.'

Kate wasn't optimistic. One of Adam's little foibles was secrecy. 'I'll ask Annie to try on the computer. If she can't come up with something, I'll have to wait until the bank statement comes in.'

Deep in thought, Liz drove the last two miles to Kate's house.

The police car parked at the curb-stone was so foreign to the quiet road its presence was alarming.

Kate's heart lurched on seeing it parked there. Her first thought was of Adam, he had been involved in an accident, or worse. It took her another five seconds to connect the presence of the vehicle to one of her children.

Kate winced, and Liz laid a hand on her arm. 'Don't panic. there is probably a perfectly good explanation.'

Liz had hardly brought the car to a standstill when Kate jumped out.

Two uniformed police officers standing on the doorstep, a man of about thirty and a younger woman, turned on hearing Kate approach.

Still several yards away, Kate shouted 'What's happened?'

'There's nothing to worry about, Mrs Fontaine,' the woman officer called back. 'We just want a word with you about your husband, Adam Fontaine.'

A net curtain moved in the window of the neighbouring house. Kate caught the movement in the tail of her eye but she was too fearful of Adam's safety to take much notice.

With a trembling hand she searched in the bottom of her handbag for the house-key. Finding it she pushed it into the lock. The door swung inwards.

Jittery, glancing at the officers, she stepped into the quiet hall. The house had been closed up for several hours and there was a faint smell of the toast cooked at breakfast on the warm air.

Liz followed the two officers inside.

Kate, several shades paler, opened the sitting room door and the two officers went in.

Hovering on the threshold, Liz said in an undertone, 'Kate, do you want to talk in private? Or shall I stay?'

The policeman turned to her, saying officiously, 'We wish to talk to Mrs Fontaine alone.'

'I'll be in the kitchen should you need me, Kate.'

As the door closed on Liz, Kate looked beseechingly. 'Would someone please tell me what has happened?'

'Mrs Fontaine, there is nothing to worry about,' the female

officer said calmly.

For an instant, Kate thought the woman was saying that Adam was found and he was safe.

The backdoor opened noisily. She pricked her ears for the sound of Adam's voice but it was the chatter of the girls that came to her.

The officer glanced at her notebook. 'You visited your husband's parents today, Mr and Mrs Fontaine.'

The words shattered Kate's hope of seeing Adam imminently. He is not found, she thought despairingly. Adam will not walk through the door at any moment. The intensity of her disappointment brought a rush of hot tears to her eyes.

Both officers were watching her, waiting for an answer.

'What do Albert and Daphne have to do with this?' Kate answered quietly.

'You paid a visit to their home today?' The man almost sighed.

'Yes, I went there.'

'We have been informed that your husband disappeared recently. For some reason you decided not to tell us.'

His accusing tone wasn't lost on Kate and she felt a tingle of apprehension. 'Why is it police matter, if my husband leaves me?'

'That rather depends on the circumstances.' He harrumphed.

'What circumstances?' Kate said, her voice rising.

Annoyed, he became more officious. 'It becomes a police matter when the circumstances of your husband's disappearance are reported as unusual.'

Glancing at him, the woman officer's eyes sparked with annoyance.

'There is no need to get upset, Mrs Fontaine,' she said quietly.'

Kate bordering on hysteria, shrieked, 'Why wouldn't I be upset? My husband leaves me. I get a visit from the police. I can only suppose that someone has telephoned you to say my husband is missing. For God sake! Do you think I have buried him in the garden?'

To defuse the situation the female officer steered Kate towards the settee. 'I hardly think it's likely, Mrs Fontaine. But it is our duty to check out anything that is reported to us.' She sent a piercing glance towards her partner.

Kate slumped down, her legs suddenly too weak to hold her. 'I went to see my in-laws to tell them that Adam left us last week.'

Raising her head, she looked up into the woman police officer's face. 'Was it my father-in-law? Did he call you?'

'I am not in a position to reveal who telephoned us, Mrs Fontaine. But if you could tell us what happened.'

It took a few moments to explain the events leading up to Adam's departure from the Shore Cottage and her eventual discovery that he had gone from home.

Throughout the narration she was aware of the officer standing behind her, making notes, his pencil scratching the paper of his black notebook.

He took a moment to read through what he had written. Flipping the book closed, he said 'We need Mr Fontaine's bank details, credit cards et cetera and the name of his employer.'

The door opened. Annie, wearing a red and blue print dress, a blue Alice band in her hair, stood on the threshold. 'Have you found my father?'

Rising off the settee quickly, Kate went to her. 'No, Annie, they haven't found him. They just want to ask questions about the day he disappeared.'

In a malicious afterthought, she said 'Your grandfather

called them.'

Fond of her grandparents, Annie's face crumpled. 'Granddad did. Why?'

Kate sighed. 'God knows. I explained everything to him and Daphne. But they're both getting a bit senile, I suppose.'

The male officer wishing to bring the interview to a close became impatient. 'The bank details, Mrs Fontaine.'

Kate was curt. 'I'll see what I can find.'

Without hurrying, she had no intention of pandering to the man's arrogance she walked out of the room.

Annie fled back to the kitchen.

Ten minutes later, the two police officers left the house with credit and debit card statements and the address of Adam's employer in their possession.

Watching the car drive away, Kate wondered if Tony Everett would report the alleged embezzlement to them. Not disclosing it herself would probably put her in a bad light. But, she reasoned, if Tony Everett were involved in the theft and using Adam's disappearance as a cover, he of course would say nothing to the police.

The police car turned right out of the cul-de-sac. As it disappeared she was sorry that she had not set the record straight. It was a lost opportunity to bring everything out in the open and reveal her suspicions concerning the chief accountant.

Turning from the window, she looked at the tidy room as though seeing it after a long absence. It was the *same* but *different*. Without Adam's personality the room lacked substance. The essence of the man was still present but the vibrancy of his personality had gone.

Everywhere she looked there were bitter-sweet reminders, to make her sick with longing. The tan leather chair where he normally sat bore the shape of his body. There was a slight darkening on the corners of the arms where he rested his hands.

The magazines he liked to flick through were in the rack beside the chair, one protruding above the others as though he had just pushed it there. A pair of cufflinks lay discarded on the small table, silver talismans of the past. On the same table, a swan-necked brass student lamp he read by most evenings still held his fingerprints, tiny relics of himself. Wherever I look, she thought, there are shadows of Adam. The sound of his voice, his laughter, is constantly in my ears.

Liz and Annie were sitting at the table as Kate came into the kitchen. A pleasant breeze was blowing through the open door and windows.

Annie had her hand on the cover of a magazine to stop the paper ruffling. 'Why were the police here so long?'

Pouring white wine into a spare glass, Liz was indignant. 'You would think they had better things to do. When did being a deserted wife become a crime?'

Kate took the glass from her. 'God knows. You would think we had enough to worry about without the local constabulary poking their long noses into our family business.'

'What did they say, Mum?'

'Oh that they'll check your father's bank account and credit cards to see when and where they are used. They have started what they call a *missing from home log*. However did it come to this, your father's name on a thing like that?'

Liz and Annie remained silent. The only sound in the room was Kate's fingernails tapping on the side of the glass.

Kate's eyes went to the wall clock. 'The police have gone to speak to Tony Everett at the bank. They should be there by now.'

'I hope you told them about the money,' Liz said quietly,

afraid that at any moment Kate would fall to pieces. She had never seen anyone so near to the edge as Kate was at this moment.

To hide tears, Kate moved to the window and looked out. The grass needs cutting, she thought, but I don't even know how to operate the mower that Adam bought recently.

'I didn't say anything to them about the money.'

'Oh Kate, why didn't you?'

'I don't want to get Adam into trouble.'

'Poor Kate,' Liz said her eyes filling.

Chapter 5

Dusk was falling, the last moments of slanting golden sunlight gilding the magnolia walls of the bedroom. There was a faint scent of wax polish coming off the warmed wood of the mahogany tallboy.

Kate was sitting on the edge of the double bed, her cold fingers plucking at the blue and red tapestry bedspread.

A second visit from the police, and a lengthy interview, had shocked her to the core. The two officers were not the same two that had called earlier. There had been a change of shift at the station. The later callers were older, brusque to the point of rudeness.

They had proof that Adam's bank account, credit and debit cards, mobile phone and internet account had not been accessed since the day he went missing.

Accused of withholding evidence, the embezzlement having come to light during the afternoon, she had reacted in an undignified way losing her head and actually ranting at one point. It had come out that she suspected Tony Everett at the bank of involvement and went as far as to say he was using Adam as a scapegoat. Adam fled because he was unable to prove his innocence.

Scornful looks passed between the two men that made her feel stupid and neurotic.

To make matters worse, she hauled Annie into the sitting room and insisted she told the officers everything, from the phone call to Adam at Shore Cottage, to their arrival back home.

Annie was terrified and her story was disjointed missing many of the relevant facts.

Kate did her best to make things clear, interrupting Annie,

reminding her of the sequence of events.

Annie became more fretful, her tears bordering on hysteria. Worried about the child's state of mind, one of the police officers dismissed Annie. Fleeing to her room she locked the door, refusing entirely to speak to anyone.

With the slamming of the bedroom door, Kate thought things couldn't get any worse. Then the officer began to inform her they were calling on Adam's friends and his golf and rugby club to get a picture of his habits.

Vainly proud, it came as a severe blow to Kate to realise she would be the talk of the neighbourhood. It was dreadful to think that women, her so called friends, would smirk at her downfall and degradation. Many of them were attracted to Adam and flirted outrageously with him, never caring if she were upset or hurt by their behaviour.

Watching the sun sinking behind the trees in the park, the first doubts of Adam's innocence began to creep into her mind. It was now proved that Adam hadn't used a bank card or cheque for days. So what was he living on? Money he had stolen and stashed away? If so, it meant that somewhere there was another bank account, perhaps abroad. The police said that he hadn't used his mobile or internet access, but how could he if he wanted to remain hidden; just one phone call would pinpoint his whereabouts.

'Where are you, Adam?' Kate cried from the heart. 'Where are you?'

Her love for Adam was so intense that to be without him was like drowning slowly. If she could die without laying a violent hand upon her body, she would. Perishing now, this instant, would be a mercy. Death would quiet her tormented mind and stop the endless pain, the ceaseless waiting to hear from him.

Adam had been her first and only boyfriend. They had met at

a weekend music rave in Oxford. Kate had immediately been drawn to his blond good looks.

No warning bells pealed on discovering that he was a lapsed catholic whilst she kept a strong faith with the Church of England. For a brief period Adam toyed with the idea of a political career; a passionate socialist he might have risen through the ranks swiftly.

Apolitical, Kate misconstrued his Labourite leanings. Fiercely ambitious, Adam made an enormous effort studying for his degree. Lazy at college, Kate barely scraped through her cookery course.

The three years between meeting and marrying were an agony of suspense for her, every moment expecting another woman to snatch her prize.

It came as something of a shock to Adam, when Kate announced she was pregnant and determined to keep the baby. Fortunately his final exams were imminent, and on leaving university he was soon employed at Brand's Commercial Bank.

They married before Annie was born, buying a small semi-detached house with an enormous mortgage. This first home was an unreasonable commuting distance from London. It took another two years before they could afford to move to a large Victorian house a few miles nearer the city. Three more moves before they had a home of choice.

Throughout the fifteen years of the marriage, Kate believed that Adam loved her. So it was utterly incomprehensible that he should choose to leave her. She didn't deserve it.

As the amber light in the bedroom faded and the walls took on a grey lifeless hue, Kate stirred, her legs stiff from sitting too long in one position.

The house was deadly quiet. The girls were in bed. She

wondered if they had locked the doors and windows. There was nothing for it but to move, to secure the house for the night.

The hall was in blackness, as she ventured out of her room. Putting her hand to the familiar switch on the wall, the upstairs hall and downstairs flooded with light.

At the top of the stairs she listened for a moment, nervous that the door may still be open, an invitation to an opportunist burglar who might still be in the house. There was silence but for the rhythmic tick of the wall clock in the kitchen. Cautious she went down, alert for the slightest movement of air.

It took her a moment to check the doors and windows, but whoever was last to bed, probably Carla, had secured the house properly. Making a mental note to thank her in the morning, Kate pushed open the kitchen door.

The room was in darkness, the blinds closed on the two windows.

A chair leg scraped on the tiled floor and Kate's heart jumped into her mouth.

Trembling, filled with terror, she flicked the light switch on.

Annie was at the kitchen table, holding a glass of cola.

'My God Annie, you frightened me to death. What are you doing sitting in the dark?'

'Sorry, Mum. I couldn't settle so when the girls went to bed I came down. It went dark as I was sitting here.'

'You look tired, Annie. You should be in bed.'

'I'll go when I finish this,' she said lifting the glass to her mouth.

Going to the fridge for milk, Kate saw an opened bottle of white wine; putting the milk back, she took the bottle out and poured the Soave into a glass propped on the draining board. Standing with her hip against the sink, she drank a mouthful. It was cold, cold enough to make her aware of her hot face and aching head.

'It's been a bad day, Annie,' she said quietly. 'I'm sorry I made it worse for you.'

'It doesn't matter, Mum. Every day is a bad day. What does one more matter?'

'Oh Annie, you're too young to think like that. You should be out having fun with your friends.'

'There's time enough for that, when all this awfulness is behind us.'

Kate sighed. 'Maybe you're right. It will not be over for me, until your father comes back home.'

Annie drained her drink. Standing, she went to the sink and ran the glass under the hot tap. Kate was close enough to catch the smell of alcohol in the steam. Glancing at her daughter's tired face she decided not to mention it until tomorrow. Then she would have a proper talk to Annie.

'Goodnight, Mum,' Annie said kissing the side of Kate's face.

'Try to sleep, Annie. You look worn out.'

Without replying, Annie went through the kitchen door.

Kate sat in the vacated chair listening to her daughter climb the stairs.

It was hard not to blame Adam for this new turn of events, Annie sitting alone in the dark drinking alcohol in her cola. God only knew what pressure had brought Annie to it. Some of the blame was hers, she had over relied on Annie to take care of Carla and Beth, cook meals, and deal with most of the day-to-day running of the house since they had returned from Shore Cottage.

The holiday now seemed a lifetime ago. It was hard to imagine that she was the same woman who had sat complacently in the car being driven by Adam to their favourite holiday retreat. She sighed remembering how she had looked forward to the two blissful weeks with Adam. The days since then had been a living nightmare. Now the police were taking more than a passing interest in Adam's disappearance, which only made the episode all the harder to bear.

Lifting her glass, she took a swallow of the wine. It was too astringent for her taste but a favourite of Liz's. She supposed Liz had brought it. She wondered how she would have survived this past week without Liz. She had been a tower of strength. Unlike her in-laws, whose meddling had made things ten times worse, she would never forgive Albert for ringing the police.

If he had telephoned and asked Annie how events had unfolded, it would have saved all this unpleasantness. It had been in her mind to phone him the moment the police left the house. But she was too worked up; her anger might well have boiled over. As it was she was still seething with indignation at the thought that the police had by now questioned their friends and the members at the rugby club and the golf club. Albert Fontaine could count himself very lucky if he ever saw his granddaughters again.

Chapter 6

Standing in the small conservatory looking out on the hot sunlit garden, Cyril Oliver was feeling every one of his seventy-eight-years. Weariness, like sluggish water, trickled through his veins.

Absentmindedly, he noted the hedge needed trimming, but he had neither the inclination nor energy to set about cutting the two elderly privets separating the garden from the two adjacent neighbouring properties.

Not so long ago he had tended the garden religiously, familiar with every square foot of soil, the design was typical of a pre-war plot, long and narrow with plenty of room for a vegetable and a fruit patch. The boughs of an ancient apple and pear tree provided shelter for winter snowdrops and the crop of primroses, bluebells and wallflowers, his springtime favourite.

A shed, his private bolt hole, was rooted at the farthest corner. Painted a dark shade of green it melted into the mature foliage.

Near to the house was a well-kept lawn. It hadn't always been as neat as it now was. When Kate and Helen, his two daughters, were young there was always a bald patch in the centre and small holes in the turf where the kids had poked sticks as markers.

Elizabeth his wife did most of the work in the garden now, bar cutting the lawn and trimming the hedge, which was generally left to him.

Elizabeth was out there now, tweaking immature weeds from beneath the azalea bushes. Stooping to pluck out a particularly resilient dandelion her grey skirt rode up her thighs and he caught a glimpse of the backs of her sturdy knees.

Fifteen years younger than he was, there was vitality about her that he no longer possessed. He envied her energy and fitness.

The substance beneath his flesh shrank by the day, the papery brown skin ceasing to fit the body it was once tailored to.

Glancing at his liver-spotted and nearly hairless forearms, folded across his midriff, he sighed. He was now no more than an echo of his former self. The firm flesh, moist muscle, strong sinew and ivory bone were a thing of the past, and most probably would be extinct in the not too distant future. He had spent his allotted time, three score years and ten, and eight besides.

Sighing again, he turned from the window. Rather overplaying the part of old-man he went to the kitchen, the heels of his slippers scuffing on the carpet. Switching on the kettle, Elizabeth had thoughtfully left it ready, he set it to boil. The biscuit tin was too much of a temptation; opening it he took three chocolate digestives out. Slightly more cheerful he spooned coffee granules into a mug.

With a twinge of guilt, he really should have offered Elizabeth a coffee; he went back into the conservatory. Putting the mug and the three biscuits on the little folding table, he slumped down in the chintzy upholstered chair.

He almost smiled dunking the first biscuit into the steaming coffee. The warm thick smell of chocolate and tang of coffee rose up and he gave a sigh of satisfaction as he bit off the sodden segment. Elizabeth called him a barbarian if she caught him dunking biscuits.

Checking her whereabouts, he glanced through the open window. She was standing at the low picket fence, which had been put there to replace a section of privet that had died

71

mysteriously, in conversation with Mrs Jones the next door neighbour.

He caught a snatch of the exchange; hearing Kate's name he supposed Elizabeth was mentioning that their daughter was visiting today.

Kate had telephoned last night, dropping the bombshell that Adam had left her. It was terrible news and so unexpected. Knowing Kate as he did, he was worried for her. Kate was highly strung. Not a bit like her mother or sister Helen. Kate favoured his mother. Victoria Oliver bearing numerous children suffered terribly with nerves.

Dunking the remainder of the biscuit, eating it quickly, he brushed the damp crumbs from the front of his shirt.

Glancing out again he saw Elizabeth had gone back to uprooting stray weeds, deftly chucking them into a black bucket on the crazy paving path.

'Indefatigable,' he said, a little resentfully.

A key turned in the Yale lock of the front door. Bracing himself for the invasion, he plastered a benign smile on his craggy face.

Kate, wearing a primrose linen dress and beige canvas sandals, the paleness of the dress accentuating her summer tan, stepped into the hallway. The air was still and warm. Meat was cooking in the kitchen and there was a slight aroma of coffee.

The scent of the house was so familiar that for a moment Kate was a child again, returning from school and not a grown woman come home to explain her husband's disappearance and the subsequent muddle of her life.

Until now she had been the shining light, the successful child. Adam's defection, the visits from the police had ground her pride into the mud. Only shame remained, a physical thing rotting in her heart.

'Hello. We're here,' she shouted with feigned cheerfulness.

Beth, wearing a blue and white striped top and blue jeans, rudely brushed passed her mother and Annie. 'Granny, Granddad. We're here,' she shouted.

'Little pig,' Annie snapped as the magazine in her hand was sent flying.

'Pig yourself,' Beth shouted over her shoulder.

'Please behave, girls,' Kate said tiredly.

Standing, brushing the few biscuit crumbs still attached to his clothes, Cyril did his best to look pleased that the quiet tranquillity of the house was broken and likely to remain so for several hours.

The kitchen door leading to the garden was wide open. Beth ran through it. With a minimal wave to her grandmother, still weeding the flowerbed, she ran towards the ancient dog sleeping in the shade of the apple tree.

Kate came into the conservatory. 'Hello, Dad,' she said, instant tears blinding her.

Drawing her into his arms, Cyril patted her gently.

Carla glancing in to the room did an-about-turn. The last thing she needed was another depressing scene from her mother.

Annie, shrugging her shoulders, followed Carla into the garden.

Elizabeth, pulling off her dirty gardening gloves, dumped them on the pile of weeds in the bucket. The occasion warranted a broad smile and she did her utmost to deliver. Not that she felt like smiling; the news that Adam had done a bunk had knocked her for six. She had hardly slept a wink all night worrying about Kate and the girls, wondering how on earth Kate would cope as a single mother.

How she disliked the term single mother. The business of

73

breeding children wasn't a solitary phenomenon. It took two to tango, but only one to pick up the pieces.

Putting on a show of delight for the benefit of the two girls advancing towards her, she called cheerfully, 'You have arrived, how lovely.'

Eyes glistening with tears, Carla ran into her grandmother's open arms.

Holding her close, sensing the despair in the small frame, Elizabeth's anger towards Adam rose up fiercely. Looking over the child's head, she glared unseeing at the branches of the innocent apple tree. The tears shining in her eyes merging the summer dry leaves with the green apples of autumn.

Sniffing, wiping the tip of her nose with the back of her hand, she said 'Mrs Jones's Labrador has had four puppies. Mrs Jones said you are to go round to see them. Isn't that wonderful? Four furry babies and they are adorable.'

As there was hardly a response from Carla, she went on enthusiastically, 'Granddad mentioned that he might like to have one of them.'

A shadow of a smile crossed Carla's face. 'That would be wonderful. Can I come and stay sometimes and take it for walks?'

'Of course you can,' Elizabeth said positively, wondering how Cyril would react to the news that they were to have another dog.

Carla broke free. 'Beth,' she called. 'Granny and Granddad are getting a new puppy. We're going next door to choose it.'

As the back gate closed on the three girls, Elizabeth made her way into the house, dreading hearing the details and the financial difficulties that Adam's defection had created.

Coming into the conservatory, she heard Cyril saying firmly, 'But I insist, Kate. It's the only sensible thing to do.'

On seeing Elizabeth standing in the doorway a look of uncertainty came into his eyes. The offer he had just made to Kate was a spur of the moment thing. He couldn't retract it now, although Elizabeth might not be pleased.

He spoke snappishly, 'I have offered the car to Kate. It's time I gave up driving. The car really needs to go.' As she didn't respond he went on rather quickly, 'You haven't driven since...' He didn't elaborate on Elizabeth's accident many years ago. The memory still had the power to upset her dreadfully.

She gave him a weak smile. 'I wondered how long it would be before you decided to stop driving.' Recently she had noticed that his co-ordination wasn't all it should be. They had suffered a couple of near misses at junctions.

Coming to Kate, she kissed her cheek, her hand lingering for a moment on her daughter's arm. 'You'll need a car if you are to find a job and run the girls about.'

Kate's eyes searched her mother's. 'But it's such a big thing to take from you, Mum.'

Elizabeth was light-heartedly scornful. 'What that old thing!'

Turning to Cyril, an amused smile on her lips, she said 'I have just promised the girls that we will get a pup from Mrs Jones.'

'A dog,' he said flabbergasted. 'We've already got a dog.'

She sniffed. 'Yes, but the old thing is on his last legs. A pup around the house will brighten him up. The girls have gone next door to choose one. I expect they'll be back any moment with the little mite.'

'Elizabeth, you really should have consulted me.'

She gave him a matter-of-fact look. 'Yes, I probably should have.'

'Kate, you poor thing' she said changing the subject, 'sit

down and tell us what's happened. The children will be back any moment and we will not have chance to talk properly.'

Tense, perching on the edge of the small settee, Kate looked at her mother. 'It's difficult to know where to start. Everything has gone so horribly wrong.'

Elizabeth patted the back of Kate's cold hand. 'Well darling, just start at the beginning. When did you last see him?'

A vision of Adam driving away from her without a goodbye came instantly into Kate's mind. She would never see him again, nor touch, kiss or smell him, his naked flesh would never more be aligned with hers. Grief, a physical pain, ached somewhere in the region of her heart.

The sound of Beth's laughter came through the open window and she imagined her daughter playing with the puppies on the lawn next door. Beth as carefree as only a child can be, living for the moment.

Whilst for her a single hour had a nightmarish longevity. The minutes shod with iron shoes creeping by. With no hope of seeing Adam before night fell again.

The extent of Kate's pain was clear to see, and Elizabeth full of compassion reached out to her. 'I know how much you loved him and how very hard this time must be for you. But Kate, you must look forward, for the sake of the children.'

Kate's thoughts were entirely negative. Is this really all I have to look forward to, months or years of being pacified by my mother and told to think of the children before myself?

Waspishly, she snapped 'I don't need a sermon, Mum. I came here today to explain. Not to be told I'm not taking care of the children.'

Elizabeth was silent, regarding her child compassionately.

Harrumphing, Cyril levered himself out of the chair and went to stand by the open window, looking out intently and seeing nothing.

Kate spoke bitterly, 'It's easy to preach from the comfort of a sound relationship.'

Elizabeth gave her a small smile. 'The last thing I want to do is preach. I want to help you Kate.'

Turning around sharply, Cyril glared. 'I suggested giving you the car to cheer you up. What more do you want from us?'

Tears swam in Kate's eyes. 'I don't want anything, other than a bit of understanding. You have no idea how hard everything is right now.'

'Life's hard, Kate,' he said harshly.

She wished she had not come today. She had dreaded facing them and the reality was worse than she had imagined. Without Adam at her side protecting her, she didn't want to go anywhere, least of all to her father who plainly didn't understand.

Cyril fixed his eyes on her, studying her intently. 'You can have the car, Kate. But I don't see how else we can help. Our own finances are not what they were. My pension, as you know, never came up to expectation. Your mother and I have had our own disappointments.'

Oh please not that again, Kate thought despairingly, I really cannot bear another diatribe on the pension swindle.

'Cyril,' Elizabeth almost barked. 'Kate hasn't come all this way to talk about your pension.'

'Or lack of it,' he said, worrying his pet subject like a dog with a bone.

Elizabeth glared in his direction.

Pushing his hands into his trouser pockets, Cyril looked fiercely out of the window. He would do anything for a cigarette although he hadn't smoked in fifteen years, and couldn't afford to, not with his old firm going bust and the government reneging on his pension rights.

'I'm sorry,' Kate said into the icy silence.

Cyril wasn't in a mood to be pacified. 'It's not me I worry about, Kate. You can upset me as much as you like. It's your mother's happiness, I worry about.'

Kate knew full well that he was far too self-centred to worry about anyone but himself. But he did have unexpected bursts of generosity, the car being a case in point.

'All the same, Pop, I'm sorry.'

Elizabeth looked up from the low seat of the settee. 'How will you manage, financially? Has Adam left anything for you and the girls to live on?'

Sighing, Kate slumped back down beside her mother. 'There's still a little money in his bank account. The direct debits are being paid out of that for the moment. If Adam doesn't put more money in, we will run out in two or three months. But I really think he will make arrangements.'

That Adam might let her down turned the blood in her vein to ice.

Her voice dropped to almost a whisper. 'If he doesn't, there'll have to be drastic changes. The girls will have to come out of private education. Carla must give up her music lessons, and when Annie's subscription to the gym and martial arts classes runs out, that'll be it.'

'But Annie lives and breathes her martial arts. She's so talented. She looks such a slip of a girl but she can throw a sturdy lad to the mat. We saw her do it several times,' Elizabeth said with pride, remembering the open day she and Cyril had gone to at the gym. 'It would be a great shame to give it up after all her hard work.' She tut-tutted.

'Needs must,' Cyril said philosophically, harrumphing.

Kate decided this was not a good time to mention the

charges of embezzlement levelled at Adam and her suspicions that Tony Everett was involved in some way.

Cyril glanced at Kate. 'Well, it's good that there's money to last you, even if it is for a short time.'

It came to Kate that her father had no notion that a wife was entitled to a portion of the family assets, house, bank accounts, pension…

Elizabeth wondered how she could possibly help to pay for the music lessons and the subscription for Annie. Cyril would never agree of course; he lived in mortal fear of an unexpected financial outlay. His pension hadn't been all he had expected, but it wasn't far from it. To hear him talk you might believe they were heading towards penury.

'Would you like a sherry before lunch, Kate?' Elizabeth said, her mind already whirling to find a solution to the problem.

Turning his face from the garden he gave his wife a withering glance. 'She can't. She's driving the car.'

The back gate opened with a clatter. The girls, puppy in tow, came in through the open kitchen door.

'Granny, Granddad. We've brought Sam to see you,' Beth bawled.

As the girls came in, Elizabeth caught Annie's eye. 'Be a darling, Annie. Pour me a sherry and your grandfather a whisky and soda.'

Surprised to be offered a drink so early in the day, usually forbidden on health grounds, Cyril looked cheerfully towards the young dog.

In the kitchen, Annie looked in a cupboard for her grandmother's favourite schooner glass. The dark brown sherry bottle was on the work surface. Picking it up, pulling out the cork stopper, she filled the glass to the rim. The rich caramel aroma was too tempting to ignore and dipping her head she sucked sherry into her mouth. The taste reminded her of past Christmases, warm mince-pies and a tot of sherry. And dad close by, laughing, opening presents, pretending to be delighted with the silly gifts they had bought or made for him. Nostalgia brought pain. Filling the glass to the top again, Annie took a large swig.

Going back in the conservatory, stepping over the puppy playing with a small ball on the floor, Annie half-heartedly offered the schooner to her grandmother.

'Can I have a tiny sip? I've never tasted sherry before,' she said eyeing her grandmother, afraid the old lady would get a whiff of the sherry she'd filched before she had a chance to cover it with a sanctioned mouthful.

Elizabeth had hardly agreed, when Annie put her lips to the glass.

Elizabeth noticed that Kate wasn't paying attention to the children or the puppy she was sitting frowning at her hands. She had lost weight and she was pale, her skin usually so healthy and translucent was now thinned and a little papery.

Elizabeth couldn't abide to remain motionless watching her daughter's misery. Vehement bitterness rose up against Adam and the woman he'd traded Kate for. There wasn't a doubt in her heart that another woman was involved. Adam needed a woman, if only to bolster his ego.

Bustling out to the kitchen, she returned a moment later with a small glass of red wine for Kate. Handing it to her, catching Cyril's disapproving look in the tail of her eye, she said. 'A small drop won't matter. It'll be hours before you drive home, Kate.'

She flashed her eyes in Cyril's direction, silencing the protest on his mouth.

It was easier to look away than match Elizabeth's wordless warning. Feigning interest in the geraniums cascading from square terracotta pots on the paved terrace, he sat twiddling his thumbs, intensely disgruntled.

Tut-tutting, Elizabeth went back out to the kitchen. In moments she was back bringing a whisky and soda. Still cross, she hardly met his eyes as she handed it to him.

Accepting the olive branch, as Cyril interpreted it, his mood lightened instantly. In a moment he was reeling off the car's maintenance record to Kate, and the date of its last M.O.T. 'It passed with flying colours,' he said cheerfully.

'You make it sound like a clever child,' Elizabeth said sarcastically.

Unable to come up with a quick witty reply, Cyril took a swallow of whisky, pretending not to have heard her remark.

Elizabeth said crossly. 'Come into the kitchen, Kate.'

'She can't come to the kitchen now, I'm telling her about the car,' Cyril said tetchily.

'Never mind all that. You can tell her everything she needs to know, over lunch.'

Accepting the inevitable, Kate rose from her chair and followed her mother out into the sunlit kitchen.

Perching on a high stool in the corner, she watched Elizabeth put water into a saucepan. The gas flared, the saucepan was put to it. The mundane domesticity completed, Elizabeth turned to her. This was the moment Kate had dreaded for days, a maternal grilling from her mother, determined to draw out the truth.

Pandemonium broke out in the conservatory.

Beth squealed excitedly, 'Puppy's weeing. Puppy's weeing.'

The small table went flying and a pottery vase crashed to the floor, a pool of water darkening the centre of the turkey rug.

Attempting to take control, Cyril yelled, 'Put the scamp out. Put him out.' The conservatory door, pulled closed to pen the pup, was thrust open ricocheting off the brickwork.

'Carla, tell your grandmother,' Cyril ordered.

Sighing, Elizabeth stooped to the cupboard below the kitchen sink, bringing out a small bucket and floor cloth.

'Keep your eye on the vegetables, whilst I mop up,' she said calmly.

With a sense of last minute reprieve, Kate slid off the kitchen stool.

***

Driving the eight-year-old Honda away from her parents' house, Kate felt guilty and rather ashamed that she hadn't told them the truth about the charges levelled at Adam, or her suspicions of his infidelity. It was a miracle that one of the girls hadn't blurted out the details of the police calling at the house to question her and Annie. If the truth had come out, she would have been forced to reveal that she believed Tony Everett was involved in the theft and had frightened Adam into fleeing. How could she have explained all this and not looked irrational or plain paranoid? No doubt both of them believed Adam had absconded with a woman.

Deep in angry thought, Kate forgot to change gear and the engine revolutions slowed and almost died.

'It's not as nice as dad's car,' Carla said, critically eyeing the stained head lining.

'It doesn't drive like a BMW automatic either,' Kate said under her breath. 'But it was very good of your granddad to let us have it. It'll make all the difference having your own personal taxi service again.'

A muttered agreement came from the back seat, but Kate wasn't listening. She was thinking of Adam.

Where is he? She asked herself for the thousandth time. Why has he deserted us without a word of explanation? Why didn't I confide everything to my mother when I had the chance?

Is Adam at this moment with another woman? An explicit image of the pair entwined on a bed filled her mind. A moment later it came as a shock to find she was still driving. She thought she may have ignored a red light, or failed to stop when she should have.

Glancing at Annie, sitting beside her in the passenger seat, she wondered if she had noticed anything amiss. But she was slumped down, arms folded, staring unseeing out of the windscreen, with hardly a flicker of her long dark lashes, waiflike, in her quiet introspection.

The two girls in the back engrossed in magazines didn't bother to look out. It came to her that since Adam's departure, conversation between them was virtually non-existent. The girls sparked off each other occasionally, but they didn't hold a proper conversation.

Navigating a traffic island she mixed up the gears almost stalling the car. Cursing, she checked to see if the girls had registered her mistake, she wasn't surprised to see that nobody took a blind bit of notice.

The road ahead was straight and the traffic light.

Kate counted the days since Adam's disappearance. It hardly seemed possible that it was so few. Time dragged torturously, waiting for the phone to ring or a letter to arrive.

Driving into the cul-de-sac, her eyes flew to the drive, but there was no sign of the BMW parked there. Her heart sank again.

The girls roused themselves, seeming surprised that they had reached home.

***

Annie and Beth were watching a hospital drama on the television in the sitting room. Uninterested in the programme, Carla lay sprawling on the floor, leafing through magazines. Her eye caught the silvery edge of something beneath the low shelf of the coffee table, and she tugged it out.

'Look, Mum. Here's dad's laptop,' she said excitedly.

Too stunned to speak, Kate stared at it.

Carla ran her hand over the smooth surface. 'I thought he took it with him when he left.'

Rising slowly out of her father's leather chair, Annie came alongside. 'Perhaps he took the bag thinking the laptop was in it.'

Carla shook her head from side to side. 'But surely he would have noticed. Laptops are quite heavy.'

Annie pushed a lock of hair behind her right ear. 'He carries so much other stuff in the bag, books, files, cables and things. It would be an easy mistake to make.'

'Dad is sure to come back for it.' Carla said optimistically.

'Can I play with it, Mum?' Beth said trying to snatch it from Carla.

Kate grabbed the child's wrist, holding her firmly. 'No, you may not, and if you so much as touch it you'll be in serious trouble. Do you hear me, Beth?'

'No need to pinch me,' Beth said frowning, rubbing her wrist.

Ignoring the child, Kate turned to Annie. 'What's his password?'

'How should I know?'

Trying to be helpful, Carla said 'It could be Nan's maiden name, or Nanny Elizabeth's, even a favourite pet.'

Kate was standing stiffly, her hands trembling slightly. 'His mother's name was Kilman. My mother was a Davies. I don't know anything about his pets.'

'We could be here all night thinking about it,' Annie said sounding bored. 'And it won't do us any good at all. The thing has been under the table for days, so the battery will be flat. As dad has the computer bag, he'll also have the charger.'

A sense of defeat washed over Kate. 'Perhaps he hasn't got it. Maybe it's in the house.'

'Fat chance,' Annie said pessimistically.

Carla glanced at her mother. 'Auntie Liz's got the same make.'

'Has she? You are a clever old thing, Carla.'

Picking up the phone, Kate tapped in Liz's number. Glancing towards Annie, she said 'Will you pour me a glass of wine?'

'Course I will,' Annie said thinking of the wine she would filch.

Beth waited until her mother had finished on the telephone before sidling up to her.

'Dad once told me that he had a white rat called Roland, who he loved very much. He was only eleven.' She giggled. 'Dad was eleven, not Roland the rat.'

'When did he tell you this?' Kate said feeling a stab of jealousy that Adam had told this personal little history to Beth but not herself.

'It was the day I saw a big fat rat near the canal. I screamed and wet my knickers a little bit. Dad told me about Roland and the funny things he used to do. It made me laugh and I forgot to be scared of the grey rat, because he was a cousin to Roland. That's what dad said anyway.'

Carla wrinkled her nose. 'How old were you when you wet your knickers?'

'About four, but I still do it now if I laugh a lot,' she said without the slightest concern.

'You are disgusting, Beth.'

Annie came in from the kitchen, holding a glass of white wine. 'Who's disgusting?'

Taking the glass from her, Kate smiled. 'Beth was just regaling us with a tale about wet knickers.'

'And rats,' Carla said a trace of disgust in her voice.

Annie wrinkled her nose. 'Yuck.'

'Roland was a nice white rat,' Beth said petulantly.

Kate took a sip of wine. 'Less of rats and knickers, let's all concentrate on the password. So far we have Kilman, Davies, and now Roland.'

'Who's Roland?'

'It's a long story, Annie. I'll tell you later,' Kate said smiling.

Slumping down on the floor, her back resting against the settee, Annie relaxed. 'So now we want the name of dad's university, and school,' she said.

A picture of a young Adam walking across the lawns of the university came to Kate and a wave of longing swept over her. How long would it be before she saw him again? Held him in her arms or felt the strength of his arms around her?

Glancing through the window, she saw a luminous moon rising in the darkening sky. Wherever Adam is he is beneath the same moon, she thought sadly.

'Let me top your glass up, Mum,' Annie said seeing her mother close to tears again.

Kate gave a little sniff and then putting the glass to her mouth she swallowed the last of the wine, handing the empty glass to Annie.

In the kitchen, Annie opened the fridge and took out a bottle of chardonnay, pouring enough in the glass to reach the rim, swigging the first half-inch off the top before refilling it.

Leaning against the work surface, eyes closed and her face contracted with emotion, Annie thought about the look she had just seen in her mother's eyes. It had frightened her. She wondered if her mother was losing it completely. If she did, her life and the girls would be in ruins. They would be shunted from care home to care home. Or foisted upon foster carers and forced to live with kids they didn't know and probably wouldn't like.

Fearful of the future, and dreading facing the present, Annie picked up the glass and swallowed a mouthful of wine.

A car pulled onto the driveway; recognising the tone as Liz's, Annie took another glass out of the cupboard.

There was a light knock on the backdoor. It opened inwards and Liz came into the kitchen. Seeing Annie, she said cheerfully, 'Hi. Who found the laptop?

'Carla did.'

Placing a canvas bag on the table, Liz took out a charger and a bottle of chilled white wine.

'What a bit of luck having the same model laptop as your father,' she said unravelling the wire from around the plug.

'It's hardly surprising, you recommended the model to him,' Annie replied in a monotone.

Liz frowned. 'Fancy you remembering that.'

Annie sniffed. 'I wanted him to buy one with a built in webcam, that's how I remember.'

'Teenagers,' Liz said to herself.

Taking the glass of wine Annie offered, Liz went into the sitting room. 'Hello, you lot,' she said cheerfully.

Morose, wishing to be upstairs in her room instead of messing with the laptop, Annie followed Liz, slumping down in one of the oversized leather chairs.

The charger and laptop were connected. There was an air of anticipation at the table where Liz, Kate and the two girls sat waiting for the screen to come to life.

Feeling excluded Annie was depressed. She wished she could walk out of the house and vanish into the night.

Kate could hardly bear to draw her eyes away from the bright screen; it was a connection to Adam, however tenuous.

'Can I try a password?' Carla said her eyes bright buttons in her pale face.

Liz gave the child a warm smile. 'Of course you can.'

Nibbling her lower lip, Carla typed in Kilman. As it was rejected she tried again with Davies.

Sprawling across the table, Beth poked at the keys. 'The password will be Roland. Bet you.'

'Who is Roland?' Liz asked puzzled.

Carla, glad of any suggestion typed in the rat's name. 'Hey look, it's worked,' she shouted.

'Told you it would,' Beth said smugly.

Carla glanced to her mother. 'There are loads of emails, but none recently.'

'When was the last one?' Kate asked nervously.

Innocently, Carla said 'Dad sent the last one on the day he disappeared. But there are loads in his inbox.'

There was only one message that interested Kate. It read - Meet me at Luigi's at lunchtime. Look forward to discussing arrangements then. Carolyn.

'Carolyn could be an old biddy that Adam worked with, or

someone he's helping with an investment,' Liz said seeing the look of dismay on Kate's face.

'But why take her to Luigi's for lunch?' Kate asked hollowly.

'If that was the only time he could see her, why not?'

Bitterly disappointed that there was no message from her father, Carla closed the computer.

'Oh don't shut it. I want to write him an email, and look through the accounts,' Kate said tearfully.

Annie, distressed, rose out of the chair. 'I'll get you some more wine, Mum.'

Hardly registering that Annie had spoken, Kate tapped nervously at the keyboard.

When Liz had gone, and the girls were in bed, Kate sat staring at the email from Carolyn, trying to read a hidden message there.

Eventually she went to bed, leaving the laptop on the coffee table. There was always a chance that he would come to collect it. If he did, she could talk to him and make everything right again.

Chapter 7

Adam stood framed in the doorway, the landing light behind him. He called her name softly, 'Kate, Kate are you awake?'

She came up off the pillow. The sheet falling away, exposing her naked breasts, pale as ivory in the dim light.

She could hardly speak, then in a hushed whispering voice she said, 'Adam.'

He took three slow steps towards her. 'I can explain everything, Kate.' His voice was low and full of contrition. 'I just want you to trust me. Believe in me Kate and everything will work out.'

She held out her arms, willing him forward. 'Oh, Adam darling, I trust you with my life.'

She sensed rather than saw the slow familiar smile come to his mouth as he took the remaining two steps to the bed.

Then he was in her arms, his warm breath brushing her cheek. Near to crying with relief, she pulled him close.

His hair held the smell of the sea and she was propelled back to Shore Cottage and the night she had stood barefoot on the cold front step, listening to the waves in the darkness. A thought flitted through her mind, that maybe he had never left the vicinity of the cottage, remaining hidden close by.

'I love you,' he whispered into her hair.

'I love you too,' she said her eyes shining with unshed tears. 'I hate being apart from you. Promise me you will never leave again.'

His lips found her, silencing her with his kiss.

In a wonderfully familiar and loving way he traced a path down her neck to the small hollow at her throat with his fingertip. Kissing her there, circling the tiny depression with the tip of his tongue.

She hardly noticed him shedding his clothes until the length of his naked body was touching hers.

As he lifted the bed sheet, the breeze coming in through the open window shimmered against her flesh and she gave a little shiver.

He smiled in the darkness, white teeth glinting in the light from the landing.

She wondered if he really knew how much she loved and desired him. The question remained unasked for his lips found her mouth and he kissed her with an urgency she had never known before. His strong hands were in her hair, holding her head.

Kate cried out as he entered her.

He paused for a heartbeat, looking into her eyes, and then closing his, he moved slowly and rhythmically and both were lost to the world.

Eventually she fell asleep, her head on his chest.

Sunlight flickered through the narrow parting in the curtain, wafting gently in a light breeze. It was quiet but for a song thrush trilling in the eucalyptus tree in the garden.

Stirring languidly, Kate reached out to touch Adam. The bed sheet was cold beneath her hand. Disappointed that he had risen early, she moved onto her back and let the events of the loving night run through her mind.

Intuitively she knew that something was absent. There was no tell-tale aroma of intimate passion, nor tang of the sea she had noticed on Adam's hair.

The truth came to her and she lay like a beautiful corpse, blank-eyed staring at the ceiling. Turning her face into the pillow, she wept bitter tears of grief as her new found happiness turned to ashes. Eventually, exhausted, she climbed out of bed and donning a lightweight housecoat, she went down the stairs.

Opening the sitting room door, she looked to the coffee table. The laptop was gone. Confused and shocked, she remained standing on the threshold, staring at the place where she had left it last night.

The dream, if it was a dream, was so realistic. Had Adam really come back and made love to her? Only to disappear before morning broke, taking the laptop with him.

Erratically she began to search for clues, seeking indentations of his body on the cushions on the settee and armchairs, before throwing them aside carelessly to hunt for any small thing he may have left behind.

With a stab of fear, she wondered if she was losing her mind, if the awful stress of the past days had rendered her incapable of differentiating between fantasy and reality. If she was going mad, or already in that pitiful state, there was no hope. Everything is lost to me, Adam, our way of life, and the children. A picture of an asylum flashed through her mind, the occupants, dispossessed humanity, pacing the long bleak corridors in colourless nondescript gowns.

'If Adam was here, then there is evidence of his visit,' she muttered to herself. Flinging the last cushion to the floor, she stood breathing shallowly and fast. Scanning the room she tried to think as Adam might. What had been here, beside the laptop that he needed so urgently that he had come back for it in the middle of the night? What was missing? Tears of frustration filled her eyes. There was absolutely nothing obvious. Nothing seemed to have been touched or was out of place.

Perhaps he hasn't gone. Maybe he just popped out to the garage or the garden. With this thought, she ran in a state of excitement towards the door to the integral garage.

'His car will be in the garage,' she cried aloud, flinging open the door at the end of the hall.

The elderly Honda looked out of place, a foreigner in the familiar garage space. Kate's heart sank as she looked at the now despised car.

'How could I forget it was here?' She sobbed.

Drawing her housecoat tightly around her, she sat on the garage step, head on her knees, rocking backward and forwards.

Sometime later, Kate had no idea of the time, though she had been sitting on the concrete step long enough to become cold, she heard either Carla or Annie coming down the stairs.

Hearing the kitchen door open and close, Kate came slowly to her feet. Sniffing, her nose was blocked from crying, she dried the salt tears from her face. Slowly, like an old woman, she drew the housecoat around her body. Closing the door to the garage quietly, she went in the direction of the kitchen.

Annie was filling the kettle as Kate came in. Shocked at the state of her mother, she stood open-mouthed for a moment, water slopping over the kettle's spout. It was obvious that she had been crying. She was shivery, as though she had been sobbing for a long time. Her eyes were dark with hollows beneath, the skin there as fragile as bruised petals. The recent weight loss had left her cheekbones prominent. The sunlight, streaming through the kitchen window, made her face colourless. Annie realised that her mother didn't look as though she had the strength to cross the room.

Turning off the tap, Annie stood on tiptoe, stretching over the sink to open the window. A light draught blew in, moving a little roll of fluff lying under the table.

Kate's eyes went to it and she thought about getting the vacuum out later, if she could muster the energy and enthusiasm.

'Why don't you sit down, Mum? I'll make tea,' Annie said softly.

As the kettle came to the boil, Carla and Beth came in. Beth wearing old beige shorts, hand-me-downs, and a white tee-shirt. She had red rather tatty sandals on her feet, the buckles were undone and the straps flapping.

'Do your shoes up, Beth,' Annie said pointing to the straps.

'Don't want to.'

Pulling out a chair from beneath the table, Kate sat down. Staring at her hands folded on the table-top.

Noisily, Beth drew a chair out from beneath the table and scrambled up onto it. 'Can I have an egg, Annie?'

'No, you can't. You'll have marmalade and like it.'

'Oh. I haven't had an egg for ages,' Beth moaned.

'You little tyke, you had one yesterday.'

Beth's small nose wrinkled. 'No I didn't.'

'Well, if it wasn't yesterday, it was the day before,' Annie shouted, losing her temper.

Unfazed, Beth looked beguilingly at her. 'Can I have one now?'

'No, you bloody can't,' Annie snapped.

'For goodness sake stop arguing,' Kate said putting her head in her hands.

Glancing nervously at her mother, Carla asked quietly, 'Can I take the laptop to my room?'

Kate gave a low sigh. 'You can, if you can find it.'

Anxious to start her school project, Carla looked askance. 'What do you mean? Where is it?'

Kate's eyes threatened fresh tears. 'I don't know,' she said on a sob. 'It was on the coffee table when I went to bed. This morning it is not there.'

'So where is it?' Carla looked from Annie to Beth suspiciously. 'Who took it?'

Without taking her eyes from the toast she was buttering, Beth said helpfully, 'Perhaps dad came back to get it. I heard something in the night. It sounded like the front door opening. And I heard a thump, like somebody bumping into something.'

Beth had Kate's full attention.

'Why didn't you wake someone? Or run down and see if it was him?'

Carla was near tears with disappointment.

Smearing marmalade on the toast, Beth said bluntly, 'I was tired. So I turned over and just went back to sleep.'

The other three chorused, 'Beth!'

'What!' Wide-eyed she stared at them. 'I was very tired. I'd been practising on the trampoline for two whole hours, yesterday.'

Afraid that she might actually slap Beth, Kate got up from the table and left the room. Climbing the stairs, hearing the three girls arguing in the kitchen, she went into the bedroom, closing the door on the noise.

Showered and changed, she came back down wearing a sleeveless blue linen dress, the heels of her strapless white sandals click-clacking on the stair-treads.

The sun slanting through the hall window cast rectangles of transparent gold on the beige wall and carpet. It was only in direct sunlight that the wide and rather nondescript hall showed any depth and colour.

Putting her head around the kitchen door, she announced snappishly, 'I'm going out for a walk.'

Beth sitting at the table looked up mutinously. 'You promised you'd take us swimming,' she whined.

Kate sighed irritably. 'I will take you later. Now I just need

95

to get out of the house.'

Annie, bent loading the dishwasher, straightened. 'You and me both,' she said sulkily.

Sighing again, wondering if any of the girls actually knew how much she was suffering, Kate turned away from the hostility in their faces.

A moment later, she banged the front door closed. Standing on the step, her back to the house, she surveyed the cul-de-sac. It was deserted. No one was out cleaning a car or weeding a front garden. For days she had avoided coming outdoors, afraid that a neighbour might ask about Adam's sudden departure.

She was holding a pair of large sunglasses; slipping them on, as she stepped away from the sanctuary of the house. The dark shades were a great screen and she walked across the short driveway a little more confidently. Anxious to get away from the small and rather nosey community, she hurried towards the outskirts of the large village towards the canal.

Once she was away from the houses, she felt no need to hurry and slowing down she strolled the mile and half. The hedgerows were dry, the leaves of the May bushes dusty after the exceptionally hot summer. Straggly pink forget-me-nots speckled the coarse grass in the verges, and tiny blue petals of birds-eye, and vivid yellow dandelions sprouted from the grass.

Coming to the bridge spanning the canal, she slipped off her sunglasses; leaning over the stone parapet she looked down. There were no boats to disturb the green coolness of the water. Only a dragonfly, its iridescent body caught by sunlight, dipped to the water creating a tiny circular ripple on the smooth surface. Even the birds were silent, somnolent in the midmorning heat.

Shaded by a towering beech tree, the burning heat of the sun filtered through its dense leaves, she thought she could stay here for ever, soaking up the peace, a perfect balm for her tormented mind.

It came as something of a shock to realise that she hadn't actually thought about Adam since leaving the cul-de-sac. Images of the children came to her. But she couldn't bear to dwell on the girls. The situation was getting too difficult to cope with. Annie was constantly complaining, sulkily. Carla had become uncommunicative and was spending too much time in her room alone. And Beth was running out of control.

Sighing, Kate turned her eyes from the water and began to walk down the slope that would take her onto the towpath.

Beneath the tall hedgerow, arching over the path, the air was greenly cool. The hedge cast long dark shadows, changing the water to a flat olive-green. In reeds, on the opposite bank, a lone moorhen drifted, its shiny blackness like an exquisite toy caught in a slanting ray of sunlight.

Taking interest in every little detail, the bird, splash of a fish, ripples on the water, the iridescence of an insect, Kate did her utmost to recapture the tranquillity of moments ago but images of Adam intruded. She felt no bitterness or anger, only great sorrow, an overwhelming sense of loss and loneliness She stood for a while watching the water, her luminous grave eyes filled with unshed tears.

Questions came unbidden and she found herself once again going over old ground. 'Why didn't he tell me he needed to go away? How could he disappear without saying a word?'

She imagined catching a plane, landing in some foreign hot place, Adam waiting for her in a small out-of-the-way makeshift aerodrome.

She found herself crying quietly. 'But I *could* leave.' It was the first time the idea had occurred to her and with it came a fleeting sense of euphoria. Running away from the mortgage, everyday bills and the embezzlement hanging over her like a sharp samurai sabre, was an option.

A pigeon flew out of a nearby tree, its sudden flight like a mini thunder clap in the dry leaves. Shielding her eyes with her hand, she watched it swoop over the trees.

I'm being totally irrational, she thought, her spirits sinking. I cannot leave. The children must be taken care of. And I must wait for Adam.

She pictured his tanned handsome face, framed by fine blond hair, and eyes as blue as the sky with a smile in them for her. 'Did you come back last night?' she whispered. 'Did I dream and yearn for you because subconsciously I heard your footsteps in the house?'

In her mind she went through the few personal possessions he had left behind in his rush to be away and wondered if there may be something else that he would return for. When she got home she would search the attic and every nook and cranny of the garage and the house. In her heart she knew that Adam would not have returned and left again without everything he came for.

A slow moving narrow boat came into view. The partly submerged hull as black as tar, the cabin painted bright scarlet with whorls of green and gold decoration. There were several adults aboard; she could hear their voices quite plainly, carrying on the water.

The intrusion broke her pensive mood. Slipping on her sunglasses, she moved on.

As the boat passed, she gave a perfunctory smile, and then averted her eyes from the approving looks of three men sitting near the tiller.

The hedge and trees petered out and Kate emerged into full

sunlight, midday the heat was at its peak, the sky too bright to look up to.

The Cut Above, Liz's bistro, lay a hundred yards ahead. Picking up her step, dust and grit creeping into her sandals, Kate walked towards it with thoughts of a long cold lager in her mind.

Liz, looking bright and cheerful in a red dress with white spots, was in the garden serving red wine to two elderly women, as Kate came through the little picket gate.

The garden was a cool haven, shaded by the branches of a tall ash. The fragrance of roses and scented stocks growing in the flowerbeds lay heavily on the air.

The appetizing aroma of toasting cheese and baking cannelloni, wafting from the kitchen at the back of the old lock cottage, stirred Kate's appetite.

Liz broke away from the table. Still holding the bottle of Beaujolais she walked towards Kate, still standing near the gate.

'What a lovely surprise,' she said beaming. 'You couldn't have timed it better. I have almost finished here. Amanda will take over in a minute or two.'

Her smile widening and she went on 'I have some news that I think will interest you.'

'Am I in the way?' Kate asked quietly.

'No of course not, it's lovely to see you. Go and sit at the table beneath the eucalyptus tree; not only does the tree smell heavenly but it keeps insects away.'

Smiling again, she asked, 'Would you like a glass of wine?'

'I'd prefer a lager, Liz. I'm really thirsty.'

'Lager, it is then.'

Kate didn't dare to think in any detail that she was here at *The Cut Above* without Adam for the first time. Her hands folding and unfolding in her lap, creasing the linen skirt of her dress, she waited for Liz to return.

Carrying a metal tray, Liz came out of the bistro door. Glancing at Kate, she cursed Adam Fontaine for the thousandth time in a fortnight. Kate's heart was broken, as was her spirit.

Liz slumped onto a chair beside Kate. Folding the corners of her white apron across her lap, she lifted a glass of lager off the tray and passed it to Kate. Taking the second glass she lifted it to her lips. 'I need this,' she said taking a sip of the ice cold drink.

'You deserve it, working on such a hot day,' Kate said.

Liz made a grimace. 'The winters are long and cold. There are hardly any customers other than the occasional boat passing through.'

Remembering her news Liz came forward in her seat. 'Mrs Tennyson brought a friend for lunch.'

'Do I know Mrs Tennyson?' Kate asked frowning.

'You probably don't. But she knows Mr and Mrs Tony Everett. Tony Everett has been fired from the bank.'

'He's been fired! Why?' Kate said her mouth opening in surprise.

'I don't know. Mrs Tennyson said she'd only heard it last night and doesn't have the details. It's very interesting though, isn't it?'

Kate pictured Tony Everett sitting on the settee in her living room, completely unsympathetic to her predicament. Pompously insisting that her home must be sold and the money used to reimburse the bank. The news that he had been fired gave her a malicious kind of glee.

'Liz, if the bank has discovered that he was behind the embezzlement, it'll be very interesting indeed.'

Picking up the glass of cold lager, Liz took a sip.

Kate was clutching her glass, turning it slowly, leaving wet rings of condensation on the table top. 'Maybe they already know Adam isn't guilty.'

'Maybe,' Liz said without much conviction.

Kate was too excited to take notice of Liz's cynicism. Sitting on the edge of her seat, her face brightly intelligent for the first time in a fortnight, she said eagerly, 'Do you think I should go to the bank and see the chief executive? Ask him about it?'

Liz was sorry she'd mentioned Mrs Tennyson. Inadvertently she had raised Kate's hopes. But perhaps by going to the bank, Kate would come to realise that Adam was as guilty as hell.

Kate was looking up at the sky. There was joy in her face. 'This may be the end of the nightmare,' she said confidently.

Liz refrained from answering.

Chapter 8

Arriving at Brand's Commercial Bank fifteen minutes before her appointment with Richard Lloyd, Kate was shown into his secretary's office. With butterflies circling beneath her ribcage, she waited nervously for Mr Lloyd to appear, her eyes constantly going to the clock on the wall. Thirty minutes passed with no sign of Mr Lloyd taking possession of his inner sanctum. Expecting him to appear at any moment, Kate's fluttering stomach jumped at the slightest sound coming from the outer corridor.

Earlier, arriving at the new and impressive building on the town wharf, it took every ounce of her willpower to mount the steps at the granite portico and enter the vast foyer. Hostile and inquisitive eyes watched her every step as she crossed to the reception desk, her heels clicking loudly on the polished black marble floor.

Approaching the immaculately dressed female receptionist, Kate tried to smile but her jaw was so stiff her expression looked wooden.

Please God, she prayed silently, let Adam be cleared of the charge of embezzlement today. Let this nightmare be behind us.

There was a trembling in her knees as she stood at the sweeping desk.

Totally ignoring Kate, the receptionist with forced nonchalance moved a vase of white lilies several centimetres. Satisfied the flowers were in exactly the right place, she gave Kate an insipid smile.

On hearing Kate's surname, the girl lifted her eyebrows sanctimoniously.

For a dreadful moment, Kate was unable to remember the name of the chief executive she had come to see and she was forced to ask for him by title. Saying rather foolishly, 'I wish to see the chief director.'

The superior smile remained on the girl's mouth as she corrected Kate. 'Do you have an appointment to see the Chief Executive, Mrs Fontaine?'

'Yes of course,' Kate managed to say without stammering nervously.

Picking up a grey telephone, her eyes penetrating Kate's, the girl asked for a security man to be sent to escort Mrs Fontaine to the top floor. Giving a small yawn, she glanced from Kate to the clock on the wall.

Being escorted by a security guard was embarrassing. It was not so long ago, only weeks, that she had walked from the reception area to the top floor to see Adam. No doubt she was now seen as a security risk. She wondered if the order had come from above or the girl had taken the decision upon herself.

With nowhere to wait but at the desk and having no wish to watch the receptionist tinkering with a pens and pencils in a stainless steel tub, Kate turned her eyes to the dozen lilies and the surrounding emerald leaves.

Several minutes later, collected like an unwelcome package, Kate was shown up to the top floor by a uniformed man, who said not a word to her.

Now, looking across at Mr Lloyd's secretary, typing professionally at the computer keyboard, she wondered if she dared go to the loo and get back before Richard Lloyd appeared. Glancing at the clock again, she saw the black minute finger on the white dial had hardly moved.

A hot dusty breeze laden with traffic fumes wafted in

through the open window. There was a sense of impatient rush on the street, in contrast to the chill and condescending atmosphere of the secretary's office. Kate's eyes alighted on the white orchid on top of a filing cabinet. She wondered if the plant was purchased out of petty cash or if it was a gift. If the latter, it was a perfect choice for the austere and rather prim Miss Robinson.

The outer door opened quickly. On tenterhooks, Kate jumped giving a little mew of surprise.

Richard Lloyd came in. Dressed impeccably in a dark grey suit, white shirt and light grey silk tie he looked every inch the successful city banker. In his late forties, his dark hair was peppered with grey. A love of sailing, he had a forty-foot yacht moored on the Hamble, kept him slim and tanned. An Englishman, educated at Rugby and Oxford, he was self-confident, assertive and direct. It appeared that the stresses of running a business as large as Brand's rarely marred his sleep.

Kate had met him previously at the staff Christmas dinner dance, but she had forgotten what a handsome man he was until this moment. On that occasion Adam had steered her away from his boss at the first opportunity. Kate now wondered if Adam had done this deliberately. Perhaps he thought Richard Lloyd too good looking and too powerful, a potent aphrodisiac to most women, to allow her to get acquainted. Did Adam really think that she would be tempted by this man? For just a moment she forgot her nervousness and gave a small smile.

'I'm sorry to have kept you waiting, Mrs Fontaine,' he said politely.

Kate came to her feet, clutching her red handbag close to the centre of her grey skirt. Tongue-tied, she mumbled 'Your secretary has taken good care of me.'

The secretary, who had almost ignored Kate's presence completely, smiled graciously.

The expensively and beautifully furnished room that was Richard Lloyd's office didn't faze Kate. The furnishing and decoration in Adam's office were sumptuous, bordering on extravagant. It was no surprise that the chief executive would go one better.

Taking the seat behind his desk, he gestured to the chair opposite.

Keeping her knees primly together, Kate sat, and placed the red handbag by the side of the chair.

Slipping on a pair of glasses, Richard Lloyd looked seriously at Kate. For a moment he was silent, which Kate found intimidating.

Slowly, as though talking to a delinquent child, he said 'What can I do for you, Mrs Fontaine?'

Momentarily tongue-tied, Kate hunted for the right words to express herself. 'I want to ask you about Mr Everett,' she said nervously.

His dark silky eyebrows rose slightly. 'Mr Everett has left the company.'

'I want to know if he has gone because he had something to do with the embezzlement that you believe Adam is involved in.'

Sounding slightly irritated, he said 'Mr Everett left the bank because he failed to keep a check on the accounts. If he had done his job efficiently, he would have detected something was wrong earlier. He could have stopped Adam.'

Tears filled Kate's eyes. 'Oh, surely you don't still believe Adam is guilty?'

Showing no sympathy, he said calmly, 'There is no doubt in my mind that Adam took more than three hundred thousand-pounds. I have the evidence.'

A rushing noise, like the torrent of a stream cascading down a mountainside, filled Kate's ears. As she spoke her own voice sounded strange, far-away and muffled. 'Surely, it's all a terrible mistake. I can't believe that Adam would do such a thing.'

His well-shaped mouth tightened in annoyance. 'There is no doubt in my mind whatsoever. Adam has seriously let down the bank.'

'But can you be sure?' she said her heart beating erratically.

Leaning forward, elbows on the desk, he steepled his fingers. 'Mrs Fontaine, I am not in the habit of falsely accusing someone of theft. Adam took that money. Mr Everett's only involvement in this debacle is that he failed to keep track of the accounts as he should have done.'

Kate said forlornly, 'And the police are involved?'

'Yes, Mrs Fontaine. The police are involved. If we ignored the theft, there would be no chance of getting our money back.'

Sighing, he leaned back in his chair. 'We are in the process of taking advice from our solicitors. If we can force the sale of your property we will do so.'

Kate's down-turned head jerked up. With a flash of fire, she said 'I own half of the house. It's the children's home. The bank surely has no right to sell what is legally mine.'

He gave the impression of being polite and in control, not the least perturbed by her burst of temper. 'As I say, we are taking advice.' He stood, signifying the end of the meeting.

As she rose from the chair, Kate eyed him defiantly. 'I wonder how your shareholders will view the eviction of three children from their home.'

'Our shareholders look to us to make a profit for them. I would be surprised if they didn't agree with the board; the stolen money must be refunded.'

Hot tears of outrage came to her eyes. Picking up her handbag, she went to the door and out into the secretary's domain.

The secretary, busy typing, didn't acknowledge her. Kate wondered if she had heard the entire conversation on the office intercom.

Out in the sanctuary of the corridor, she resisted the urge to sit in an upholstered chair to regain her strength. Instead she made for the elevator, the doors were open. Quickly she crossed the slate-grey carpet, the tips of her high heels tugging at the thick pile, and stepped in. With trembling fingers she pressed the red button to descend. Reaching the ground floor, the doors slid open onto the palatial foyer.

There was no avoiding crossing the expanse. The massive double doors leading to the outside portico seemed acres away, as she click-clacked across the floor.

With only a few yards to go, hurrying footsteps came up behind her. She didn't dare look round. Confrontation with a member of staff was unthinkable. As was the possibility that some person she had known in the past may show her sympathy, the way she was feeling right now she was likely to break down and make a complete idiot of herself.

Outside the air was heavy with traffic fumes. Although it was still early, the heat of the morning trapped in the brickwork and pavement, leached into the polluted air.

Quickly she walked to the car park. Her father's old blue car was conspicuous parked with flashy new Mercedes, BMWs, Jaguars and Porches. Rifling through her handbag she found the car keys. Opening the door, sliding in, throwing her bag in the well of the passenger seat, she turned the key in the ignition. It took two attempts before the tired engine coughed into life.

Inching the car forward, careful of the new paintwork of a silver Mercedes, she pulled out of the parking bay. Driving slowly she passed the area reserved for the directors of the bank. The name plate on Adam's slot had been removed.

The first parking bay held a new Bentley, the black bodywork like polished Whitby jet. Glancing at the registration plate she read RL 2. So there was no need to guess who the car belonged to. A devil on her shoulder urged her to give the Bentley a sideswipe with the old Honda. She imagined a cruel dent in the pristine paintwork. Fortunately vandalism wasn't part of her make-up. Putting her foot gently on the accelerator, she passed the limousine.

Out of the car park she made for home. The old car, misfiring occasionally, threatened to stall at every red traffic light.

At the beginning of the journey, Richard Lloyd's words went around in her head. But at the first red traffic light she concentrated all her efforts on keeping the engine running.

Turning into the driveway, the automatic garage doors lifting as she approached, she drove straight in. The doors came down as she killed the engine.

Beth dashed into the garage. 'Mum. Mum. Carla fell off the trampoline. Mrs Bell has taken her to hospital. Blood was pouring out of her head,' she said in a panicky rush.

Climbing out of the car, Kate took hold of Beth. 'Calm down and tell me what has happened, slowly.'

Beth took a noisy breath. 'Carla fell off the trampoline.'

'Yes, you said that. How long ago was it?'

'Oh it was hours ago. There was blood all over the path.'

It flashed through Kate's mind that the safety net couldn't have been attached, 'Where's Annie?'

'Don't know. She went out just after you. I think she's gone to Millie's house.'

'You're here all on your own?' Kate said irately.

'Yes. I have been for a long time. I was a bit frightened,' Beth said not losing an opportunity to get Annie into trouble.

'Get into the car, Beth. We must find Carla.' As she spoke Kate pressed the button on the remote control to lift the garage doors.

Driving too quickly, almost running a red light, she couldn't afford for the car to stall now; Kate drove into the accident and emergency parking bay, risking a fine, or worse, being clamped.

Hurrying Beth out of the back of the car, they dashed to the emergency unit.

Carla and Mrs Bell were walking along the corridor towards the exit. 'Mrs Fontaine,' Mrs Bell said looking slightly guilty. 'Don't worry it is only a small cut.'

Hugging Carla close, Kate said 'Are you all right, my darling girl?'

Carla promptly burst into tears.

Tears welled in Beth's eyes.

Drawing both of them towards a seating area, Kate gently sat Carla down.

'I want to go home, Mum,' Carla cried.

Handing her a tissue from her jacket pocket, Kate was sympathetic. 'We'll go the minute I know that you are all right.'

'I am, honestly, Mum.'

Frowning, wondering if she should check with a member of the medical staff, Kate stood indecisively.

'I really am okay,' Carla whined plaintively. 'Can we go now? I hate it in here.'

Following Mrs Bell out of the hospital building, Kate wondered how much the woman knew of the family's predicament. The old Honda would give a clue to the change in their circumstances.

'The doctor suggested she comes back if she feels the slightest bit woozy or sick,' Mrs Bell cautioned Kate.

'Are you really feeling okay, Carla?' Kate asked unlocking the car door.

She gave a weak smile. 'Yes, Mum. I have a headache but it's better than it was. The nurse gave me a painkiller.'

Mrs Bell stood beside the old car, gazing at the suspicious bubbling beneath the paint on the bottom of the passenger door.

Tight-lipped, Kate unlocked the car and ushered the girls in.

Back at the house, Mrs Bell parked behind them on the driveway. Getting out of her car, a smart new model, she came alongside Kate. 'Will you let me know how she is? I'll worry myself sick thinking about the poor mite.'

Kate replied snappishly, 'Yes, of course I will. In fact I'll call around later. You can tell me exactly how the accident happened. How Carla managed to fall onto a concrete path.'

Kate's mood wasn't lost on Mrs Bell. Answering in a similar vein, she said 'I will be in all evening, Mrs Fontaine. My husband will be at home too.'

Wondering if Mrs Bell had put a deliberate emphasis on husband, Kate scooped the two girls forward, leading them into the house.

Putting Carla onto the settee to rest, Kate went to the kitchen to make a snack. Preparing a salad, she questioned Beth. 'What time did Annie leave the house?'

Beth, not averse to landing her sister in trouble, said in a babyish voice 'We all went out at the same time. Annie made us go and play at Samantha Bell's house. Carla and me didn't want to, but she said we must or else.'

'Or else what?'

'Dunno. A slap, I suppose.'

Kate's eyes sparked. 'Has Annie slapped you before?'

Aware she may have gone a bit too far, Beth backtracked. 'I can't remember if she actually hit me.'

As Beth was obviously bending the truth, Kate changed the subject. 'Wasn't there a safety net on the trampoline?'

Beth nibbled her bottom lip. 'The big boys, Samantha's brothers, took it down. They said it was babyish.'

Kate stopped slicing the tomatoes. 'Carla could have been killed. I'll have a word with Mr and Mrs Bell. We'll see who still thinks safety nets are babyish when I've finished with those lads.'

Jumping off the chair, Beth grabbed Kate's sleeve. 'Please don't say anything to them, Mum.'

'Why?' Kate asked astonished.

'Cos there bigger than us.'

Stooping to the child, Kate looked into her eyes. 'Are you saying that they are bullies? Are you afraid of them?'

'Yes, a bit. But only because they're so much bigger than me.'

'If they bully you or Carla, you must tell me at once. I can stop them being nasty. But only if you tell me.'

Beth's lower lip trembled. 'You're not going to say anything to them? Are you, Mum?'

Kate hugged her close. 'I will be very careful what I say. You mustn't be afraid.'

Annie strolled into the house at five o'clock. Throwing her bag down onto the kitchen table, she went to the fridge for a cold coke.

111

Hearing her, Kate came into the kitchen. 'And where have you've been to?' she said icily.

'I'm allowed out, you know,' Annie said petulantly.

'You're allowed out, when I say so. Because of your selfishness today, Carla ended up at the hospital.'

'What happened?'

Kate ignored the question. 'You promised me you would take care of the kids whilst I went into town.'

Slightly drunk on vodka, Annie shouted, 'Oh, so it's alright for you to go out enjoying yourself, but not me.'

Images of the meeting with Richard Lloyd flashed into Kate's mind.

'Oh so you think going to meet the chief executive at Brand's is having fun do you?'

Kate's voice rose hysterically. 'I went there to get at the truth, to find out why Tony Everett has been fired. And how much Everett is involved in the missing money and your father's disappearance.'

Annie's face fell.

Kate shouted, 'Aren't you even going to ask how Carla is? Are you now so selfish that your younger sisters are of no concern to you?'

Matching Kate's temper, Annie shouted back, 'No of course not. But you expect me to do everything around her. I've practically cooked every meal, cleaned up and looked after the kids. Whilst all you have done is sit in a dark corner and cry. Well, it's not good enough. You should pull your weight too.'

Enraged, Kate slapped Annie's cheek.

Annie's hand flew to the mark, instantly turning bright red. Dashing out of the room, she thumped upstairs.

Mentally exhausted, Kate slumped down on a kitchen chair. The palm of her hand stung, she rubbed it gently on her skirt.

Venting her anger hadn't helped; she was still taut with resentment for Richard Lloyd, Mrs Bell and her stupid boys, and Adam.

It didn't occur to her that this was the first time since his desertion that she had admitted to herself that she was angry with Adam.

A light tap sounded on the back door. It opened and Liz stepped in.

'I popped round to see how you got on at Brand's.'

'Not very well,' Kate sighed.

Pulling off her white jacket, Liz hung it on the back of a chair. Sitting down, elbows on the table, she said 'What's wrong?'

'Oh everything is. Richard Lloyd still believes Adam took the money. Carla fell off the Bell's trampoline and cut her head open. Mrs Bell took her to A and E.'

'Oh no, is she alright?'

Kate sighed. 'Yes. The poor kid has got a bump the size of a plum and it'll be the same colour tomorrow, and a cut which isn't too bad. But we have to keep an eye on her in case she's a bit concussed.'

Liz was truly concerned as Carla was her favourite of the three girls. 'Poor old Carla,' she said making a mental note to bring her a present tomorrow.

'That's not the half of it,' Kate went on crossly. 'I purposely told Annie to mind the kids, whilst I went into town. What does she do? She goes wandering off the moment my back is turned. Poor little Beth was here on her own. What Mrs Bell was thinking of leaving a child so young alone in the house, people can be so thoughtless.'

'Oh dear,' Liz said.

'To cap it all, Annie rolls in just after five. I'm not sure she

113

isn't half-cut. She starts to berate me for not looking after the kids. God, she can be a vicious little bugger at times. Anyway I slapped her.'

Liz eyebrows rose. 'Did you feel better for it?'

'No, I'm just as angry as I was when I left Brand's bank earlier. It all got on top of me, Liz. Perhaps tomorrow I'll feel differently about slapping her face. But this evening I'm still fired up with anger.'

In her room, Annie took a bottle of vodka from beneath old clothes stacked at the bottom of her wardrobe and poured a measure into a glass of coke. Taking a mouthful, she let it linger on her tongue to get the full taste of the spirit.

The anger she was feeling for her mother was so potent it made her breathless. Why did it have to be her mother who was so flaky? Neurotic Katie Fontaine, always thinking of herself. She deserved to be alone.

Hearing the back door open, her bedroom window was above it, she guessed that Liz had arrived. Imagining them sitting together, drinking wine, she took a slurp out of her own glass. She was thirsty; the vodka she drank during the day had given her a slight hangover. Her head felt thick and heavy, her tongue furry. She thought another drink might help. She lifted the glass again.

Chapter 9

A terse letter from Brand's bank demanding the house be put on the market and a buyer found, galvanised Kate into action. Telephoning the local firm of solicitors who had dealt with the house purchase, she made an appointment for the following day.

Doulton and Marsh were housed in an old Victorian redbrick building in the town centre. A relic lodged between Marks and Spencer and a new restaurant built from little more than chrome and glass.

Parking the old Honda in the municipal car park, she rooted in her bag for change for the Pay and Display, checking that the letter from Brand's was still safe. Organised, the parking ticket on the windscreen, she checked her watch. She still had fifteen minutes, so there was no need to rush, but glancing at the sky, it looked like rain, she hurried towards the exit.

A light wind was blowing down the street. Two abandoned polystyrene chip boxes drifted passed her shoes. At the corner they caught in the eddy of the breeze and tumbled end over end before scooting away on the next gust.

Because of its incongruous situation, Doulton and Marsh were easy to locate. Five minutes after leaving the car, Kate stepped into the open porch. The inner door was propped open, held back by an antiquated six inch brass lion. It passed through her mind that the first occupant of the building had probably bought it for just that purpose.

Walking into the office, doubling as a reception area, Kate had the distinct thought that she was taking the first step that would ultimately lead to her and Adam's divorce.

A secretary sat at an oak, partners-desk. Behind her there

was a blocked off black marble fireplace, the mantelshelf a depository for all kinds of articles, files, a half-dead potted ivy, an old clock, and a brass letter holder brimming with torn open envelopes. The furniture, two large glass fronted bookcases lining the walls were from a previous century, filled with legal books bound in maroon leather. The desks, immensely large, were cluttered with files bound in pink ribbon.

A woman in her late forties, wearing a short sleeved navy blue dress with tiny white spots, was sitting behind one of the desks, a computer screen to her left. Her bobbed hair, the colour of a new penny, was held back from her face by two tortoiseshell combs. Slipping off her rimless spectacles, she smiled at Kate as she approached the high wooden reception counter.

'I have a nine-thirty appointment with Mr Doulton,' Kate said trying to sound confident and failing.

Checking the appointment book, the woman said 'Mrs Fontaine. Mr Doulton is expecting you. Please take a seat for a moment.'

Several old, cracked leather chairs were against the wall. Sitting on the centre one, Kate untied the belt on her jacket, and then was tempted to retie it on seeing a deep crease in her cream silk blouse. But afraid to be caught fidgeting by the efficient looking secretary, she left it open and tried to keep her hands still.

The front window was at her back; most people passing seemed to be in a hurry and just kept walking by, but a few looked in and Kate felt exposed, vulnerable to their curiosity.

Picking up the internal phone, her eyes going to Kate, the secretary spoke quietly. Replacing the receiver, she was apologetic. 'Mr Doulton asked if you'd mind waiting for a few minutes.'

Kate sensed a man passing the window, caught the shadow through the tail of her eye. She wondered if she would appear foolish if she changed seats with only a few minutes to wait.

Without looking at Kate, her eyes on the appointment book lying open on the desk, she said 'Can I get you a coffee?'

'No thanks. I had one a few minutes ago,' Kate lied, afraid she'd be caught with it unfinished and not know what to do with the cup when called into the solicitor's office.

Harry Doulton stood, looming over his desk, as Kate was shown in.

She had forgotten how extremely tall he was. Rather like an overgrown schoolboy with his unruly brown hair flopping onto his forehead and hazel eyes hinting of mischief.

'Thank you for seeing me at such short notice,' she said politely.

'Take a seat, Mrs Fontaine,' he said gesturing to the dark blue upholstered chair placed opposite his own.

The sun shone through a chink in the clouds; the beam lit up the room, reflecting in the glass doors and polished mahogany of the old bookcase, drawing Kate's attention to the hundreds of books within, each a different colour. The light died and the room became nondescript again, the glass doors almost black.

Kate opened her handbag and withdrew the letter from the bank. Reaching across the desk she handed it to him. His lips moved as he read and the frown on his otherwise smooth brow, deepened.

'This is nothing to do with repossession because the mortgage is in arrears?' he said puzzled.

She saw the necessity of explaining everything clearly, but it was embarrassing to admit that a charge of embezzlement was directed at her husband. She truly didn't believe Adam was a thief, but Mr Doulton probably would see it differently, as Liz

117

did. She felt the colour rise in her face and could do nothing to stop the bright pink blush.

'Mrs Fontaine,' he said kindly, his brown eyes searching hers. 'Just start at the beginning.' The letter was still in his hand, held between thumb and forefinger; he waved it gently. 'How did this come about?'

Unable to meet his candid eyes, she looked at the littered desktop. 'We were on holiday…'

'We?' he said with a slight lift of his eyebrows.

Glancing up, Kate replied 'My husband Adam, me, and our three children were on holiday. Because of a problem at the office, Adam drove back home. My eldest daughter travelled with him, so I know he arrived, but then he just vanished.'

He frowned so deeply his dark eyebrows came together. 'And the police, what do they have to say?'

'Initially they were very helpful. But when they discovered…' She could hardly bear to go on.

Unfazed by tears, he had dealt with too many people steeped in grief and anger over the years. 'Just take your time, Mrs Fontaine.'

Taking a tissue from her pocket, Kate dabbed her tears. 'His employers are accusing Adam of embezzlement. I don't believe that Adam stole the money.'

He spoke so softly his voice was barely audible, 'The bank expect you to give them the money back?'

'Yes,' she said forlornly.

He tapped the letter with his left forefinger. 'This is a try on,' he said cynically. 'They expect you to run scared and put the house on the market.'

'They have succeeded in scaring me, Mr Doulton.'

'That's hardly surprising,' he said. 'I will reply to them today. Just put it out of your mind. I would be surprised if they

118

wrote to you again, but if they do, just get in touch with me and I will deal with them.'

It seemed too good to be true and Kate said uncertainly, 'So they can't touch the house?'

'They cannot.'

Although Harry Doulton explained the legalities, Kate hardly took in his words. Her entire thought was directed at the house and the burning question of how she was to keep it.

The meeting with Mr Doulton inspired her to begin to make decisions. Before she left town, she called at the Citizens Advice office on the high street. Armed with information she walked from there to the Social Service building near the new precinct.

Arriving home, more relaxed than she had been since Adam's disappearance, she felt more able to confront problems.

Beth came running to the door as Kate came into the house.

'Mum. Annie broke my tennis racket.'

'No I didn't, you little pig,' Annie shouted in retaliation.

'Yes you did.'

'I did not. You left it at the top of the stairs and I fell over it.'

Kate felt her good mood evaporate. 'Girls, will you please stop arguing!'

Beth folding her small arms defiantly, glared at Annie.

'Where's Carla?' Kate asked trying to sound cheerful, to recapture her mood of a moment ago.

Sulkily, Annie crossed from the fridge to the draining board. 'She's in her room, as usual.'

Placing her hand on Beth's bony shoulder, Kate pushed the child gently in the direction of the door. 'Go up and get her. Tell her I have something to say to you all.'

Beth's grubby face lit. 'Is daddy coming home?'

Kate's mood dipped. 'No, I'm afraid not,' she said sadly.

'Perhaps he'll be home soon,' Beth shouted cheerfully, dashing through the kitchen door.

Running up the stairs, she called 'Carla, Mum wants you.'

There was a muttered reply and the closing of a door. The two girls came down together, noisily bickering.

Sulkily, Carla slumped onto a chair. Elbows on the table, chin in hand, she waited uninterestedly for Kate to tell the news that Beth seemed to think so important.

Kate stood with her back against the work surface. A small smile on her mouth enjoying the moment, she expected the girls to be thrilled with her news. Her optimism dissolving as they fell short of her expectations. 'The bank can't take our house,' she said for a second time, hoping to conjure up some enthusiasm.

Annie, fiddling with her nails, muttered 'I don't expect we'll be able to stay anyway. We can't afford it.'

Blaming Annie for ruining the moment, Kate said a little childishly 'You could be wrong. I intend to get a job and with help from social services we might be staying put.'

Carla, a bruise the size of a tablespoon on her forehead, was close to tears. 'We have to stay, Mum. If dad came back and found us gone he would be sad. He would not know where to look for us.'

Squeezing her shoulder gently, Kate said 'You're a good girl, Carla.'

Wrinkling her nose in disgust, Annie muttered, 'Goody, goody two shoes.'

Irritated, Kate snapped 'You can stop that at once, Annie. You are still not in my good books, in fact far from it. So behave, before I get really cross.'

Short-tempered, Annie shouted 'Oh and what you going to

do about it, slap me again?'

Curbing her tongue, Kate glared.

'Don't spoil everything again.' Carla's eyes filled with tears.

The anguish in her sister's voice pulled Annie up. Feeling guilty, she began to unload the dishwasher.

The phone rang, Beth picked it up. 'It's Auntie Helen,' she said grinning.

Dreading the conversation with her sister, Kate took the phone from her. With forced brightness, she said 'Helen, how are you?'

Dying to hear the news, Helen barely gave Kate time to finish, 'I'm fine, but what about you? Mum tells me that your Adam has done a bunk.'

Stung, Kate thought, how like Helen to wallow in my misfortune. What sort of sister is she to be pleased to see my life in turmoil?

'Are you still there?' Helen said fractiously, disappointed at Kate's calm reaction.

With a slight wobble in her voice, Kate replied 'Yes. Course I am.'

'Is it true, then?' Helen said beginning to believe her mother had got the wrong end of the stick or Adam had returned to the fold.

'Adam is away from home,' Kate said falsely serene.

Kate's composure rattled Helen and her voice rose, 'Mum said he'd disappeared off the face of the earth. Has he taken off with another woman?'

Annoyed that the pair had gossiped, Kate snapped 'Mum shouldn't have said anything.'

Angered that Kate thought she should be excluded from the family drama, Helen was brusque 'Why shouldn't my own mother tell me what's going on in my sister's life? My only sister, I might add.'

'Because I don't like being gossiped about,' Kate replied sharply.

'Why is it, when I say something it's gossip, but when you say anything it's taking an interest?

'Oh let's not fight, Helen. I haven't the energy.'

Glad she had got to the truth at last, Helen was triumphant. 'Oh, so it is true then. Who's he gone off with?'

Kate sighed. 'He hasn't gone off with anyone.'

She was thankful that she hadn't said anything about the embezzlement to her mother; what Helen would have to say about that wasn't hard to imagine.

Since childhood Helen had been jealous, with rarely a good thought or word concerning Kate, the younger by three years. Helen's position was eroded with the arrival of a new baby. Kate had done better at school, gone on to college, and then eventually married Adam.

Whilst Helen married Jack Dillon, a lay-about who had hardly done an honest day's work in his life. The family, five children, three boys and two girls, lived in a rundown council house on a crumbling estate on the edge of town, five miles away from Kate's and Helen's parents. Jack's mother often lodged with the family, she was a woman as feckless as her son, and equally moronic. This conversation was payback for Kate's apparent success in life.

'Adam always has his eye on other women,' Helen said spitefully.

Kate remained silent. A picture of Jack Dillon came into her mind and she thought that Helen need not worry on that score. No one with a brain was going to run off with Jack.

Getting no response from Kate, Helen launched into the reason for the telephone call.

'Jack, me and the kids are coming over to see you on Saturday. We're coming to cheer you up. We can have a proper natter. You can tell me everything,' she added cheerfully.

'Oh, we're out on Saturday,' Kate lied. 'I've promised the girls a trip to... '

With a touch of malice, Helen broke into Kate explanation. 'Mum said Dad has given you their car. I do think it's a bit ripe of you to take it off the poor old buggers.'

Kate sighed. 'He offered it.'

'Well he would. You're his favourite child, the bright eyed girl that married so well. But all the same I think you should have said no to it.'

'Mum didn't mind. In fact it was partly her idea.'

'Well, all the same, the old Honda is a terrible come-down for you after the swanky BMW.'

With her teeth clenched, Kate remained silent.

'If we can't come Saturday, we'll come Sunday instead,' Helen said cheerfully.

Kate's heart sank.

'See you at about two or thereabouts. If you want a natter you know my number,' she said, her mission accomplished.

The three girls were no more enthusiastic than Kate, when told of the visit from their cousins.

Annie wrinkling her nose said 'I hope they don't want to stay for a meal. The kids are disgusting, like pigs in a trough. Uncle Jack's not much better.'

Kate didn't bother to chastise her.

Saturday she drove the girls into town and they spent a couple of hours rifling through the clothes in Next and Topshop. To compensate them for not being able to buy anything new, she took them to MacDonald's for an early supper. It was in the back of Kate's mind that Helen would disapprove of the extravagance of eating out.

Chapter 10

The girls were out; Carla and Beth were at the nearby park and Annie had gone to town with Millie and a few school friends.

Upstairs, Kate was changing the bedding on Beth's bed when she heard the rattle of the letterbox. Expecting a bank statement for Adam's account, she instantly felt sick with anxiety. If the statement showed that all the recent transactions were in the debit column and none at all in credit, she had to face the awful truth that Adam had truly abandoned her. That soon there would be no money to meet the household bills was a serious but secondary dread.

Throwing the duvet across the bed, she straightened it, brushing the creases with the palm of her hand. Biding her time, putting off the moment of opening the post, she tinkered with the tiny ornaments on the small chest of drawers.

Beth, she thought, would soon outgrow the room; she would want the furniture changed, new curtains, carpet, and wallpaper. The Mr Men on the pink wallpaper would not satisfy her for much longer. Sighing, Kate wondered where she would find the money to make the changes.

A glance in the mirror showed her that the strain of the last few weeks was taking a toll. She had lost weight, too much. Her mouth, once ready to smile, was now down-turned and sombre. Her eyes lacked life, and with no make-up her face was sallow.

She thought of the envelopes lying on the carpet in the hallway. The one from the bank, if indeed it was there, could sentence her to a life without Adam.

As a bout of fresh panic seized her, she leaned on the chest of drawers for support.

The morning had started so well. For the first time in weeks she actually had some energy, enough to tackle the sticky finger marks that Helen's brood had daubed on the paintwork and furniture, during their visit yesterday afternoon.

Perhaps I'm just being foolish, she thought, glancing in the mirror again expecting to see traits of madness in her expression. The face looking back was drawn and unhappy.

Examining the eyes, she said softly 'What does it prove if Adam hasn't put any money in? Perhaps he hasn't any to give.'

Desperate to find excuses for him, her mind went down a now familiar track, her thoughts growing more feverish. Her mouth moved but there was no sound as she said, 'If Adam ran away because of something Tony Everett did, where would he get money from to put into the account?' For a moment she stood quite still, deep in thought. Then she went on, 'If he has money he will put it in the bank to meet the mortgage and direct debits. So if there are no credit transactions, it proves that Adam hasn't got any money, so he couldn't be involved in the embezzlement.'

The jumbled thoughts brought instant dilemma; she needed money desperately, but if none was there it was a reason to celebrate.

The suspense was too great to ignore. Leaving the bedroom, she came downstairs, her eyes on the three white envelopes on the doormat.

One was definitely from the bank. The address of the customer service department was printed on the back. Taking the post into the kitchen, she switched on the kettle to make tea.

Resting her hip against the top of the work surface, she slit open the envelope, her heart pitter-pattering horridly in her chest as she withdrew the statement. Her eyes flew to the credit

126

column. It was totally blank. Not so the debit, money had been drawn against the direct debits. There was just enough remaining in the account to pay the bills for one more month. She didn't know whether to laugh or cry.

Throwing the paper onto the kitchen table, she made a cup of tea and sat at the table to drink it.

This was the first time she had been broke since college days. Back then it had been easy to pick up a job and earn enough to get by. But now there was the upkeep of a fairly expensive house and four people. Whatever salary she might earn would not come anywhere near to paying the bills.

Leaving college early, pregnant with Annie, she had failed to get the diploma in cooking she had aimed for. Now, without qualifications, she knew it would be difficult to get any worthwhile employment.

Envisaging working in a factory on an industrial estate on the edge of town, Kate's depression took hold.

Helen, who hadn't done a day's paid work since she was a teenager, would really enjoy seeing me working in a factory for a living, Kate thought miserably.

For several hours yesterday, Helen harped on about the change in the Fontaine family fortunes. Whilst her brats rampaged through the house and garden, traipsing in mud and leaving sticky marks everywhere. Even the new wallpaper in the hall suffered, young Jordan splashing it with blackcurrant juice.

Adam would go spare if he saw the damage. 'But he isn't, neither is his salary,' she said talking to herself.

Picking up the bank statement, she glanced again at the blank credit column.

Biting the metaphorical bullet, she decided that tomorrow she would go to the job centre and see what was available.

127

Whilst she was there, she would ask how the family's housing benefit would be affected if she worked. Tax credits were a complete enigma, as were the other benefits she might be entitled to.

Sighing deeply, she rose. Throwing the remainder of the lukewarm tea into the sink, she rinsed the mug under the hot water tap.

We must start saving money, economising drastically, she thought positively. They could start with the hot water; it was always available, from now on the immersion would only be switched on when hot water was a necessity. Other times they could boil a kettle. If she could persuade the girls of the importance of going green they were likely to be more cooperative.

Going upstairs, opening the airing cupboard door, she switched off the water heater. It's a start, but it's hardly likely to save the planet or this family from poverty, she thought despondently.

***

The job centre was virtually deserted. Feeling horridly out of place, until a few days ago she didn't even know the location of social services or the job centre, Kate entered the rather austere government department.

The office was open plan, with more than a dozen identical desks surrounded by a red screens to give the impression of privacy. Having no idea of the procedure, and anxious not to make a complete fool of herself, she went to the nearest desk.

A fierce premonition that Adam was at this moment walking into their home almost made Kate turn and run. There was no need for her to be here, if Adam had returned. Everything would immediately be back to normal. All the fear and uncertainties would disappear as if by magic. There would be no pressing anxiety about money. No reason to drive around in an ancient, unreliable car. Their home would be safe from repossession, and the girls would be happy again and so would she.

'Can I help you?' Adrianna Phillips asked politely.

Kate was suddenly aware that this question had already been put to her twice.

Shaking the image of Adam from her mind, she said 'I'm sorry. I was miles away.'

She wondered what sort of impression she was giving to Ms Phillips. No doubt she already saw her as an unemployable daydreamer.

The form filling lasted more than thirty minutes but at the end of that time, Kate had an interview arranged for the position of cooking assistant at the local comprehensive school.

With a sense of relief she walked out of the government building and down the long sloping pathway to the pavement. Afraid of meeting a neighbour, or worse still someone from the golf club, she hurried to put distance between herself and the social services office.

At the bottom of the short hill, she slowed down. Anyone she now met might assume she was coming from Morrison's, the butcher's, or the deli. She knew it was just silly pride and didn't mind admitting it. For the past fifteen years, married to Adam, she'd had status, a financially secure existence where the norm was the golf club, holidays, nice car, beautiful home, no debts, unlike so many of their acquaintances. Now all that was washed away and she was ducking down the street away from the benefits office, hot under the collar with embarrassment.

On the main road, feeling less conspicuous, she made a dash for the car park. She was desperate to reach home to see if Adam really was there. If her telepathy proved to be accurate, it wouldn't be necessary to visit the job centre again, or turn up for the interview at the local comprehensive.

Convinced Adam would be waiting at home for her, she broke the speed limit several times getting there. Looking forward to seeing him didn't seem the least bit illogical; she had often anticipated his phone calls and on several occasions predicted his early arrival home from work. With mounting excitement, she turned into the cul-de-sac. The empty driveway was a minor let-down. Adam has garaged the car, she thought cheerfully. Pulling onto the driveway, grabbing her handbag, she climbed out of the car, slamming the door closed. Jittery, her limbs trembling slightly, she opened the front door and stepped over the threshold.

The house was curiously silent, but for the tap drip-dripping into the stainless steel kitchen sink.

Standing at the bottom of the stairs, she called 'Adam,' her voice echoing slightly in the empty house. There was no returning cry, only the sound of a dry ceiling joist creaking.

A great sense of loneliness swept over her.

She was sitting in Adam's chair, an almost empty wine glass in her hand, when Beth and Carla returned in the late afternoon. She didn't mention the job interview at the local comprehensive. She had no enthusiasm for it and didn't really expect to attend.

It was late when Annie came noisily through the door, slightly intoxicated and ecstatic with it.

Standing in the doorway of the living room, she glanced over to her mother, saying 'I'm whacked. See you in the morning.'

Two minutes later her bedroom door closed.

Kate sat on alone, trying to recapture her vision of Adam entering the house. It had seemed so real, she had seen him so clearly; it was hard to believe that he hadn't actually been in.

During the afternoon she had checked the house thoroughly, going into each room looking for something, however small and insignificant, to be out of place. The disappointment at finding everything in order was crushing, and she sank into total despair.

With the children in bed, she went to the kitchen to refill her glass, bringing a bottle of Merlot back into the living room.

Again she sat in Adam's chair. For the thousandth time she went over recent events convinced that there was something about Adam's disappearance that she was missing, a small detail that was really important. The answer to why he had fled was within her grasp. All she had to do was put her tumbling thoughts in order to solve the mystery.

The light from the table-lamp beside her cast a glow on her greyish complexion, but it failed to lighten the dark shadows beneath her eyes or eradicate the emptiness in the jade irises.

Hours later she woke on the chair. The light streaming in through the window hurt her eyes. Liz was close by and a man, she recognised as her doctor, was holding her wrist.

'Mrs Fontaine,' he said gently. 'Do you know who I am?'

She gave a small nod. 'You're Doctor Mackenzie. But I'm not ill, doctor. I'm just very, very tired.'

Liz gave a breathless little sob. 'Why didn't you call me, Kate, you didn't have to be alone if you were so low. I would have come at once.'

'I know, Liz,' she said trying to get out of the chair. Her limbs were leaden and she wondered if she really was ill.

'Mrs Fontaine, do you remember how many of these pills

131

you took?' He was holding a white box labelled diazepam.

Kate recognised it as Adam's, prescribed for him when he injured his back playing rugby. 'They're not mine. They belong to Adam.' Her eyes filled with tears.

'How many did you swallow Mrs Fontaine?'

Kate tried to remember if she had brought the pills down from the bedroom. She had taken one, or maybe two, when she got home. Perhaps she'd swallowed another when the girls had gone to bed. But she couldn't recall bringing the packet downstairs.

'Maybe three,' she said, expecting the doctor to be angry with her.

Turning to Liz, he said softly 'I think it would be a good idea to get her checked over at the hospital. They may want to keep her in overnight. Could you get a few things together for her? I'll telephone admissions.'

Liz touched Kate's arm. 'Don't worry about a thing. I'll stay with the girls. Everything will be perfectly all right.'

Kate, near sleep again, nodded.

She woke again in a hospital bed. Liz standing beside her, smiled wanly. 'How do you feel, Kate?'

Lethargic, Kate struggled to sit up. 'I'm very tired.'

She didn't mention the violent headache or that her limbs ached with fatigue. The void in her memory was too disturbing to admit to. Several hours were completely lost.

Like a dark blanket, sleep was overwhelming her. Liz's voice was coming from far-away.

When she woke again it was dark outside. White globes of light were burning in the corridor. A small oblong reading light on the bedhead was illuminating her pillow.

That she was in a hospital bed came to her immediately on opening her eyes. The room was two-bedded but the bed opposite hers was unoccupied, for which she was grateful. Conversation was not what she needed right now.

Lying still, she looked at the shadows and the reflected lights from the hospital traffic on the ceiling.

A young man in a white coat stood in the doorway, a file in his hand. 'Kate Fontaine?' he asked.

Kate inched up the bed. The hospital gown she wore rucking around her middle.

Coming into the room, his walk loose-limbed and relaxed, he sat on the edge of the mattress. Folding his arms, the green medical file held against his midriff, his dark brown eyes searched Kate's face.

'I am Doctor Singh,' he said with a trace of a Delhi accent. 'I will be taking care of you whilst you're here and when you come to the outpatient department.'

'I'm not sick,' Kate said quickly. 'I am just terribly tired. I don't belong here at all.'

There was a long pause, and then he said softly, 'We can't ignore the fact that you took several diazepam tablets, Kate.'

'I didn't,' Kate said incredulous. 'I might have foolishly taken three, but not more than that. I wasn't trying to kill myself.' She was horrified that he might think this had been her intention.

Opening the file, he looked at the result of Kate's blood test taken on admittance. 'There's evidence of too much alcohol and enough diazepam to knock out an elephant.' He gave a small smile. 'Albeit, a fairly small elephant.'

Kate stared hollow-eyed. 'I wasn't trying to kill myself. I took two or maybe three and then had far too much to drink. I don't remember taking any more.'

That she had come close to death was frightening. Pain beat in her temples as she shook her head. 'I wouldn't do that. I have the children to think about.' It came to her that her parents, or God forbid, Helen, may have taken the girls in, had she died. She began to cry.

Drawing a neatly folded clean tissue out of his hospital coat pocket, he put it into her hand. 'You mustn't distress yourself, Kate.'

Her eyes glittery with tears, she cried 'I can't help it. My husband has disappeared. My heart actually aches for him. Do you understand that?'

He nodded solemnly. 'Yes, I do.'

She didn't believe him. He hadn't the look of a man consumed with frantic cravings for someone lost to him. His eyes were not blank with hideous grief and longing. No, she did not believe that he had suffered as she now did. A smile had come too easily to his lips.

Although feeling wretched, she answered his questions attentively, knowing how important it was to convince him that she had not meant to harm herself. It was in his power to section her. If they lock me in a mental institution, I will go mad, she thought, her hands sweaty and her heart racing frantically.

The following morning he came into the room intending to discharge her.

Liz, arriving ten minutes before him, was waiting to be told she could take Kate home. She was propped against the window sill, the morning sun streaming through the window expanding the pupils in her tired eyes, making them appear glittery and glassy.

A full day was ahead of her, an appointment with the accountant, a trip to the wholesalers, and a late shift at the bistro. Anticipating a lot of running around, organising Kate her priority, she had dressed casually in a denim jeans and white tee-shirt. Her dark-blonde hair was pulled back into a ponytail. Large sunglasses, generally at the bottom of her handbag, were perched on the top of her head.

Handing Kate an appointment card, the doctor looked into her eyes his expression serious. 'I would like you to return next week for a counselling session. It's important you attend.'

Glancing at the card, Kate saw the appointment was at the day clinic in the psychiatric unit and her heart did a little somersault in her chest.

'But I'm not mentally ill,' she cried out, tears brimming in her eyes.

The reaction was fairly usual; he'd seen it a thousand times before. 'There's no shame attached to mental illness,' he said patiently. 'Many of us are disturbed by events in our lives.'

'Disturbed,' Kate said hotly. 'I am not disturbed. I am hollowed out. Empty. Cavernous. I am sorrow.'

It flashed through Liz's mind that Kate had already stepped over the barrier between sanity and madness.

Kate's revelation, how she perceived herself, was over in an instant and she answered the psychiatrist quite calmly, 'I am not disturbed. I am just very unhappy because my husband is not with me.'

Looking imploringly towards Liz, she said 'Are you ready to leave?'

'I'm ready. But do you think you are well enough, Kate?'

'The doctor thinks I am. So I must be,' she answered with forced cheerfulness.

He was debating whether or not to hold her for another night, recheck her mental state. But as she said how much she missed the children and looked forward to seeing them, he decided to let her go.

'I will write to your GP,' he said. 'But I want you to come to that appointment.' He pointed with a pen to the small white card Kate was holding.

He followed them out into the corridor and accepted Kate's words of thanks with a mild smile.

Glad to be outdoors, feeling as though she had escaped prison, Kate breathed a sigh of relief.

Liz had parked the car nearby. They walked to it in virtual silence. Climbing in, Liz put the key in the ignition and drove out of the car park.

Troubled by Kate's revelation and her lost hours, Liz was determined she would return for the appointment, even if it meant playing the guilt card, telling her just how traumatised Annie and Carla were at finding their mother unconscious.

'Do you think I'm losing it, Liz?' Kate asked a few days later, as Liz walked into the Fontaine sitting room.

Taking care how she replied, Kate had been fragile since her return from the hospital, Liz said 'You're not mentally ill, but I do think you're deeply unhappy.'

'Oh, I'm that all right. But I reckon I have a plan that will help.'

Expecting something constructive, Liz was hopeful. 'What's the plan?'

Kate smiled craftily. 'I'm going to get Annie to send an email to Adam's email address at least once a day, perhaps even twice.'

Before Liz could reply, Annie and Carla came into the sitting room.

Kate's feverish face brightened. 'Just the person I want to see,' she said looking at Annie. 'I was just telling Liz about my plan. I want you to send your father an email each day.'

Disdainful, Annie snorted. 'Are you mad?'

Kate giggled. 'I don't think so. Liz doesn't think so either. I just asked her if she thought I might be.'

With a smirk in her voice Annie said 'Nobody asked me. And I reckon you're bonkers. Why do you want to send an email to him at all? Never mind, every day.'

Kate spoke as though to a small child, her voice rising on the last two words, 'Because I want a reply from him. I would like to know where he is. Why else?'

Slowly shaking her head from side-to-side, Annie tut-tutted. 'You've lost me. I can't see that anyone in their right mind would want…'

Having heard enough, Kate interrupted her, 'Less of your rudeness and less of the jibes about being mental, bonkers, barmy, or anything else.'

Annie's face was mutinous. 'Well, you can count me out. I am not sending messages to him.'

Though she feared her mother would reject the offer, Carla said softly 'I'll do it, Mum.'

'Thank you, Carla. You can always be relied upon,' Kate said patronisingly.

Her mother's mood swings frightened Carla. Afraid to be alone in her company, she suggested quietly 'I'll show you how to do it. Then you can email him anytime you want to.'

An artificial smile spread across Kate's lips. 'You see, Annie, not everyone is as unhelpful as you are.'

As she couldn't stand her mother in this mood, Annie turned to leave the room. Brushing passed Carla, she glared spitefully.

Liz thought emailing him at all was a complete waste of time. In her opinion, Adam did not wish to be found. A thief, he had bolted with more than three hundred thousand pounds. There was probably another woman in tow. But Kate would not listen to reason. She had made up her mind that Adam was guiltless and he would return to her the moment his name was cleared. She was living in a dream world. No change that to a living nightmare, she thought despondently. It was sad that the kids were dragged into the sorry mess. They were desperate for love and support. Annie was learning to stand up to Kate. But if Kate took too many liberties, the kid would revolt.

On a sudden impulse, Liz called Annie back. 'Would you like a Saturday job in the bistro?'

Without looking at her mother for permission, Annie replied at once 'I certainly would. I could do with the money.'

Liz was aware that Kate's questioning eyes were on her. She has every right to be cross, she thought. Kate would have expected to be consulted before the offer was put to Annie. But she wasn't sorry she'd asked. A fifteen-year-old girl has to buy things for herself, get her hair done, and go out with her friends. Kate was relying on the children too much and not giving very much back. Kate was too wrapped up in her own misery to see the girls were also suffering.

'What shall I wear?' In her mind Annie was flicking through her wardrobe and finding nothing suitable to wear for the bistro.

'Black pants and a white blouse will do, plus very comfortable shoes.'

Annie's face was animated for the first time in weeks. 'Thanks, Liz,' she said with a broad smile.

A car pulled up outside. Kate jumped up to look through the window. Seeing a grey saloon parked at the kerb, the dreary sense of let-down swept over her. Staring at the car, she wished Adam's was parked there instead. Turning her head, robot-like, she looked at Carla.

'Come with me,' she said, disappointment evident in her tone. 'We can write the email to your father. Annie and Liz can discuss hours and things.'

Although she didn't feel like talking to anyone, least of all Carla, the child's eyes were generally sad and slightly accusing, Kate tried to chat lightly. 'I don't know why I didn't think of emailing him before today,' she said leading the way upstairs. 'If he has access to a computer, there is every chance that he will still read his emails.'

Carla pent up with emotion remained silent. Her eyes were on the slightly dry skin of Kate's heels clacking on the soles of her plastic flip-flops.

The computer the girls shared was in Annie's bedroom. Going in, seeing that it was switched on, the colourful screen-saver looping across the glass, Kate gave a passing thought to the economies she was planning on making.

Obediently Carla sat at the computer table. With a look of intense concentration, her small brow with the fading bruise puckering in a frown, she opened the email page.

Her mother was standing at the side of the chair. Her jaw clenched with nervous tension. Her fingers holding her red silky cardigan tight across her midriff, bone white.

'If we had a webcam we could see him.' Carla spoke so quietly her words hardly broke the silence.

A great longing sigh oozed from Kate. 'Let's just hope to God we can contact him. I would be happy just doing that. Finding out where he is.'

Carla envisaging the scene her mother would make if her father answered sat with her back upright, tense and full of anxiety. There'll be tears, she thought fretfully. She's sure to shout at him and scare him off. Then I'll never get the chance to email him secretly and tell him how much I really miss him and how hard it is just living with mum.

Her hands slightly sticky, she typed in Adam's email address. Glancing up at her mother, she said uneasily 'What do you want me to put?'

Kate bit the tip of a nail. 'Tell him to call home. Say it's very, very, urgent. Make it look like you're doing this on your own.'

Dismayed, Carla's dark hazel eyes widened. 'But he might think there's something terribly wrong.' Sorry for her dad her eyes filled with tears. 'What if he thinks you are terribly ill, or that you have died? That would be awful for him.'

'Your imagination is running away with you,' Kate said crossly. 'Just do as I tell you. I know exactly what I'm doing.'

Hoping her father would never find out she had deceived him, Carla typed, 'Daddy, please phone home quickly. It's very, very, urgent. Love Carla. Clicking on, send this message, before her mother insisted she add anything more to it.

'What happens now?' Kate said staring at the screen.

Carla pushing aside the mouse remained silent.

Kate touched the child's narrow shoulders. 'Can we find out if he's got the email?'

'No.' Carla said flatly. 'We have to wait. Just keep checking the inbox.'

Nibbling the very tip of her fingernail, Kate stared at the computer. 'We'll give it ten minutes and then look again. In the meantime, show me how to use the email.'

She glanced to the bed and the far wall. 'I'll move the computer into my room. It's a bit cramped in here for Annie.'

Dreading the argument this would create, Carla remained silent. Annie emailed her friends at all hours and surfed weird sites in the middle of the night. When she wasn't too drunk or spaced out on pills.

Before five minutes elapsed, Kate checked the email box.

No New Messages, flashed up, mocking her impatience.

The row Carla predicted happened the moment Kate came

into the living room. Annie, outraged at losing a privilege for no reason, refused to help move the computer. Carla taking herself off to the kitchen, sat at the table her head in her hands, wishing that school would start, her daddy would come home, and Annie would stop being so frighteningly angry.

Liz tried to calm Kate and Annie. But coming close to losing her own temper, she left them to sort it out.

Satisfied that she had got her own way, Kate wheeled the computer desk into her bedroom. Set up in her own room, she switched it on somewhat apprehensively unsure of the correct button to click. Her heart skipping as the screen came to life.

It was good to accomplish something, she thought, even if it caused friction between Annie and herself. The girl was still banging about in her bedroom, venting her anger by slamming the cupboard and wardrobe doors.

There was a drawback to the arrangement; the girls would flit in and out of her bedroom to use the computer and when the new school term began it would be used even more frequently. But it was worth the disturbance, just to check for emails from Adam at any time of the day or night.

She spent the evening in her bedroom, the girls fending for themselves for supper. Perching on the bed, her back against the headboard, her eyes never far from the computer screen, she watched the mesmerising colourful swirls looping across the glass. Several times, cramped, she rose and walked to-and-fro between the door and the window, coming back to the computer every few minutes, unable to resist checking for a reply from Adam. Becoming more anxious as the, No new messages, signals flashed up.

Suffering a virtually sleepless night, she rose to check several times; finally she fell into a fitful dose and woke shortly after dawn. With consciousness came a sense of

141

expectation. What is it that makes me feel eager for the day? Has something happened? Did Adam phone?

The time by the alarm clock, still on Adam's bedside table, was almost five o'clock. Too early to do anything but just lie still, waiting for a return to sleep.

There was a dull thumping in her head, caused by tiredness or too much wine. She would really have to stop drinking every evening, she thought with mild contempt for herself.

Closing her eyes against the brightening sunlight, she tried to capture the sense of anticipation of a moment ago. Perhaps it was nothing more than a tail of a dream, she thought beginning to drift off. But no, it was more urgent than that.

Remembering, she opened her eyes and turned to face the computer. The green on-off switch was still flickering, the colour hardly registering as the room took on the yellow lustre of sunlight.

Adam may be only a mouse click away; the idea brought a brief upturn to her lips.

Flipping back the duvet, she slipped from the bed, her tangled nightdress unravelling to cover her tanned slender legs.

A light breeze blew in through the open window, the air chill for the time of year. A reminder that the girls would soon be starting the September school term. They were sure to need books and stationery. As this term would be Annie and Carla's last before starting at the local comprehensive, she wouldn't buy new uniforms; she couldn't afford to anyway. Somehow they would just have to manage, unless of course, Adam returned home. Then everything would be different, the girls would stay where they were. If Adam cleared his name at the bank, everything would go back to normal.

'Please reply, Adam,' she prayed, picking up the computer mouse and clicking on email. Her heart pitter-pattering madly as she waited for the page to come up. She gave a little mew of disappointment as the, No New Messages, flashed up.

In a haze of misery she went back to bed, pulling the duvet over her head. Eventually she dozed off.

She was running through the streets of London, crowded with men in filthy threadbare clothes. Shoulder to shoulder they filled the doorways. The gutters were overflowing with unkempt humanity, sleeping head to toe in the dirty wet open sewers.

She was searching for Adam, but every face that turned to her had dark stubble and deep cavernous creases pitted with dirt. 'Adam,' she shouted until hoarse. 'Adam, for the love of God, see me.'

She woke drenched with sweat and her heart pounding so fiercely in her chest she wondered if she were on the brink of a heart attack. Drawing herself up, arms on her knees, she buried her face in the soft duvet. It took long moments before she began to recover, the images of the filthy men playing in her head like a video on rewind. Is Adam on the streets? The idea brought her upright. Shaking the dream from her mind, she concentrated on the thought that he could be hiding on the streets of London, safe from the law and the directors of the bank.

Getting out of bed, she sat on the edge of the mattress, looking at the computer. How could she search its intricacies for the answer when she hardly knew how to use it?

Carla's bedroom door opened. Kate called to her as the child passed her own. Opening the door, standing on the threshold, Carla looked meekly towards her mother.

'Do you want me?' she said rubbing her eyes.

'Show me how to get on the Net.'

Barefoot, Carla crossed to the computer. 'It's easy. What do you want to find?'

Uncertain, Kate was hesitant. 'I suppose missing persons is the place to start.'

Almost immediately a list of organisations involved in searching for people across the world appeared on the screen.

Carla turned to go.

Hardly aware that the child had left the room, Kate sat on the office chair and began to search. The images of the men in her dream not far from her mind.

Late morning, whilst Kate was cleaning the worktops in the kitchen, the telephone rang. Perhaps it's Adam. The thought always sprang into her mind on hearing the 'phone. Recognising Clare's voice, she hid her disappointment well.

Clare was the wife of a member of the golf club. As Kate didn't like her particularly, never becoming friends during the six years of their acquaintance, she was surprised to receive an invitation to lunch the following day.

'The girls,' Clare explained 'are going to the Ambassador. We are meeting there at one o'clock. Say you'll come.'

'I don't think I can,' Kate said pensively. 'I have already made arrangements for tomorrow afternoon.'

'Come for one teeny weenie drink.'

It passed through Kate's mind that Clare had already had her first drink of the day.'

'Say you'll come. Brenda, Lydia, Sylvia and Frances are going to be there.' She giggled.

'Lydia is recovering from a bit of a fling. She actually left Jonathan and went off with someone else. She only returned a few days ago. Isn't Jonathan a darling for taking her back?'

Kate instantly recalled catching Lydia and Adam standing very close together on the veranda at the golf club. It had been pitch dark, indoors a party had been in full swing. She had come outside to find Adam. He had been missing for some while. Seeing them together silhouetted by the darker shadows, a pang of jealousy so fierce stole Kate's breath. Adam had moved towards her, putting his arm loosely around her shoulder in a possessive gesture. But his action had not suffocated the dreadful suspicions that Lydia and Adam were having an affair.

Now hearing Lydia's name, learning that she had abandoned her husband, the old uncertainties rose up. It was impossible to ignore the possibility that Lydia had fled with Adam. Fast on the heels of this thought came another, if Lydia had gone with Adam, she would know his whereabouts.

'On second thoughts,' she said quickly 'I would like to come. I can rearrange my appointment for another afternoon.'

'Oh good,' Clare said cheerfully. 'It will be really nice to see you. One o'clock at the Ambassador.'

'I'll be there,' Kate replied trying to match Clare's bright tone.

Putting the receiver back, Kate stood thoughtfully for several moments, going over the episode at the golf club, searching her memory for similar incidents between Adam and Lydia.

For one mad moment she considered calling Jonathan and went as far as picking up the telephone. But at a loss of how to begin a conversation, stopped her dialling the number.

Beth and Carla came rattling in, swinging badminton rackets, arguing about which one of them had lost most games.

Beth coming into the kitchen, abandoning her muddy racket on the kitchen table, asked 'What's for tea? I hope it's not pizza again. It's all Annie gives us.'

'Sausage and chips,' Kate answered mechanically. 'Move that dirty racket off the table. Put it in the garage or in your room.'

Beth gave a loud theatrical sigh. 'It's not really dirty. It's just a bit of grass and mud from the Jones' lawn.'

'Well clean it,' Kate said getting a packet of Cumberland sausages out of the fridge.

Beth smiled cheekily. 'There's no need. It'll only get mucky again tomorrow.'

Kate's mind was too full of Lydia and Adam to take much notice of Beth's logic.

She knew without a doubt that Adam was innocent of the theft at the bank. But she had always suspected him of womanising. To be honest, she thought despondently, throughout my entire married life I have suspected him of having affairs and it has spoilt our time together. I could not look at him and wonder if he was lying, sleeping around behind my back, coming home to me with the smell of another woman on his body.

'I don't really fancy sausages,' Carla said plaintively.

'Oh, for goodness sake, Carla, stop being so bloody fussy,' Kate snapped.

Upset, afraid her mother was about to lose her temper, Carla ran out of the kitchen and up the stairs to her room.

Kate, her jaw tight with stress, slapped a bag of oven chips onto the work surface. 'Bloody hell,' she shouted for the entire household to hear.

The back door opened and Annie came in. 'What's going on?'

'Don't you bloody start,' Kate yelled. 'Here,' she thrust the bag of chips into Annie's hand. 'You cook the bloody tea.'

The kitchen door banged closed behind Kate.

'Fucking hell,' Annie cursed, throwing the plastic bag onto the table.

It took Kate most of the morning to decide what to wear for

lunch to the Ambassador Hotel. Finally she settled on a red trouser suit, with red sling-back sandals.

Fortunately, she thought, whilst applying her make-up, Carla and Beth had an invitation to the Jones' house to play on the trampoline. Mrs Jones, ever the hostess, was putting on a barbeque for a handful of kids. The girls being occupied and perfectly safe, was just one less thing to worry about.

Rummaging in her make-up bag, discovering she didn't have the correct colour of lipstick to go with her outfit Kate smoothed lip balm onto lips. A dab of Dior and she was ready.

In the kitchen, Annie, disgruntled, was emptying the dishwasher, practically throwing the cutlery into a drawer.

Coming down the stairs, hearing the clatter, and not wishing for another confrontation, Kate took her keys off the hook by the front door and went out of the house.

From the kitchen window, Annie watched her mother reverse the car out of the garage.

'All right for some,' she muttered throwing a tea towel down on the draining board.

The garage door dropped down and locked automatically. As the car left the drive, Kate gave a final glance at the house before driving off.

Seeing a puff of dark grey smoke coming from the exhaust, Annie was hopefully optimistic that the car would break down, stranding her mother in some godforsaken place, in the pouring rain. Wishing for a cloudburst, at the very least her mother might end up drenched she glanced at the cloudy sky. Unfortunately it didn't look as though it would rain anytime soon.

An open bottle of Merlot was tucked between the breadbin and the sandwich maker. Pulling off the plastic stopper, Annie poured a generous measure into a wine glass.

The foyer of the Ambassador was marble and glass, hard edges and artificial light. The Georgian building had been massively altered during the winter months. Walking in for the first time since the renovation, Kate wasn't sure she liked it. Previously the décor was cosy, red plush, old wooden picture frames, brass lamps and huge bevelled mirrors reflecting the radiance of a central chandelier. Now it was stark and impersonal. She wondered if Adam would prefer it this way. His taste was contemporary, Scandinavian wood floors, plain décor, fabrics without designs. He was the only person she knew whose favourite colour was beige.

Coming into the lounge area she saw Brenda, Helen, Sylvia and Frances sitting on a grey leather banquette.

Clare playing hostess, rose, beckoning to her.

The women's conversation stopped instantly and they watched Kate cross to them, her high heel sandals clacking on the highly polished floor. Feeling horribly conspicuous, Kate wished she hadn't come.

Clare, looking immaculate in a dark brown silk shirt and black trousers, a string of black and brown beads lying in the V of the shirt, was poised to kiss Kate continental style on both cheeks.

Kate caught the fragrance of expensive perfume as her face brushed Clare's.

Straightening, Clare tucked a strand of silky ebony hair behind her ear, exposing a jet and tourmaline earring, with a glittering diamond at the centre.

Elegantly, Clare descended onto the banquette. 'Lydia will be along any moment, she's just gone to titivate herself.'

She laughed glassily. 'Perhaps she's worried about the competition.' She laughed again. 'You're looking particularly good, Kate. Have you lost weight?'

'A little,' Kate replied with a self-conscious smile.

No one spoke for a moment and to bridge the gap, Kate said without thinking, 'Is everything just the same at the golf club?'

'Not quite,' Frances said facetiously.

Of course everything wasn't the same, Kate thought blushing with embarrassment. Adam, the captain of the club, was no longer there. Absconding, he had let the club down badly.

'Frank Jefferson has taken over as captain,' Clare volunteered. 'But what sort of job he'll make of it, is anyone's guess. He hasn't the charisma for a start.'

'Pretty awful golfer too,' Brenda laughed. 'His wife's a dreary woman. She hasn't come up with one original idea for the end-of-year entertainment. It'll be beetle-drives and more beetle-drives, if it's left to her.'

Clare gestured to a passing waiter. 'Can we have bottle of Beaujolais and another glass, please?'

Answering half-heartedly, he sloped off in the direction of the bar.

'Ah, here she comes,' Clare said seeing Lydia walk in.

From beneath long dark lashes, Lydia's eyes flashed to Kate.

Kate's hackles rose. She had never liked Lydia. Ever since the occasion she had caught her standing suspiciously close to Adam on the club veranda. Remembering how she had felt at that time, so full of spiteful jealous rage, she watched Lydia's approach resentfully. There was no doubt in Kate's mind that Lydia had flung herself at Adam. Men acted stupidly over women like Lydia, their dark sensuality, come-on-eyes, attracting them like bees to flowers. Such women are blight on humanity, she thought, with murderous intent.

Reaching the table, Lydia sat down on the banquette elegantly. Crossing her legs, her short skirt rode up, revealing perfectly shaped knees and slender thighs.

Watching her, listening to her silly prattle, Kate's jaw clenched tightly. How she wished she had the courage to ask outright, were you with my husband? What a fool she would look if Lydia denied it and named another man. And if she admitted it was Adam, what action could she take? She could hardly wrestle the bloody woman to floor and clout her, as she so wished to do.

Frances, having few scruples when it came to gathering gossip, asked Lydia outright, 'So how long have you been back from your little escapade? Where did you and the fancy man runaway to?'

Lydia's eyes flashed again to Kate and a blush rose on her face. 'We only got as far as London.'

'So what brought you back?'

Lydia picked up her almost full glass, twirling the contents around the bowl. 'You're full of curiosity, Frances. Don't tell me you're jealous of my little fling.'

Frances shrugged her shoulders. 'Hell no, I can't see the fun in getting into the emotional mire of an affair. You were lucky Jonathan took you back. Not many men would.'

Worried that Lydia would take offence and the afternoon be ruined, Brenda tried to change the subject. 'Let's decide what we are going to have for lunch.'

None of the woman, least of all Kate, took any notice of her.

Sylvia, married to the wealthiest member of the golf club, was at a loss to understand why anyone would risk their financial security. 'Lydia, whatever possessed you to leave your husband and go away with this man?'

Lydia, twirling the wine in the glass again, took a moment to answer. 'When an affair begins, it's exciting. There's something particularly thrilling about meeting clandestinely.

150

Chasing around the country just to see each other for an afternoon is fun. But going away together, cutting yourself off from friends and family and being in each other's company twenty-four-seven, is a different matter entirely.'

Her eyes flashed again to Kate. 'One night, lying beside him, I thought what the hell am I doing here?'

'So what did you do?' Brenda asked her eyes wide with curiosity.

Lydia shrugged. 'Got up, went into the loo and rang Jonathan on my mobile.' Her voice softened, 'I just asked him if I could come back home.'

'And he said yes, just like that?' Brenda gasped.

'Yes, more or less. But that's Jonathan for you. He's basically very kind. He didn't want me to be unhappy.'

'Lucky you,' Kate chipped in sourly.

'Yes, I suppose I am. But sometimes, married life can be pretty boring.'

'Mine wasn't boring,' Kate snapped. 'It was exciting. I love my husband.' Tears filled her eyes.

Returning, the waiter placed another bottle of wine on the table. The atmosphere brittle, he retreated without waiting for a tip.

Lydia touched Kate's shoulder compassionately. 'I'm sorry you are unhappy, Kate.'

Kate shrugged her off. 'Are you? Were you sorry when you were with my husband?'

Furious, Clare stood. 'Lydia has absolutely nothing to do with Adam's disappearance. You really are out of order, Kate.'

Jumping up, Kate glared. 'Defend her if you want to. I know differently.' Hearing herself, Kate knew she was out of control.

Brenda came to her side. 'Kate, we understand that you are upset. Lydia isn't the guilty party.' She sighed. 'Adam went off

151

alone. He went because of the money,' she said trying to calm the situation.

It came as a shock to hear someone talk of the theft so easily. Kate gave a cry of anger. Grabbing her bag, she flounced away from the table.

Trying to stop her, Brenda caught her arm, but Kate threw her off.

'Let her go,' Clare said sighing. 'There's nothing you can say that will change her mind.'

Reaching the open door, Kate dashed to the sanctuary of the ladies loo.

Watching her disappear, Frances said sotto-voce, 'Thank God the room is empty, but for us. What a spectacle she made of herself.'

'I think she's losing it,' Sylvia said without compassion.

Clare sniffed. 'Kate was always somewhat neurotic.'

'Perhaps that's the reason Adam flitted,' Frances speculated.

Clare laughed. 'I think it had more to do with embezzling than living with a mad woman.'

They laughed together.

Kate, opening the door of the ladies room, heard them and vowed to have nothing to do with any of them again. They were a stuck-up crowd. The only reason they invited me was to gloat, she thought, crying again.

Locking the door of a cubicle, she sat on the lid of the toilet seat, drying her eyes. After a while, in control again, but afraid if she went into the rest room she would meet one of the other women, she remained in the cubicle, repairing her make-up using the tiny mirror in her eye-shadow compact.

The outer door opened and Lydia and Clare came in, chattering.

Clare said 'Whatever gave her the idea that you were

152

involved with Adam?'

'Oh, I don't know. She was always a bit neurotic and jealous around him. Terrified that a woman would snatch him away from her. You know what she's like.'

'Hush. There's someone in the cubicle. It might be her.' Clare warned.

'No. She left ages ago.'

Two of the toilet doors opened and closed.

Tense, terrified of making a noise putting the make-up back into her bag, Kate sat tensely waiting for them to leave.

'Do you think he went off with someone?' Clare asked over the sound of peeing.

'No. He ran because he knew he'd been found out about the money.'

The toilet roll reeled round. 'So where do you think he is?' Clare said curious.

'He's in London. Frederick Banks swears he saw him there last week. He was walking into one of the posh hotels in Mayfair.'

Both toilets flushed and the cubicle doors opened.

Kate, her heart racing, listened to water running from the taps.

'Which hotel was it?'

Two hand driers came on simultaneously, drowning Lydia's words.

Kate wasn't breathing, her entire being concentrating on the lost answer.

The outer door swung open and closed. Alone again, she waited until her heart stopped racing before getting up and pulling across the bolt on the door.

Hurrying across the foyer, praying that none of the women would look up as she passed the doorway of the bar area, sure that she would hear them titter if they caught sight of her; she made it outdoors without being noticed.

Driving the Honda out of the car park, she debated whether to go straight home to think about the overheard conversation or to go to Liz's bistro. It was still lunchtime, she could get a bite to eat and talk it over with Liz. The other option was to go home, pack a bag, and head for London. The girls could manage without her for a day or two.

Stopping at the first set of traffic lights, she considered the expense; it wasn't just the journey, but a bed and breakfast too.

The old car threatened to stall. It's stupid, she told herself, to consider spending money when the car needs fixing. The light turned green and she drove on, deciding to make the decision after lunch. Although food was not a priority, she was too excited to really think about eating. Perhaps after all these weeks she was getting closer to finding Adam.

Parking the car in the small car park a short walk away from the bistro, Kate got out and retrieved a brolly from the boot. Heavy rain looked imminent, bellying black clouds threatening thunder ranged across the sky. Locking the car, she made her way to the canal towpath. Her high heel shoes were not designed for walking on rough ground; mindful of the stones, the last thing she needed was a turned ankle, she went along cautiously.

The first drops of rain fell, making circular ripples on the faintly green water. Stopping, Kate put up her yellow and white striped umbrella.

A drooping fond of cow parsley brushed her leg. Splattered with rain the plant had a slightly sickly fragrance.

Overhead silver-blue lightning forked down from the clouds. Caught half-way between the car and the bistro, Kate was undecided if to go on, or get back to the car. Thunder rolled and in an instant rain fell horizontally from the laden sky.

Doing her utmost to take care, but to hurry, Kate made for the safety of the bistro. The rain bouncing off the stones, wetting the bottom of her flapping trouser legs.

In a moment the towpath was a quagmire, rainwater running down from the high verge, the drenched vegetation giving off a smell of mushrooms and the musty stench of rotting wood. Her shoes were a mess, covered in wet grit and dark brown mud, as were the hems of her trousers.

Just as she opened the picket gate, a roll of thunder clattered across the sky.

The deserted garden was drowned; water flowing down the crazy paving pathway had nowhere to go but the flowerbeds and closely clipped lawn.

The wind carried on the fringe of the storm, caught beneath the raised parasols, water sluicing off the flapping red canvas in tiny rivers.

Using her brolly as a shield, Kate avoided the cascades. Anxious to get indoors before the next clap of thunder, she almost ran down the path to the porch door. Finding it ajar, she collapsed the brolly and dashed in.

Water overflowing a guttering was running down the outside wall, drenching the whipping tendrils of the climbing honeysuckle, the downpour spilling into a terracotta pot of lavender, splattering peat and rainwater onto the pebbles.

The garden will be ruined, Kate thought, glancing through rivulets of water running down the quaint gothic style window, to the drooped roses.

A slight change in wind direction blew the rain into the porch. Closing the door, hoping the storm would pass quickly, she poked her umbrella in amongst several others parked in the old-fashioned umbrella stand.

155

Drenched, feeling a complete wreck, the bottoms of her trouser legs were sodden and her shoes ruined, Kate pushed the inner door to the restaurant open and was greeted by a pleasant smell of cooking.

An elderly couple were sitting at a nearby table, their faces turned to the window watching the rain. Lost to their own thoughts neither looked up as Kate entered.

At a corner table, shadowed by the inglenook fireplace, Liz was sitting with a man.

Not wishing to intrude, Kate turned to go back out into the rain. But just at that moment, Liz looked up and beckoned her over.

The man half-turned and his dark eyes met Kate's. He was startlingly handsome, a young Sidney Poitier.

Embarrassed, interrupting what was obviously an intimate lunch, Kate hesitated before walking over to them. 'I'm not staying more than a moment,' she said quickly. 'I only came in out of the rain.'

'Well at least stay until it eases off,' Liz said gesturing to a chair.

The man stood, towering over Kate.

'Greg, this is a friend of mine, Kate Fontaine,' Liz explained.

'Nice to meet you, Kate. Liz mentioned you earlier.' he said pulling out a chair for her.

Wishing she had gone straight home, she could now be on her way to London, Kate sat.

Liz, twiddling a fork, part of the place setting, said 'Greg is a very old friend. We go way back.' She smiled, her eyes meeting his. 'We bumped into each other earlier and I talked him into having lunch with me.'

He gave a friendly smile, his plum-brown lips accentuating

the whiteness of his perfect teeth.

Kate wondered how much Liz had told him. No doubt her abandonment had been discussed and possibly the embezzlement. The idea only went to increase her awkwardness. Three is definitely a crowd, she said to herself. Wondering how quickly she could make an escape, she glanced out of the window; the rain was easing, she could go in a moment.

Liz stilled the fork in her hand and then placed it beside the cork tablemat. 'Greg lived locally until ten years ago,' she went on to explain. 'He went off to Ireland and set up a garage in Limerick.'

Anxious not to be drawn into a long explanation, desperate to make a start on getting to London, Kate didn't reply.

Greg filled the void created by Kate's silence. 'I sold up recently and started looking for something similar here.'

Liz wondered what it was that brought Kate to the bistro on such an appalling afternoon. But she didn't want to ruin the lovely time she was having with Greg by focusing her attention on Kate. Being polite he would leave them to discuss Kate's problems. Making a definite choice, Liz put her hand on Greg's.

'Luckily, he has found the perfect place to set up a business. We met as he came out of his solicitor's office after signing a contract on Thompson's Garages. It's amazing, seeing him again,' she said smiling broadly.

Dolly, the waitress, came out of the kitchen carrying two plates of steaming lasagne. Bringing them to the table, she set them down.

Greg sniffed appreciatively. 'Looks and smells good.'

'We aim to please,' Liz said frivolously, her smiling eyes on him.

'Can I get you something, Kate?' Dolly asked, taking a small writing pad from her apron pocket.

Glancing out of the window, the rain had almost stopped; Kate said positively 'No thank you, Dolly. I should be getting back. I only meant to come out for a little while and then got caught in the storm.'

Standing, leaning over to plant a brief kiss on Liz's cheek, Kate said 'I'll ring you later.'

She touched Greg on the shoulder. 'Nice meeting you. I hope you settle in all right.'

She gave him the briefest smile. 'Must fly. I promised the girls we would do something this afternoon,' she lied.

Halfway down the room, she looked back intending to give a small wave, but they were engrossed in conversation, the food on their plates forgotten. Kate retreated hastily.

The porch door was open, framing the drenched garden. A ray of watery sun slanted from a breach in the grey clouds. Here and there a raindrop glinted, catching her eye.

Negotiating the tiny rivers running down the path, Kate made for the gate. The mud on the towpath was glutinous, pocked with uprooted stones. Less mindful of her red sandals, they were beyond redemption; she went as quickly as she could back to the car park.

Driving home, Kate was pleased that she hadn't had the opportunity to talk to Liz alone. Liz would have done her utmost to dissuade her from racing to the city to begin a search for Adam. Liz was a good and loyal friend. But it was time she made her own decisions and not run to Liz every time a problem needed solving.

Pulling the car onto the driveway, she sat for a moment looking at the house but not really seeing it. She wondered if she should telephone Lydia and apologise. If she could speak to Lydia, she could ask her which hotel Frederick Banks had seen Adam in. Telephoning Mr Banks wasn't an option; he was a crabby old man with a high opinion of himself, and not much of a one for women. He wouldn't be any help. Probably tell her to mind her own business. She remembered him once saying 'Women only get involved in committees and meetings because they are curious creatures. Cheeky bastard! I don't suppose any woman has ever been curious about him, Kate thought crossly getting out of the car.

In the kitchen, flinging off her shoes and putting her bag onto the table, she reached for the empty kettle. Filling it, she put it to boil. Changing her mind, she took a bottle of wine off the rack and poured herself a glass.

Going to her bedroom she put the computer on and checked for emails and then began searching for hotels in Mayfair. In a moment she discovered there were seventy five hotels in the district. Nibbling the tip of a fingernail, she printed out the list.

Annie came through the front door with Millie.

Opening her bedroom door, Kate shouted down the stairs, 'Where's Beth and Carla?'

Irritable, Annie shouted back 'How should I know? They were here when I went out.'

Kate sighed with annoyance. 'Couldn't you have asked them where they were going or taken them with you?'

Coming out of the kitchen, Annie stood in the doorway looking up the stairs. Her eyes flashed ice. 'Why? They're your children, not mine.'

Huffy, Kate started down the stairs.

Turning back into the kitchen, Annie said to Millie 'Let's get out of here.'

Before Kate reached the last tread, the back door slammed closed. Looking through the long window in the hall she saw the two girls hurrying away from the house.

'You selfish little bugger,' Kate said under her breath.

It was almost nine o'clock in the evening before Annie returned. Her jacket wet with rain, and her damp hair hanging limply. Petulant, anticipating an almighty row, she came in through the back door hoping her entrance would go unnoticed and she could get to her room before an argument with her mother kicked off.

Kate, listening for Annie's arrival for hours, jumped up from the chair on hearing her footsteps.

Opening the sitting room door, she saw Annie half-way up the stairs. 'I want a word with you, young lady,' she said doing her utmost to curb her temper.

Annie gave a long drawn out sigh. 'What have I done now?'

'You know full well what you've done. You ran off, when I needed you.'

Annie came down each tread, deliberately slowly. 'You always need me. I can't be expected to spend my entire summer holiday looking after Carla and Beth. It's not fair.'

'I'll tell you what's not fair, lady. It's not fair that your father is no longer here. That I am so unhappy is not fair. All I am asking you to do is look after the girls once in a while.'

Annie's breath exploded from her. 'Once in a while? Are you having a joke? I look after them more than you do. You're hardly ever in. And when you are, you're on the computer, sending messages that will never be read.'

'I'm warning you, Annie. Keep a civil tongue in your head, or else!'

'Else what? You'll slap me again?' Without waiting for an answer, Annie flew up the stairs and ran into her bedroom, slamming the door behind her.

Deflated, Kate stood for a moment. She expected Carla or

Beth; both in their rooms, to come out, but the silence remained.

Turning, she went back into the sitting room. Picking a glass of wine up off the small table, she went to the window and looked out onto the wet grey night. What had it come to when she and Annie were constantly at loggerheads? They no longer had a normal conversation. Annie was becoming too demanding. She expected too much. Living without Adam was difficult enough without Annie making a scene every day. Typical teenager. There was only one thing important to them. Themselves!

The orange street lights flickered on. The pavement slick with rain glistened bronze.

The cold fear she felt so often, came to her now. She stood motionless for a long time.

The next morning she left the house before the children were awake. Leaving a note for Annie on the kitchen table. Reversing out of the garage, praying the Honda would not falter, she joined the early rush-hour traffic.

Arriving in London mid-morning, she found an expensive parking space in a private car park and slotted the Honda in.

Catching a bus to Mayfair, she sat in a window seat, looking out on the pedestrians, scanning every male that looked vaguely like Adam. Wondering how she would react if she saw him. Would she bang furiously on the window? Hope the bus stopped so she could run back to him? Or jump off, praying she landed safely? Finding him, holding him close, was worth a broken ankle.

After several hold-ups, the traffic snarling up twice on Victoria Street, a broken water main blocking off a side road, Kate alighted from the bus on Grosvenor Place.

Standing on the edge of the pavement, people intent on their

161

journeys rushing past, a reminder of a stampede of wild animals, she tried to get her bearing. Past visits to the city had been day-trips made during the Christmas holidays to see the lights on Oxford Street. She wasn't familiar with the hotels in Mayfair and Belgravia.

Ahead was the Unicorn Hotel, an impressive building, the architecture pure art-deco. The wide frontage a semi-circle of white rendering and long windows. Wide steps swept up to immensely tall double doors, painted dark green and embellished with gilt.

A uniformed doorman, the shoulders of his green jacket sporting braids of gold, lifted his hat to Kate as she came up the steps.

Acknowledging him with the briefest of smiles, Kate passed into the reception area. The desk, manned by four receptionists, seemed an acre away. Silently, the green and gold carpet was luxuriously thick, Kate headed for the only female standing behind the desk.

Three young male receptionists, wearing lightweight dark green suits and ties with pale green shirts, glanced up as she approached but then went back to what they were doing.

The woman, in her late twenties, smiled professionally. 'Can I help you, Madam?' she said, the smile revealing perfect pearly teeth, framed by coral lipstick.

The woman looked so utterly in control, her green suit and silky shirt impeccable, Kate felt suddenly travel worn and somewhat provincial in her dark grey trousers, cream shirt, and grey jacket. The shoes she had chosen for comfort, black and in need of a buff, were in such stark contrast to the receptionists green stilettos, Kate felt frumpy, heading for middle-age.

Throughout her journey, Kate had pondered on what line to take with hotel staff. Should she ask outright if Adam was a guest? Or pretend to be delivering something for Mr Adam Fontaine?

Although she hadn't made a conscious decision on what tack to take, she said sounding fairly confident, 'I am meeting my husband here, his name is Adam Fontaine. Has he left a message for me? Or given a time when he may return to his room?'

'Wait one moment,' the young woman said referring to a computer screen.

A minute passed slowly. Nervous, Kate took a leaflet from the counter top. Although she appeared to be reading the information, she took none of it in.

Taking her hazel eyes off the screen, the receptionist looked blankly at Kate. 'I'm afraid there is no one of that name registered at the hotel.'

Feeling a complete idiot, a blush rising to her face, Kate stammered 'I...I must have the wrong hotel.'

With barely a lift of her dark pencilled eyebrows, the receptionist turned to greet a bona fide guest.

Kate retreated to the sanctuary of the street and the nearest coffee shop, sure that the woman had supposed her to be a prostitute, doing the rounds of the expensive hotels, hoping a man would accost her before being required to state her business.

With a polystyrene cup of coffee before her, she glanced at the Unicorn Hotel leaflet. The tariff was beyond the means of most people, okay for oil rich Arabs and members of parliament, she supposed somewhat enviously.

How many people she wondered could actually afford to pay almost a thousand pounds a night for a room, noting this actually excluded breakfast? Certainly not Adam. Unless he had run away with a millionairess. If these prices reflected the hotel tariffs in Belgravia and Mayfair then she hadn't a hope of finding Adam in one of them. Perhaps he was staying locally. Frank Jefferson sighting of him walking into a Mayfair hotel was just a fluke. Maybe Adam was boarding economically but visiting a five-star hotel. If so, there was a chance she would see him on the streets or the parks.

Buoyed by this idea, she picked up her bag and went to the door. If he was here, she was determined to find him, however many miles she had to walk to do so.

Annie came out of her bedroom after an almost comatose sleep; she had drunk too much vodka the day before. Cautiously she went down stairs hoping to avoid her mother. Today, she would do her best to put things right. She would not lose her temper, nor make aggravating comments about her mother's state of mind. Somehow they had to pull together to keep the family, such as it was, together. And in some sort of harmony.

Coming into the kitchen, the floor cold beneath her bare toes, she saw the note on the table. For a terrible moment her heart lurched in her chest as the idea that her mother had killed herself flashed into her mind. Certain that her mother was hanging from the beam in the garage, her body blue, lifeless and pitifully dead. As the eldest she had to deal with the situation, cut her mother's cold and limp body down, call the police, and keep Carla and Beth from seeing her. With trembling fingers she unfolded the sheet of paper, truly expecting to see herself named as the reason for her mother's suicide. Reading the real reason for the note, tears of relief and anger filled her eyes. Throwing the note down, she covered her face with her hands. Sobbing as though her heart would break.

After walking for more than an hour, looking in café windows and through the glass doors of shops, Kate sat in the park to eat an egg and cress sandwich. Aware that the price of it would provide a simple supper for four.

Every park bench was occupied, the pathways filled with people taking a lunchtime stroll, making the most of the sunshine. Autumn would soon descend and a crisp coolness would come to the days.

Adam entered the park with a woman on his arm.

Stupefied, Kate felt a surge of malicious jealousy so strong she wanted to kill him and the woman, and even his children had they been close by.

The bread of her sandwich stuck in her dry mouth; she hadn't the saliva to swallow it.

The woman giggled, tucking her neat brown head into Adam's shoulder; a mini-second later he burst into mirthful laughter and Kate knew that it wasn't Adam. Adam had never laughed with joy as this man did.

Shaken, she felt sick, trembling with emotion.

Throwing the remains of the sandwich to the pigeons, she sat staring at the grey and iridescent pink and green feathers of the city birds.

***

'When is Mum coming home?' Beth demanded to know.

Annie was still shaken by the vision of her mother hanging in the garage. The steam of her anger towards Kate had turned to sad depression.

'The note didn't say, Beth. But I expect she'll be back before

165

your bedtime.'

'Seems funny to me,' the youngster said frowning. 'You don't think she's gone off, like dad did?' Tears of uncertainty and fear brimmed in her eyes.

Annie ruffled Beth's hair. 'Don't be silly. She'll be back.'

Carla morose sat pulling the cheese on toast Annie had made for lunch, to pieces. 'I thought we were going to the shops today to get new school blouses. Mine hardly fits me. The buttons won't do up properly.'

Annie's tone brightened. 'We can go to the shops and find out how much they cost. Find the cheapest for mum to buy.'

Having something else to think about blurred the awful image that had played in her head for the last few hours.

Beth got down off the kitchen chair. 'I'll wash my face. And put a clean jumper on.'

'You do that,' Annie said suddenly feeling very protective to her small sister.

'I'll come with you,' Carla said.

'You can get changed in a minute, Carla. First, you can put this lot into the dishwasher. I shouldn't have to do everything around here.'

'Sorry, Annie,' she said piling the plates and cutlery together.

Annie, near tears herself, was sorry she'd snapped. Speaking softly, she said 'If we each do a bit, it won't be so bad for me. You do understand how hard it is doing practically everything round here, don't you?'

'Yes, Annie. I understand. I'm sorry I haven't helped you more. I'll try very much harder from now on, promise.' She gave a wan smile.

Catching the bus at the end of the road, they came to the shops in the town centre. The pavements were packed, parents

166

and children shopping for the back-to-school uniforms and stationery.

Chatting lively, Beth held tight to Annie's hand.

Quiet, Carla walked shoulder to shoulder with Annie; afraid she would get lost and have to get the bus back home alone. Being alone outside had started to frighten her. Wishing she could hold Annie's hand too, she kept a careful step close to her.

***

Searching faces the entire day had made Kate's eyes ache.

Walking back to the car park to retrieve the Honda, she wondered if seeking Adam by day was the right thing to do, when in reality he had always been something of a night bird. Perhaps she would have a better chance of finding him after dark. Drinking in expensive hotel bars came naturally to him. As director of the bank he had been expected to entertain prospective wealthy clients.

Fishing in her handbag for the car keys, she wondered why she hadn't thought of searching for him after nightfall.

The black iron gates of the car park were open. Only a few cars were parked. The Honda was in the furthest corner, beside a high red brick wall, almost in total darkness. Checking her watch, seeing it was already past ten o'clock, she walked towards the shadowed car nervously. Had she known the place wasn't manned after dark, she wouldn't have used it. Deserted, in darkness, every car and the spaces between them made perfect hiding places for muggers. To make herself as inconspicuous as possible she trod lightly, masking her footsteps on loose stones.

Nearing the car she fished in her handbag for the keys. It

took two attempts to get the right one into the lock of the driver's door.

Climbing in, she locked the door quickly. Thanking her lucky stars that she was safe, she let out the breath trapped in her lungs.

A light tap on the driver's window startled her so fiercely she cried out in fright.

A filthy man, a vagrant, stood with his trouser flies open, his penis in his hand. Paralysed with fear, her limbs refusing to move, though her brain alive with terror was urging her to flee. Kate knew exactly what she should do, get the key in the ignition, start the car, drive away as fast as the elderly Honda could go in a low gear. But she was shaking so badly she was unable to put the key in the slot.

Outside the man was grunting like a pig. Scooping his dirt encrusted balls out of his tattered trousers with his other hand; he held them tightly, his penis almost touching the window. His filthy face froze in a wild grimace as a stream of white semen shot from him and ran down the glass.

Sickened, Kate cried out in shock. Too late she pushed the heel of her hand onto the horn on the steering wheel but the blare didn't wipe out the man's laughter as he retreated into the blackness.

Shivering, she turned the key. The engine fired and for the first time Kate saw the elderly car as something to be grateful for. Driving out of the car park, she steered towards the main road.

The disgusting incident wiped away any thought that she would stay the night in the city and search for Adam in the better hotels.

'Where are you, Adam?' she wailed, tears flowing down her cheeks.

Out of London, off the M25, the roads were fairly clear. Kate driving automatically, hardly registering when she changed direction or joined a new junction, the disgusting episode too fresh in her mind to concentrate properly.

The house was in complete darkness but for the porch light. Relieved to be safe home, Kate blessed the child that had thoughtfully left it on.

Getting out of the car, avoiding touching the mess now dried on the window, she went indoors. Tomorrow, she thought looking back at the car; I'll take it to the car wash. It's about time the poor thing had a spruce up. Entering the house, unnaturally quiet, she put her bag on the hall table. Going to the dining room she carried out a decanter of brandy. Taking it to the kitchen she poured herself a large measure.

Before eight o'clock the following morning, Kate dressed hurriedly and casually in blue jeans and a pale blue jumper and drove the Honda to the car wash. Watching the great wet soapy brushes swirling at the windows was cathartic, the water washing away all traces of the vagrant. Surprisingly she hadn't dreamed or suffered a nightmare after the incident; perhaps the two very large brandies helped her to sleep. She was going to do her utmost to put it out of her mind; she had enough to think about. Finding Adam was top of her agenda and she would not let a dirty old pervert divert her from that task.

The wash completed the brushes lifted clear of the car. Pleased to have accomplished something, even if it was only washing the car, Kate drove towards home.

Seeing Liz's car parked outside the house, she decided not to mention the incident with the tramp. She really wasn't up to listening to a lecture about walking the streets of London, alone and in the dark. Parking, she went into the house through the back door.

169

Liz and Greg were sitting at the kitchen table drinking coffee with Carla.

Liz was positively glowing with radiance. 'Greg has volunteered to look at your car, Kate,' she said smiling in his direction.

Taking a mug off the draining board, Kate poured coffee from the still warm pot. 'I would be really grateful, 'she said graciously.

Standing he drained his mug. 'Are the keys in it?'

'No. I have them here.' Kate fished them out of the back pocket of her jeans, handing the bunch to him.

'Back in a jiffy,' he said cheerfully, going through the back door. .

'Where's Beth?' Kate asked Carla.

'She's gone to the Bell's. Annie went out to get some eggs. We haven't any for breakfast.'

'Oh,' Kate said feeling she had failed again. She should have known there were no eggs and brought some back from the garage shop.

'I'll make some fresh coffee,' Kate said to no one in particular.

Liz's eyes were on the window, she was listening to Greg tinkering with the car. 'I'll take one out to Greg. Poor dear's a caffeine addict.'

Kate smiled. 'You've got it bad.'

Liz gave a tinkling laugh. 'No, not really,' she lied, grinning.

'It's just that me and Greg go back a long way. Unfinished business, perhaps.'

'Enjoy it while you can,' Kate said with irony.

The Honda fired into life, running irregularly.

Kate peered out of the window. Greg's head was hidden by the open bonnet. A few doors away, Mrs Wilson was watering hanging baskets, her eyes turned in Greg's direction.

Kate was grateful for the help; getting the car running properly would be a minor miracle. But it worried her to think that the neighbours might suppose Greg to be staying with her. She wasn't proud of herself knowing that Greg's presence on her drive made her uncomfortable.

'Handsome, isn't he?' Liz said misinterpreting Kate's interest in Greg.

'Yes, he is,' Kate replied but her mind was elsewhere. The school term begins next week, she thought. She would have more free time. She would travel down to London by train and search for Adam.

Annie could take care of the girls. Get the supper for them after school and see that they did their homework.

She would hunt the streets until she found him. She had no intentions of giving up, however long it took.

Money was the main drawback. There wasn't any to spare for travelling back and forth. It was hard enough to make ends meet on benefits.

The job at the school, had she taken it, might have helped. But working interfered with her search. She and the girls would just have to make further cut-backs to make the money go further.

Liz had berated her last week; she had seen Annie and Carla in a charity shop looking for school blouses and a skirt that would pass muster as school uniform. Well, it couldn't be helped, they were hard up. She was pleased that Annie was turning out to be such a good little manager. It had annoyed Liz, but for the life of her she couldn't see why, Annie was only using her initiative. What was wrong with that?

The following Tuesday the girls went back for the first day of term. Annie was furious that it had been left to her to explain to the Head that at the end of term neither she nor Carla would be attending again. At break time, making for the Head's office, the letter from her mother in her skirt pocket, Annie knocked on Mrs Turley's door.

Hiding her distain for a parent who left it to a child to explain the circumstances of recent difficulties, Mrs Turley heard the child out. Offering a cup of tea to Annie when she became tearful.

'This is an important year for you, Annie,' she said calmly watching the young girl wrestle with her emotions. 'It's imperative for your future to get good GCSE results.'

Wiping her nose, Annie nodded. 'I'll miss being at this school. Carla feels the same. She cries a lot.'

So do you, I shouldn't wonder, the elderly woman thought compassionately. 'Leave it with me, Annie. I will see what can be done. Maybe as you are so close to GCSE's the board will look favourably upon foregoing the fees until you have completed the course.'

'It's very kind of you Mrs Turley but it wouldn't work. I couldn't possibly stay here when Carla has to attend the comprehensive. It wouldn't be fair. She knows no one there. I think it would make her unhappier.' She paused. 'I must look after Carla and Beth. Though I'm grateful that you are trying to help.'

Mrs Turley gave a long drawn out sigh. 'I am impressed by you sisterly concern. If Carla is so unhappy perhaps you should have a word with your mother. See what she suggests.'

Annie smiled bleakly. 'There would be no point in that at all. We hardly ever see her. She is searching London for our father.' Her voice dropping, she said softly 'I think she is going mad.'

'Annie,' Mrs Turley said seriously 'the best thing you can do is get to your doctor and ask for help. Not only for Carla but your mother too. The alternative is to seek help from a relative. Perhaps your grandmother could help.'

'I hadn't thought to ask granny,' Annie said grateful for the suggestion. 'Gran would certainly talk to mum and make her see things more sensibly.'

Looking over the rim of her spectacles, Mrs Turley said earnestly 'I want you to keep me informed of the situation especially if it changes for the worse, Annie. Will you promise me you will do that?'

'Yes, Mrs Turley. I promise.' Sensing the interview was at an end, Annie stood. 'I'm glad I confided in you, Mrs Turley. Things seem a bit clearer now.'

After Annie had gone back to her lesson, Mrs Turley sat for a while thinking about the family, especially Carla; she was a quiet sensitive girl. She feared for her future.

Kate walking through the park wondered how the girls had got on during the first day back at school. Beth, the little tyke, couldn't wait to get to her classroom to tell everyone she was going to the Osborne Junior, the school for poor kids.

As far as Annie was concerned, moving would be like water off a duck's back. Resilient, Annie would be happy at the local comprehensive as she was at Highgate Ladies College. Her GCSE's would be disrupted, but Annie was a bright girl; she would cope with a little bit of upheaval. God, hadn't they all had to cope with a bit of that, especially herself.

Coming to the pond, Kate stopped to watch the moorhens, black as jet, skimming by, swimming effortlessly. A small boy, holding a paper bag tossed small pieces of bread to them, chuckling babyishly as the birds swam towards the edge of the pond, devouring the morsels in one greedy gulp.

Although Kate watched the small child her mind was on

Carla. Adam had spoilt her, given in too readily to her tears. Coaxing and cajoling the child out of her small depressions and insecurities. Carla was a lot stronger than Adam had given her credit for. Beneath the façade, Carla was a manipulative child. She'd had Adam wound around her little finger.

Adam, Adam, Adam, she thought desperately, looking towards the far trees as though the power of her yearning would make him appear.

Longing for nightfall, she planned on visiting several hotel bars before catching the late train home, convinced it was in the plush surrounding that she would find Adam. Nervous excitement was already uncoiling in her belly.

She glanced down at her watch-face. It was just after four, the girls would be making their way towards home.

Hopefully, Annie wouldn't be too angry at being left in charge. But she really had no right to be, it wasn't as though she hadn't left food for them; there was a Tesco's lasagne in the fridge, which only needed baking in the oven for thirty minutes.

People were coming into the park in droves, office workers shortcutting to the underground. Glancing at her watch again, Kate saw that an hour had passed without her realising it.

Her cell phone buzzed in her pocket. Eagerly, it could be Adam, she drew it out. But it was one of the children on the home phone. Guiltily she pushed it back in her pocket wishing she could turn it off, but she couldn't, Adam might phone. Tomorrow, she told herself, I will stay home and make it up to them. If she should find Adam tonight, it would vindicate her absence.

Coming out of the park, she headed for the small café she had noticed earlier in a side street. The menu in the window was reasonably priced.

Kate emerged from the *Silver Spoon* to a grey damp early dusk. The low light brought the street lights on, the glow accentuating the dreary drabness of the alleyway. Earlier, in the intermittent sunlight, the ancient walk-through was thronged with people cutting through to Grosvenor Place. With the closing of the working day it had taken on a different aspect entirely; it was eerily quiet, the back door of the shops closed and locked for the night. She was horribly aware of the click-clack the heels of her shoes made on the dirty pavement. Behind her footfalls matched hers, the stride long and purposeful. Imagining a mugger, or worse, Kate started to run.

Out of breath she emerged into the brightness of Grosvenor Place. Several passers-by gave her inquisitive looks. Heart racing, she glanced over her shoulder, but whoever had shared the side street with her was gone, vanishing into the labyrinth of alleyways.

Beneath her clothes she was clammy with perspiration. Her heart rate pulsing rapidly and the food she had just eaten lay greasily in her stomach.

If it wasn't for her need to find Adam and to bring him home to safety, she would turn her back on London and never return. A dark undercurrent was flowing through the city streets, which had not been there a few short years ago.

Several teenage boys, their faces hidden by hooded tops, came out of a doorway. Jostling one another, they slipped into a darkening alleyway. Their vulgar calls and the chinking of a kicked bottle reverberating down the bricked passageway.

Feeling vindicated for her pessimistic view of the city, Kate joined the flow of pedestrians.

Park Lane, she had already decided, was probably the most likely area to find Adam; the exclusivity and elegance of the hotels would appeal to his sense of style.

On her left was Hyde Park, the trees had lost colour with the darkening evening and now were tall soft blurs against the dark-grey sky. People were still walking across the grass, singly or in couples, the shifting figures black smudges until they were lost to the shadows.

In the darkest hours, women are raped in parks, she thought. Raped and murdered. Their bodies undiscovered until daylight, when a passing pedestrian stumbles over the wreckage of a life.

It began to drizzle. The headlights of the traffic gleaming on the road surface. If she didn't get indoors her hair would lose its bounce entirely. Flattened hair, tired and untidy wasn't the way she wanted Adam to see her on this, their first meeting in nearly two months, she thought gloomily.

Reaching the Marsh Hotel she went inside, crossing the foyer; skirting passed the reception area she followed the discreet signs to the ladies rest room.

Once inside, leaning over the shiny surface surrounding the washbasins, she looked at her hair in the mirror. It wasn't as awful as she feared it might be. Pity the same can't be said of my face, she thought despondently. There were hollows beneath her eyes the colour of old bruises. I am beginning to look old, she wailed silently, touching the fine lines that ran from nose to the corners of her mouth. Delving into her bag, finding foundation cream and lipstick she started to make repairs.

Several minutes later, emerging from the rest room she made her way to the restaurant. The only thought in her mind was of Adam, wondering what his reaction would be if she found him.

With her heart beating quickly with excitement, she stood at the pillared doorway looking in. The opulent restaurant was busy. There was an aroma of gourmet food in the air. The slight clatter of porcelain and cutlery, and a gentle hum of conversation. Crystal chandeliers glistened diamond bright, shimmering on glass and silver ware. Kate's eyes flashed from one damask draped table to another. There were several men of Adam's age group, some of a similar build, but the face she craved to see was not there. Her sense of disappointment turned to despair.

The head waiter came and stood beside her, stiff and self-important. 'Can I help you madam?'

'No,' she said despondently. 'I was just looking for someone.'

'Enquire at the reception desk, Madam. Maybe a message has been left there.'

Turning away, her heart beating a great deal slower, Kate followed the sound of a piano playing softly in the cocktail bar.

The white middle-aged pianist at the ebony grand piano glanced fleetingly towards her as she came into the bar.

In contrast to the restaurant, the large square room was glass and brushed aluminium. The fabrics the colour of grey slate and granite. Subtle wall lamps casting beams of white light on several contemporary sculptures.

She took the room in at a glance. Ignoring the paunchy bald man watching her as she made her way to a corner table. She felt out of place, like an uninvited and unwelcome guest at a party.

There were several youngish men, city types, and a smattering of slightly older males propping up the bar, but Adam wasn't in the room. How naïve of me, she thought hopelessly, to think I might find him in the first hotel I walk into.

As she took a seat, a waiter appeared at the table. With a slight bow, poised to write her order on a small notepad, he said 'What can I get for you, Madam?'

Kate answered in a monotone, 'A gin and tonic, please.'

Dipping his head, he placed a paper coaster before her.

Aware that she stuck out like a sore thumb, the few females present were sitting at tables with male companions, Kate rummaged in her handbag as though searching for something important. It was preferable to raising her eyes and confronting the interested and rather suspicious glances she was arousing.

Returning, the waiter placed the glass with the gin and tonic and the bill on the table. Giving her a small smile before heading back to the bar.

Picking up the glass, running with condensation, Kate took a mouthful of the chilled drink.

An expensively dressed man, clean shaven and almost completely bald, broke away from a group of men at the bar.

With a stab of panic, Kate realised he was heading towards her; hoping to discourage him she dropped her eyes.

In a moment he was standing beside the table. There was a slightly mocking smile on his mouth as he looked down at her. 'May I buy you a drink?'

Stricken with embarrassment, Kate's face reddened. 'I'm waiting for my husband.'

There was a momentary pause, then without making a reply he retreated to his companions at the bar. The men hooted with laughter at something he said.

Acutely embarrassed, Kate grabbed her bag, intent on retreating as quickly as possible.

Light on his feet, the waiter came to her table. With a sardonic smile he said 'The gentlemen at the bar have asked if you would like to join them whilst you wait for your husband.'

Eyes blazing with anger, Kate opened her bag and took out a brown leather wallet. Throwing a ten pound note onto the table, she snapped 'This should cover the price of my drink. Tell the so-called *gentlemen* that I prefer to wait in the foyer.'

Woman's lib, she thought crossly. Who are we kidding? Men still take us for whores if we have the courage to enter a bar alone.

Irritable, dissatisfied with life, disgruntled that she'd fled the Marsh Hotel at the first hurdle. And although she accepted that it was unlikely, she might have found Adam if she'd persisted.

With a feeling of complete failure, she caught the earlier train back home.

Looking through the darkened window, houses and streets flashing by, she came to the conclusion that visiting hotels just wasn't sensible, it was too expensive, and she hadn't the nerve to hack it. Driving down, sleeping in the car on Friday nights was the solution. This way she could search the Saturday antique markets that Adam so loved visiting.

An hour into the journey, the snack and beverage trolley was wheeled around. Kate refused a coffee. A small economy after the extravagance of the gin and tonic in the hotel bar.

Chapter 11

Beth, sitting at the kitchen table, kicking the leg of a chair, watched Annie stack dishes into the dishwasher. 'It'll be my birthday next week,' she said with an anticipatory smile.

'You've told me a dozen times already,' Annie said indifferently. Tucking her tee-shirt into the waistband of her green skirt.

'Sorry,' Beth answered cheekily.

Annie tut-tutted. Deliberately remaining silent, she waited for Beth to mention a party.

'I always have a party on my birthday,' Beth said, drawing out each word slowly.

Annie hid her smile.

'So, will I have a party?'

'Don't know. You'll have to ask mum.'

Beth harrumphed. 'Fat chance of me having one, then.' Mimicking her mother's voice she said 'You know we can't afford it. Money is tight.'

A frown wrinkled her small brow. 'It's not fair. Mum goes to London every Friday. There's money for that. But not money for me to have a birthday party. Suppose there'll be no cake or anything. I'll just sit at home. It'll be just like a normal day.'

Annie gave a long drawn out sigh. 'Don't be so silly, Beth. Of course it won't be like a normal day. For a start, it'll be your birthday.'

'Big deal,' Beth replied sulkily. 'If dad was here, he'd let me have one.'

Losing her temper, Annie said sharply. 'Well, he's not bloody here, is he? So for God sake, stop talking about him.

180

It's bad enough that mum runs off to search for him at every opportunity, without you going on about him as well.'

Tears filled Beth's eyes. 'You are a cow, Annie,' she said breaking into a sob. 'I'm allowed to talk about daddy, if I want to.' Climbing off the chair she ran out of the kitchen, her small feet thumping on the stair treads as she rushed to her bedroom.

Annie sighed.

Kate, dishevelled and tired, came in through the back door.

'Oh, you're back,' Annie said coldly, slamming the dishwasher door closed.

'Yes, I'm back. But I can't say I think very much of the welcome.'

Annie's eyes narrowed. 'What do you expect, a royal bloody fanfare?'

'Less of your cheek, my girl. And for your information, I do expect a bit of courtesy when I come in.'

Breathless with indignation, Annie stared at her mother. 'I too would like a bit of courtesy. The courtesy of being asked if I will look after the house and the girls whilst you disappear overnight, again.'

'You make it sound as though I am doing something indecent, instead of looking for your father. Do you think its pleasant napping in the car? Searching the streets for him for hours on end?'

Annie gave a sigh of exasperation. 'Then why do it? Give it up, Mum.'

Kate's voice trembled. 'I can't Annie. I have to find him.'

'And in the meantime, whilst you go on wild goose chases, what's left of the family, falls apart.'

'Don't be so dramatic, Annie.' Kate replied sharply. Reaching for the kettle, she filled it under the cold tap. She was dying for a cup of tea.

Frustrated, Annie walked out of the room.

In her bedroom, sitting on the edge of the bed, she thought of Beth. It really wasn't fair that she had to miss out on her ninth birthday. It wasn't Beth's fault that everything had gone wrong.

Opening the tin box she kept the tips she earned from her shifts at the bistro, she tipped the coins onto the bedcover. She had a good idea how much was there, and already knew that it wasn't enough for a decent birthday present and a party.

Dispirited she contemplated a shoplifting spree with Millie. They had done it before. In the beginning they had done it for fun; now it was more of a necessity. Sighing, she returned the eighteen pounds to the tin box.

***

Millie was caught. A surveillance camera in the Austin Sport Shop, recording her placing expensive trainers into a brown leather bag, brought the owner of the shop to her side. He was brisk, officious and extremely angry. Snatching the bag from Millie, he held her firmly by the arm.

Flecks of spittle peppered her face as he barked, 'This store has a policy of prosecuting all shoplifters.'

His face burned with outrage. For a terrible moment, Millie thought he might actually hit her.

Unaccustomed to being treated harshly, Millie tried to shake him off. 'Let me go,' she snapped haughtily.

Tightening his grip, he spoke through firmly clenched teeth, 'The only place you are going to is to the police station.'

A young female assistant stood beside a clothes rack, ogling the scene.

'Don't just stand there acting like a fool. Call the police,' he shouted rudely.

Millie tried to shake herself free of him. 'If you don't let go of me, I'll sue you for assault.'

He gave a short, mocking laugh. 'Tell it to the judge. I'm sure he'll take my word over a thief's.'

Standing beside a rack of winter jackets, Annie, heart in her mouth, watched the scene unfold. She had been trying on a skiing jacket, when the manager grabbed Millie. She was fully expecting him to grab her too, as they had come into the shop together. If he searched her bag he would discover two tee-shirts, a waterproof stop watch, and a wind-up torch, stolen from his stock. The watch and torch were birthday presents for Beth.

Her first instinct was to flee, to run to the open door and disappear into the Saturday shopping crowd. But she couldn't abandon Millie. Deserting her friend now would be just too mean.

Through the plate glass window she saw a police car pull up, parking on the double yellow lines. Two uniformed officers climbed out, both looking towards the shop.

The blood in Annie's veins turned to ice.

The assistants, manager, and Millie were standing like statues, their eyes on the two approaching police officers.

Slowly and silently she slipped out of the skiing jacket, lowering it gently to the floor. No one but Millie seemed aware of her presence, hiding behind the racks of garments.

Using the moment the manager started to shout again, Annie stooped down, and slinked towards the open door. Terrified that she might accidentally touch something and a hanger would rattle, she held herself taut, forgetting to breathe.

From the voices, she knew that neither the manager, Millie nor the police had moved; they were still standing in the centre aisle of the shop.

She got near enough to the door to feel the light breeze rippling down the street. Two second from freedom, Annie froze. There were several yards of open space lying between her and outdoors, crossing would expose her to the manager and the gawping assistants.

The phone rang and all eyes but Annie's turned to it.

It's now or never, she thought, breaking from cover, making a dash for the pavement.

Every ounce of her being expected a shout, a demand that she remain exactly where she was.

Rushing across the street, darting between slow moving traffic, she raced to the sanctuary of a coffee shop.

Standing in the doorway, she glanced back to the shop, but she couldn't see Millie or the police. There was too much paraphernalia in the window to get a clear view of the interior.

The coffee shop was familiar to her, a spiral staircase led to an upper floor. Climbing it, the bag with the stolen items thumping her thigh, she came to the top. Fortunately a window table was vacant, going to it, she perched on the edge of the seat, craning her neck to watch Austin's shop front.

An uninterested waitress came to her, taking her order for a latte, before ambling back to the counter to join a pair of girls operating the stainless steel equipment.

Annie, watching the shop door intently, was unaware of the cacophony of the coffee grinder, rattling crockery, and the hiss of steam boiling a jug of milk.

She didn't have to wait long before Millie appeared, walking between the two police officers. They both had hold of Millie's arms, as though clutching a desperate criminal.

Several pedestrians stopped to stare, others turned to glance at the spectacle before moving on. Annie gave an involuntary sob of shock witnessing Millie's humiliation.

The trio reached the car, the back door was opened and Millie was bustled in, one of the officers following, to sit beside her. Moments later she was driven away.

The latte arrived; Annie sipped the hot coffee without tasting it. Mentally numb, shocked at what had happened she sat holding the hot mug between her hands, unaware that it was scorching her palms.

The bus ride home was a nightmare, the worry that Millie might shop her to the police turning her insides to jelly. She needed a drink and thanked her lucky stars that there was an unopened bottle of vodka, nicked from the bistro, hidden at the bottom of her wardrobe.

As it was Saturday, and still fairly early, there was a good chance that her mother wouldn't be at home. For the first time ever, Annie prayed that her mother's mission, searching the hotels and antique markets in London for her husband, would last for as long as possible.

She had to get drunk. It was the only way she was going to stop the image of Millie spilling her guts to the police, spinning in her brain.

Nervously, searching for police cars, Annie got off the bus. It was a short walk to home; as she got nearer, her nervousness increased. What if her mother was home and the police were there?

A small involuntary twitch was tugging at the outer corner of one eye. She really had to get to the vodka before she became a nervous wreck. After all, she thought grimly, I am my mother's daughter, and my mother is as mad as a hatter. Perhaps madness is in my genes.

The driveway was empty, the house looked closed up, unoccupied. Relieved, Annie let out a long held breath.

185

Her hands trembled as she unlocked the door and went inside.

'Is anyone at home?' she called, her voice echoing through the empty rooms.

Thankful the house was empty, she ran up the stairs heading for her bedroom. Opening the wardrobe door, she raked through an assortment of old jumpers. The vodka bottle came to her hand. Sighing with relief and pleasure, she broke the seal.

Putting the bottle to her mouth, she swallowed three times. The alcohol hit her empty stomach. Her head reeling slightly, she sat on the edge of her bed, and drank again.

***

Annie dragged herself out of a deep slumber on hearing Carla and Beth come clattering into the house.

'Hey, you two, where have you been?' Kate called to them from her bedroom door. 'And where's Annie?'

Startled hearing her mother's voice, Annie climbed off the bed quickly, her coordination clumsy. Grabbing the bottle of vodka off the bedside table, she hid it at the bottom of the wardrobe.

'How should I know?' Beth answered her mother cheekily.

'Less of your lip, young lady,' Kate said sharply. Trying to look casual, Annie came out of her room, yawning. 'Who's looking for me?'

Surprised, Kate said 'I didn't know you were in.'

'Yeah. I wanted to finish my homework. But I must have fallen asleep.' She yawned loudly again for effect.

Still drugged from the alcohol, the events of the morning escaped her. It took another thirty seconds to recall fully the shoplifting and her retreat from the shop. Suddenly she felt sick and faint.

The phone rang.

Panicking, it could be the police, Annie's voice cracked, 'I'll get it.'

Running down the stairs before Beth could overtake her, she almost stumbled on the last tread.

Picking up the phone, she walked into the sitting room. 'Hello,' she said meekly.

'Annie, its Millie.'

'Jesus, Millie where are you?'

'Home, and grounded for ever according to my dad.'

'What happened?' Annie was almost afraid to ask.

'The cops called my dad. He turned up at the station. There was a frightful row, he's furious with me. We both have to go back there again tomorrow. I'm going to be given a caution. Oh, and I'm banned from all of the Austin stores. As though I care. Their stuff's rubbish.'

Annie giggled, more from relief than amusement.

'And is that all?'

'Yeah. I don't give a damn about the caution. Listening to my old man you'd think it was the end of the world.'

She giggled. 'The shame of it. My daughter a shoplifter. What will the neighbours say if it makes the local paper? Dear mother went to bed for the afternoon, after drinking several martinis to steady her nerves.'

She sighed. 'Being grounded is not so bad. The oldies are out most of the time, so they'll never know if I'm in or out. Text me tomorrow. We can meet up in town.'

'Yeah. Okay,' Annie said half-heartedly. Not really sure if she wanted to hang around with Millie, if she was getting known to the police. She was becoming dangerously wild, taking drugs too. Her older brother always had a stash of coke. He stole cars for fun. Some nights, when she was sleeping over at Millie's Clark would drive them to out-of-the-way car parks and let them get behind the wheel. It was good fun, racing the cars. Clark had taught her handbrake turns, hearing the tyres squeal really got her pulse racing. If she stopped being Millie's friend she'd miss that, but for the moment, until the fuss died down, she'd tell Millie that she was taking care of Beth and Carla. Millie would buy that; she knew what a nightmare her mother had become. After all, they did refer to her as Mad Kate.

Three days before Beth's birthday, a pile of post dropped through the letter box. Kate rushed to pick it up off the doormat.

Shuffling through the envelopes she checked for Adam's handwriting. Surely, she told herself for the hundredth time, he would not let Beth's ninth birthday go by without contacting her.

The child was anxious for a card from him. Little Beth was convinced that he would turn up for her party.

Sighing with disappointment she put aside Beth's cards. Taking the other envelopes she went into the kitchen.

Her mother, thoughtful as ever, had sent a cheque for a hundred pounds. No doubt she had guessed that money was too tight to give Beth a proper birthday present and party. Slipping the cheque into her wallet to take to the bank later, she smiled.

Turning over the second envelope she discovered it was addressed to Adam. Her heart lurched. Tearing it open, seeing it was nothing more than a letter from the bank, her disappointment was so great she felt utter despair.

'There are insufficient funds in the account to meet this

188

month's direct debits,' the manager wrote, 'If the bank are to honour the payments, funds should be deposited into the account within twenty-four-hours.'

Kate's heart sank. Now she would have to rely entirely on the social service benefits paid into her own account. There's nothing for it but to go to the bank and explain the situation, she decided in a rare moment of resolve.

The other envelope was a circular, tearing it in half; she sat at the table wondering what she was going to do to meet the bills.

Giving up her search for Adam would certainly save money. The cost of petrol to drive to London and the price of food when there were financially crippling. Although she did eat cheaply, or skipped meals entirely. But bringing an end to the search was admitting defeat. Giving up on Adam. How could she possibly do that?

If she got a job it might help, but not by much; she wasn't qualified or trained to do anything. The options were limited; she couldn't expect to get paid more than the minimum wage.

A care home, shop, canteen, or working on a supermarket checkout was about the nub of it. The local supermarket would be awful. Imagine weighing carrots for a member of the golf club. The come-down didn't bear thinking about. 'It's all vanity and pride,' she said aloud. 'But that doesn't make it any easier.' Adam's defection was causing enough pain without going looking for more.

She glanced out of the window. Duets of cars were parked on several driveways. Emblems of shared households. A landscape gardener, his sign-written pick-up truck parked alongside the curb, was cutting back the shrubbery at the Bell's house. Easily affordable, she thought, for the chief partner of a firm of solicitors.

Last night she had a terrible dream about Adam. He was floundering in a fast flowing river. Whilst she stood on the river bank, completely paralysed, unable to jump in and save him. He floated away, staring back at her with a dreadful look of hatred on his face.

On waking, sweaty, and heart racing, she reached out for him, but the other side of the bed was cold and empty. And like a child, she wept tears of disappointment into her pillow.

I must go on looking for him, she thought. I can't give up.

Chapter 12

The day of Beth's ninth birthday dawned.

Rising early, donning a blue silky dressing gown, Kate went downstairs barefooted. Aware that the slightest sound would bring Beth running out of her room. Bursting with noisy excitement, anticipating her presents and the birthday party this afternoon.

Kate wanted to enjoy the peace and quiet for as long as possible, just to sit in the kitchen in the bleak fragile morning light, watching the sky lighten. Sure in her heart that this was the day that Adam would come. That she had survived his absence was some sort of victory.

A sense of excitement kept bubbling up. Perhaps this would be the first day of a new life together. Because she was determined to convince him that together they could clear his name and lay the blame for the embezzlement where it belonged, at Tony Everett's door.

Adam, she knew without a doubt, had only run away because he could see no way to prove his innocence. His disappearance had absolutely nothing to do with their relationship. The bond between them was strong, would be made stronger still, when they were together again.

Preparing a pot of tea, a treat from the usual bag in the mug, she wondered if he would appear unannounced during the party, or come earlier, be here when the girls came home from school.

Her anxious excitement was like the feelings of a child on Christmas morning, wonderful, joyful, tinged with dread and fear that the much longed-for gift would not materialise.

Sipping the hot tea. Scenarios of his arrival gradually

unfolding in her mind, the moment when he took her in his arms and kissed her, re-invented several times, Kate sat daydreaming, as the sky lightened to pearl.

The girls began to move around upstairs.

Kate gave an odd little grimace of disappointment. Divorcing herself from Beth's laughter and the cheerful noisy shouts of 'happy birthday,' she tried to hold onto the images of Adam returning.

The moment the girls departed for school, Beth creating a row about being forced to go on her birthday, Kate went to hunt in her wardrobe for something to wear. Planning to be dressed and made-up well before the party started, in case, just in case, Adam came early.

Flicking through a rack of clothes she found a red silk jersey dress, Adam's favourite. Happy with the choice, singing, she went to shower.

As arranged, Liz came around at lunchtime to help decorate the hall and dining room with balloons and streamers. Outdoors, braving the chilly breeze, they tied several pink and silver helium balloons to a shrub at the corner of the drive and draped a fluorescent pink Happy Birthday streamer on to the front of the house.

Throughout the preparation, laying out the party food, sticking the nine sparklers into the pink and white cake, it was obvious to Liz that Kate's mind was elsewhere. Initially she put Kate's distraction down to her recalling past birthdays, when they were a complete family. Beth's birthday being the first family celebration since Adam's departure, was sure to be upsetting. But as the afternoon wore on, noticing how often Kate glanced out of the windows, or jumped at the slightest sound, Liz began to wonder if she was expecting Adam. If he in fact had made contact. The closer the time came to the girls returning home Kate's mood was hyper, almost febrile. Which worried Liz; Kate was mentally fragile, another disappointment may crush her completely.

Expecting Beth at any moment, Kate checked her watch for the umpteenth time. 'She's five minutes late,' she said, craning her neck to look out of the hall window.

'I shouldn't worry.' Liz smiled. 'The little minx will be making last minute arrangements with her friends. Checking they're bringing presents.'

Ten minutes later Carla and Annie came walking up the drive, bickering. As they came through the door, Kate seriously worried, snapped at the pair, 'Have either of you seen Beth?'

Annie tutted. 'No. Why would we? Beth doesn't come home the same way as us.'

Carla was more helpful. 'She'll be talking at the school gate.'

'She's never late,' Kate muttered, glancing once more at her watch.

The two girls clomped up the stairs heavily.

Kate sighed. The galumphing was all for effect, a small rebellion for being forced to wear old fashioned black lace-up shoes for school.

'I think I'll wear my lavender dress for the party,' Carla said to Annie as they both reached the head of the stairs.

'Why bother?' Annie sighed. 'They're only a bunch of kids.'

'It's Beth's birthday. It's special.'

'Whatever,' Annie answered disinterestedly.

Annoyed, Carla went into her room, slamming the door.

Entering her own bedroom, Annie kicked the door closed. The impact making a loud thwack.

Kate raised an eyebrow in irritation as she shrugged into a cardigan. 'I'll drive down to the school. See if I can find her.'

Grabbing her car keys off the hall table, Liz said 'I'll drive. Then you can look out for her.'

The phone rang.

Kate's heart somersaulted. Something awful has happened to Beth, she thought with dreadful premonition. For an instant her hand hovered over the phone, as she gathered courage to answer.

Watching Kate's face as she spoke to the caller, several thoughts, none of them good, came swiftly into Liz's mind.

Kate uttered a little cry, her hand flying to her mouth. 'I'll come immediately,' she said shakily down the phone.

The suspense was unbearable and Liz said over loudly, 'What's happened?'

Kate's breathing was irregular, she looked dazed and fragile. 'Beth has been run over by a car outside the school gates.'

Liz's blood turned to ice. 'Is she badly hurt?'

'I don't know. They've taken her to St. Mark's,' Kate answered feebly.

Grabbing her bag off the hall table, Liz scrabbled for the car keys. 'I'll drive.'

In a trance, Kate climbed into the car. Oblivious to how Annie and Carla had come to be there before her.

As Liz reversed off the driveway, all eyes turned to the bright pink balloons floating above the shrub. The crisis making a mockery of the cheerful display.

Morose, looking out of the side window, Annie felt terrible. Why had she been so derogatory about little Beth's party? She was nine-years-old, for God sake. Now she might be dead and there would be no future parties for her. Why was she always so mean and horrible? Thinking of Beth's excitement earlier, tears welled up in Annie's eyes.

Carla wanted reassurance from her mother that everything was going to be all right. But she was afraid to speak for fear that Kate would snap her head off, tell her not to pester. But it was hard to be silent when she wanted to know if Beth was still alive.

Turning right into Buckingham Road, Liz drove onto the dual carriageway that would take them to the outskirts of the town, to the newly-built hospital.

The rush hour traffic was beginning to build up. Liz glanced at the clock on the dashboard; it was four-thirty. With luck, it should only be a ten minute journey. She would drop Kate and the girls off at the A and E entrance. Park the car. By the time she joined them, they should have news of Beth.

She tried her damnedest not to think of Beth lying lifeless, the joy, the cheeky smile wiped out for ever. If she allowed those images to take root, she would cry. It's hard to drive in floods of tears, she told herself. She had to be strong. Kate and the girls needed her to be there for them.

Silent, a huge terrible hole where her stomach should be, Kate kept her eyes on the traffic ahead, willing it to move faster. Liz's left hand lay warmly comforting on her thigh.

'She might have got off lightly,' Liz said glancing sideways at her.

Kate didn't reply, just kept staring ahead.

Changing gear, Liz looked in the rear view mirror, then moving into the outside lane she overtook a truck.

Seen from the approach road, the hospital was huge, several floors of rectangle windows reflecting the grey sky.

An ambulance, blue light flashing, overtook the car.

Ignoring the car park, Liz drove straight up to the main entrance of the A and E unit.

Snapping off the seatbelt, Kate opened the door and jumped

out. Without waiting for the girls, she went inside quickly.

'I'll park the car and come and find you,' Liz said to Annie and Carla as they got out.

Running, the girls caught up with Kate in the main reception area.

A short queue was waiting at the sweeping reception desk. Dashing to the head, Kate in mounting desperation waited for one of the three women sitting behind computer screens to look up.

Resisting the urge to thump the top of the desk with her fist, Kate cried out 'My little girl has been in an accident. I have to find her.'

With a minute sigh, one of the receptionists shifted her large bottom on the seat of her chair. 'Name?' she said over-sharply.

Kate rushed her words. 'Bethany Fontaine. She was run down outside…'

Deftly moving the computer mouse, the receptionist glanced at the screen. 'There is no Bethany Fontaine registered. Are you sure she came to this hospital?'

Kate's voice rose hysterically, 'Where else would she be taken to? For God's sake. She was knocked down nearby.'

The receptionist's grey eyebrows arched disapprovingly. Flintily she stared at Kate. 'Try in the casualty unit.'

Turning away quickly, missing the woman's tight lipped riposte, Kate dashed towards the corridor signposted to Accident and Emergency. Carla and Annie mournfully following in her hectic wake.

Somewhere in the background an ambulance siren wailed. The flashing light casting a cold blue shadow on the dull windows.

I must find Beth. I must find Beth, Kate thought, the words repeating like a mantra in her mind.

Unable to bear the suspense and uncertainty a moment longer, Annie rushed to the nursing station where two white female nurses were checking a medical file.

'Can you tell me where Beth Fontaine is? She was brought in here a short time ago,' she said nervously.

The younger of the two, a chubby brunette with bright hazel eyes, glanced at Kate. 'Are you the child's mother?'

'Yes,' Kate said fearfully.

The nurse's face softened in sympathy. 'Beth was taken to the x-ray unit a few minutes ago, Mrs Fontaine.'

Kate blurted 'Is she badly hurt? Can I see her?'

'We're taking very good care of her. As soon as she's brought back here, you can see her.'

Frightened, Carla clung to Annie's arm.

Seeing the small tableau as she entered the corridor, Liz's heart filled with dread.

The nurse came from behind the desk. 'I'll take you to the Family Room. I'll come to get you as soon as little Bethany gets back,' she said, steering the family away from the nursing station.

Desperately lonely for Adam, needing his strength more than ever, Kate walked into the comfortless room. Someone pressed the light switch and the plain magnolia walls were made stark under the overhead light. Away from the natural noise of the hospital, or sound of the ordinary outside world, the room had stillness akin to a wake. Silent, remote, Kate stared unseeing at the rectangular window. The agony of waiting for news of Beth and grief for Adam, twisting within her.

'Carla, come with me,' Liz said quietly. 'We'll get everyone a cup of tea. There's a machine down the corridor.'

'Do you think she'll die?' Annie said to her mother as the door closed on the other two.

197

'All we can do, Annie, is wait. Until we know how badly she is injured, we can only guess.'

Annie began to cry. 'I wasn't very nice about her party. I feel awful now. I may never be able to tell her I'm sorry.'

'We all feel that way when something horrible happens. Wishing you'd told someone you love them.' Kate, thinking of Adam, said flatly.

'But I haven't been very nice to her lately.' Annie wiped her reddened eyes with a tissue.

The door opened, the spring squeaking. Putting her hip to it to stop it closing, Liz waited for Carla to enter.

'There's tea for everyone and biscuits if you want them,' she said not expecting anyone to take the small packets off the tray.

A slow, miserable hour passed. Dusk came suddenly, a grey misty veil, blurring the lights of the traffic driving in and out of the car park.

In the corridor there was a sound and all four glanced at the little window in the door.

A tall slim man, wearing a white coat, walked in. 'Mrs Fontaine?' he asked looking from Kate to Liz. His voice had a slight Irish lilt.

Filled with dread, Kate looked at him earnestly. 'I'm Kate Fontaine. Beth's mother.'

His magnetic grey eyes fixed on her. 'Beth took a nasty knock. She has an injury to her lower right arm. But more importantly her skull,' he touched the side of his own dark head,' has a small fracture here.'

Kate's hand flew to her mouth.

A small involuntary sob escaped Carla. Liz reached for the child's hand and held it tightly.

For a split second the doctor's eyes were drawn to Carla and then his attention came back to Kate. 'It may be necessary to

198

operate. For the moment we are keeping a very close watch on Beth. She is sedated, but awake.'

'Can I see her?' Kate asked her voice breaking.

'Yes, of course. A nurse will show you to the ward and also arrange for you to stay in the hospital overnight, Mrs Fontaine.'

Beth was in a side ward, close to the nursing station. The small room was quiet but for the drone of conversation coming from the nearby children's ward. The pale blue window blinds were drawn against the darkening sky. The only light in the room was a small one above Beth's bed, casting a dim circle on the bedclothes. She looked small and vulnerable. Long eyelashes fanning on the pale blue hollows below her closed eyes.

Very lightly, Kate kissed the whorl of hair at the child's temple.

Beth's eyes fluttered open and she smiled drowsily at her visitors.

'Are you in any pain, sweetheart?' Kate asked taking hold of her uninjured hand.

Beth's voice was almost a whisper, 'I am a bit tired. I'm sad I missed my party.'

The party, Liz thought horrified. Whatever had happened to the kids dropped off at the house? Their parents possibly not returning for at least two hours. Glancing at her watch she saw that it was too late to do anything about it; the party should have started almost three hours ago.

A similar thought didn't occur to Kate. Squeezing Beth's hand gently, she promised that they would have a belated party when she came home.

Remembering something much more important, Beth said hopefully 'Is Daddy outside?'

Startled, it hadn't occurred to Kate that Beth's memory

might be affected, she started to explain Adam's absence as gently as she could.

Cutting her mother off, Beth said 'Daddy was waiting for me outside school. That's why I ran out into the road and got knocked down by the car.'

Kate's heart leapt with excitement. Somewhere in the hospital, maybe only yards away, Adam waited.

With almost manic intensity, she clutched Beth's arm tightly. 'Did he come to the hospital with you?'

The exact sequence of events after the accident was lost to Beth. Afraid her mother was about to lose her temper, she said tearfully 'I don't know.'

Liz touched Kate's shoulder. 'Shall we leave Beth to sleep for a little while? The nurses at the desk or in the emergency unit should know who came in with her.'

Turning quickly, Kate made for the open door. 'I'll ask.'

As an afterthought, she glanced at Carla and Annie still standing beside the bed. 'You two girls stay with your sister.'

Liz's heart sank. Adam was still Kate's number one priority. Even though her youngest daughter lay in a hospital bed, her mental health uncertain.

Angry but hiding it well, Liz looked back on their friendship, wondering when Kate had become so self-centred and neurotic. Was it before Adam did a runner? Or had the devastating betrayal thrown her off-track?

Unaware of Liz's train of thought, Kate glanced frantically down the long corridor expecting to see Adam walking towards her. Trembling with anticipation, sick with excitement, she dashed towards the nursing station, to question the young woman sitting behind a computer monitor.

Bitterly disappointed in Kate, hardly believing her friend could be so heartless, Liz turned back to Beth's room.

Eyes drooping from tiredness and medication, Beth looked piteously vulnerable in the bed which was too big for her.

Liz's eyes threatened to fill with tears. If Adam had witnessed the accident, surely he would now be at his daughter's bedside. Adam, swine that he was, surely wasn't capable of walking away, not knowing if his little girl lay dead or alive.

Silent, Carla and Annie stared out of the window, their eyes fixed on the headlights in the car park. Liz wondered if they were waiting for their errant father to appear. If the sickness that ran through Kate's veins had infected them too.

Dispirited, she opened her bag. Bringing out a small notebook and pen she wrote a note for Kate, explaining that she was driving the girls' home and would stay with them overnight.

With hushed goodbyes to Beth, they left the small room.

Kate was no longer at the nurses' station. Liz assumed she had started a search of the hospital. Strangely, when she thought about it later, neither girl asked the whereabouts of their mother.

Shoulder to shoulder they went down the empty corridor to the lift, the soles of their shoes squeaking faintly on the rubbery floor. Exiting the grey elevator, joining people milling around in the hard radiance of the reception area was like coming back to the real world. The floors above, in the palace of hushed corridors, time moved differently.

Departing through the oversized revolving door, standing briefly under the outside canopy breathing the chill air of nightfall, Liz looked over the heads of the girls to the car park, lit with orange streetlamps.

Slinging the strap of her bag over her shoulder, she took hold of Carla's hand and put her arm around Annie's bare shoulder;

neither girl resisted.

Reaching the barrier, walking around it, they went single file between the rows of cars before finding Liz's saloon.

Inside, turning on the ignition, Liz reversed out of the parking bay. Following the arrows painted on the tarmac, she drove towards the exit.

Glancing in the rear view mirror seeing the lights of the hospital, she felt like crying. Beth was in the enormous building. Most probably alone.

The dual-carriageway was busy. Annie, sitting in the front passenger seat, unfazed by the blindingly bright headlights, stared through the windscreen. Her expression unreadable.

Carla on the back seat was silent. Liz wondered what was going on in her mind. As soon as they were warm and settled at home she would talk to her, try to reassure her that all would be well. But would it ever be well again, Liz wondered. Probably not, if Kate didn't start to see sense.

The balloons on the shrub were still flying, the silver motifs glistening in the car headlights as she drove onto the driveway.

The banner wishing Beth a Happy Birthday fluttered in the breeze, mocking them with its cheery message.

Climbing out of the car, the girls hugging themselves against the cold waited on the front step whilst Liz locked the car.

Entering the house, met by the aroma of party food lying untouched on the dining room table, Carla wept, hiding her eyes behind her forearm. Liz, tears blurring her vision, held the distressed child close.

Passing the pair, Annie with a touch of testiness tut-tutted. Going into the kitchen she took two cans of cola from the fridge. Shouting in the direction of the hall 'Do you want a coke, Carla?'

Liz, taking a clean tissue from her pocket, wiped Carla's

eyes. 'No more tears now. Little Beth will soon be home. In no time at all we'll be having that birthday party.'

Sniffing, Carla gave a weak smile.

Liz steered her into the kitchen. Filling the kettle, she switched it on. 'Tea, I need a cup of tea,' Liz muttered to herself as she got milk from the fridge.

Annie disappeared upstairs. In her room, swallowing most of the cola from the can, she topped it up with vodka. Sitting on the corner of the bed, she took a swig from the bottle. Hearing footsteps on the stairs, she screwed the top on quickly and hid the bottle beneath the pillow.

The toilet flushed.

Carla put her head around Annie's bedroom door. 'Are you coming to help put the food away?'

'Yeah. I guess so. I'll be down in a minute,' Annie said, lifting the can to her mouth.

'You'll kill yourself, drinking as much as you do.'

Annie's eyes flashed with vehemence. 'Mind your own business.'

'I am. You're my sister. It would be awful if you died,' Carla said bravely standing up to Annie's anger.

'Perhaps it'd be a good thing.' Annie heaved a sigh.

Carla's eyes filled with tears. 'How can you say that, when Beth ...'

Languidly, Annie rose off the bed. 'Keep a sense of proportion, Carla. Beth will be fine.'

Liz was putting small quiches into plastic freezer bags when the girls came into the kitchen.

Stopping for a moment, she took a sip from the mug of tea. 'Are you girls' hungry?'

'Not really,' Carla said turning up her nose, crinkling the freckles flecking the bridge.

Liz's eyebrows arched in surprise. 'That's a pity,' she said teasingly, 'I thought we might have a Chinese takeaway, to cheer ourselves up.'

The girls glanced at each other, a silent thought passing between them; treats such as takeaways had been non-existent since their father's departure.

'Decide what you'd like. I'll pick it up on my way back from the hospital.'

'Are you going back?' Carla asked quietly and uncertainly.

Liz touched the girl's cheek lightly. 'Not for long. But I do need to drop stuff off for your mum and Beth. Perhaps you would get a few things together for Beth. Her best teddy, pyjamas, anything you think she might like to have. And don't forget her toothbrush, will you?' Liz called as Carla dashed off, pleased to be useful.

Intent on finding Adam, Kate didn't notice Liz turn away from the nurses' station and go back to Beth's room. Impatient, the tips of her fingernails tapping on the desktop, she waited for the junior nurse behind the computer screen to acknowledge her. Completing whatever it was she was doing, the young woman turned, bestowing a genuine smile on Kate.

Discovering her wait was a complete waste of time, the shift had changed since Beth's admission Kate gave an irritated sigh. 'Surely a record is kept of who comes in with a child?' she said disdainfully.

There was the merest pause, then sounding slightly less cordial the nurse answered, 'Perhaps someone in the accident and emergency unit on the ground floor, could help you. They may have…'

Too impatient to listen to the young woman's explanation, Kate abruptly turned away and walked towards the lifts, the heels of her sandals click-clicking, with every rapid footfall.

Exiting the stainless steel elevator, she hurried down the bright emptiness of a long wide corridor. The bland magnolia walls were interposed with rectangles of double glazed windows, but there was nothing to see, only the darkness beyond, pierced with the orange streetlamps and the dazzle of car headlights.

Tense, not aware that she was breathing with only the upper part of her lungs, Kate made a beeline for a uniformed member of staff as the man came out of a side room. In his hand he had a stainless steel dish with dressing debris in it.

Averting her eyes from the bloodstains, Kate said 'Can you help me. I need some information about my daughter, Bethany Fontaine. She was admitted here this afternoon following a road accident.'

She seemed so nervous, her eyes darting from place to place, he wondered if she too had been involved in the accident. 'Ask at the reception desk. It's just around the corner,' he said already walking away from her.

In the main unit there were more than a dozen people waiting on blue plastic chairs for medical attention. Kate's eyes flicked from male to male. Although she knew that it was irrational to think that Adam might still be here, it was impossible to stop searching. It seemed that she did little else now but look for Adam. The supermarket, post office, street, train, in the car at traffic lights she scanned the drivers of other cars. There were few places she could relax her gaze and there were none outside the house. Even at home an invisible antenna was at work, picking up every unexplained sound from within and without. Every creak, scrape and rasp became the sound of his key in the door, his footfall on the hall carpet. There was hardly a night she didn't rise from the pillow to identify a sound. Some were inside her head, small echoes of a happier life.

A door opened and a man's shadow darkened the shining floor. Automatically Kate assessed his height and weight, dismissing him as Adam a second before he walked into the corridor.

Mentally distracted she went towards the reception desk.

Everyone, male and female, looked busy, occupied with computer monitors or handling files.

Grasping the edge of the counter with her finger tips, nails whitening from the pressure, she purposefully raised her voice over the clatter. 'Can someone tell me if Bethany Fontaine was brought here by her father this afternoon?'

Kate's distraught voice got the attention of several people and for a moment eyes were on her.

A woman in a white coat put down a brown folder. 'Who is Bethany Fontaine?'

'My nine-year-old daughter, she was knocked down by a car,' Kate explained hurriedly.

'What time was she admitted?'

'At about four o'clock.'

Picking up the folder in her short blunt hands, the woman glanced at the clock on the wall. 'This shift has only just started.'

Two spot of high colour burned fiercely on Kate's cheekbones. 'Surely a record is kept. Especially when a young child is admitted,' she said failing to keep indignation out of her voice.

With exaggerated politeness, the young registrar, Doctor Tamsyn, Kate had read her name badge, replied 'I will make enquiries. Where can I find you?' Her dark eyebrows rose questioningly, 'On the children's ward?'

Kate intended to search for Adam in the café and restaurant, before returning to Beth. Now with all eyes upon her, she could do little else but say she was going back to the children's ward immediately. Feeling outmanoeuvred, she walked back towards the elevator.

Beth was asleep, a globe of soft light falling on the coverlet, as Kate came back into the otherwise darkened room. Taking care not to wake Beth, she retrieved her bag from beside the bedside locker and went out again.

Standing at the entrance of the spacious busy café, her eyes roamed the tables searching obsessively. He has to be here, she thought in quiet desperation. Her mind in turmoil she was unable to make the simplest of decisions, like walking to the counter to order a coffee, or leaving to search elsewhere. A few interested looks were thrown at her, which only went to increase her anxiety. A man and woman came through the open door, passing so close the man's elbow brushed Kate's upper arm, turning his head to apologise he saw the anguish written in her expression. In a second she was gone, fled back into the corridor, returning to her agonising search.

After parking the car, Liz came into the hospital. As it was still visiting time, there were several people in the elevator. Most eyed the canvas bag she carried, the fluffy heads of a pink rabbit and a worn teddy-bear poking out of the top.

Slipping into Beth's room, surprised to see that it was still in darkness and Beth was alone, her mouth tightened in anger. So Kate is still hunting the errant Adam, she thought, pulling out the two cuddly toys from the bag. As she placed them near to Beth's hand the child woke.

Sleepily, Beth looked into Liz's eyes. 'Where's Mummy?' she asked softly.

'Not far away, darling girl,' Liz said stroking stray strands of hair off Beth's hot brow.

207

A shadow fell across the doorway. For an awful moment, as she turned, Liz expected to be confronted with Adam. In that instant she wondered how she could show the slightest civility towards him when the urge to hit out was so overpowering.

The doctor they had spoken to earlier stepped into the room. His eyes went to the sleepy child. 'Hello Bethany. How are you feeling?'

'I'm okay. Do you know where my mummy is?'

The young man gave Liz a questioning look.

'She's just popped out for a moment.' Liz lied, glancing guiltily at the doctor.

'I'll come back in a little while, when Mrs Fontaine returns.' He smiled reassuringly.

He was gone in an instant and Liz kicked herself for not asking if she could pass a message to Kate. At least that way she would have discovered Beth's scan results.

'Did your Mummy say how long she would be?' Liz asked Beth gently.

'Don't know. I was asleep.'

Typical, Liz thought angrily. What has happened to the Kate I used to know? There was no way in the world the *old* Kate would have deserted one of the kids under such circumstances.

Her eyes went to the bedside locker and she saw the note she had propped up against the water jug earlier. So she hasn't been here at all, Liz thought with mounting misgivings. Kate had to be seriously disturbed to have preferred searching for Adam instead of taking care of her sick child.

'I'll pop out and find mummy,' she said calmly. 'I'll be back as quickly as I can.' She smiled to reassure Beth.

'Can't you phone her?' Beth asked her eyes filling with tears.

Liz bent to kiss her cheek. 'I'm afraid not. The doctors and nurses don't like us using our cell phones in hospital.'

'Okay,' she said, accepting Liz's explanation.

Although she was reluctant to leave Beth, Liz thought it really important to find Kate. God forbid, she might actually be suffering from some sort of breakdown; perhaps Beth's accident was the last straw, on top of everything else that had happened, she thought hurrying towards the lift.

Checking the restaurant and the café without success, Liz eventually discovered Kate sitting perched on the edge of a blue plastic chair in the main reception area. Close enough to the revolving door to catch the cold draught of air wafting in. Alert to everyone passing by, she sat like a tensed spring, ready to jump up if she should see Adam.

Liz crossed to her, coming up slowly, afraid she would startle her out of her wits if she spoke too loudly or suddenly.

Putting aside her anger, she spoke softly, 'Kate. Will you come to see Beth? She's asking for you.'

As though woken from a dream, Kate looked up blankly. 'I'm waiting for Adam. When he arrives, we can go to see her together.'

Coping with Kate's enfeebled mood was exasperating. Hiding a sigh of irritation, Liz forced herself to speak calmly. 'If he turns up, he'll go straight to the children's ward. If you stay here, and he arrives through another entrance, you'll miss him.'

The possibility that she may have already missed him made Kate cold with fear. Rising unsteadily, she grabbed her bag from beside the chair. Walking ahead of Liz, the presence of her friend already forgotten, Kate made her way quickly towards the elevator.

The wait was less than two minutes but in that time, Kate's stress grew visibly. Staring intently at the stainless steel doors

209

she willed them to open. All the time whispering, 'What if I've missed him? What if I've missed him?'

When it arrived she was unable to wait for other people to get out and she brushed passed them rudely, several looked at her coldly. Once inside, she stood tensely, her hand hovering on the display panel, ready to press the button for the third floor at the first moment. An audible sigh of relief escaped her as the doors closed and it began the ascent.

Cross, Liz glanced at her several times on the short journey.

Exiting, Kate was certain that she heard Adam's voice. Imagining him flirting with one of the young nurses, a flash of angry jealousy gleamed in her eyes. 'But if he's here,' she asked herself 'what does it matter if he's momentarily distracted by a pretty face?' She would see him. Be with him. Feel his warm mouth on hers. His strong arms encircling her body would banish the cold and empty feeling that never left her now.

Almost running, Kate dashed to the room where Beth lay. But it was almost in darkness, just a dull bubble of light falling onto the cotton counterpane.

Her breath caught in her throat and she made a sound like a woman deep in grief.

Coming up beside her, Liz cradled her shaking shoulders. 'Little Beth is sleeping so peacefully,' she said softly, consolingly.

There was nothing she could say to wash away Kate's grief. She had been so sure, positive, that Adam was sitting in the room with their daughter.

It was hard for Liz to comprehend why Kate was still so obsessed with a man that had abandoned her so heartlessly. Why she went on torturing herself believing that at any moment Adam would make a sudden appearance and put everything right.

Clutching the metal cot-side, Kate tried to catch her breath, to stop the room spinning like a top around her. She heard Liz say something but couldn't comprehend the words through the black fog filling her head.

Holding her firmly, afraid she would collapse at any moment, Liz eased Kate down into a comfortable, high backed chair. 'You sit there, I will go and get you a cup of tea,' she said anxiously.

Kate didn't respond, but sat with her shoulders hunched forward protectively.

From the doorway, Liz glanced back. Although she felt compassion for Kate, she couldn't help thinking that she was behaving like a woman possessed. Without giving a thought to her daughters welfare, particularly Beth.

Bringing two polystyrene cups of tea, she handed one to Kate. Then sitting on the foot of the bed, careful not to disturb Beth, she glanced at Kate.

'This has to stop, Kate. You are making yourself ill. It's time to put your life back together, not only for your own well-being but for the girls too.'

Drawing a hand through her already tousled hair, Kate fixed Liz with an uncompromising stare. 'I don't understand what you mean. Are you saying I should give up on Adam?'

'Yes, Kate. I think it's time to let go.'

Rising swiftly out of the chair, Kate took the two strides to the window, looking out onto the blackness.

'How can you even think that way, Liz? You heard Beth say she saw her daddy outside the school.' Her voice rose shrilly, 'For God's sake. He was there because he wanted to see her on her birthday.' Tears of frustration filled her eyes. 'My little girl was almost killed trying to reach him. Does that been nothing to you?'

Liz spoke softly 'It matters the world to me. That's why I'm here.'

Kate remained quite still, the cold of the glass chilling her face.

'Kate, if Adam was there, waiting for Beth, he would have seen the accident.' She paused waiting for Kate to say something and then went on, 'If he saw it, and walked away not knowing if she was alive or dead, is he the sort of man you want to be with?'

Kate turned. Her face vicious, she said 'It just shows how terrified he must be. If he had shown himself, how long do you think it would be before the police picked him up? He risked jail just to see Beth. Does that count for nothing?'

'Kate, Kate, just listen to yourself. He wasn't there! Beth was mistaken. Perhaps she wanted to see him so much, her mind played tricks.'

'You're wrong,' Kate replied vehemently. 'Adam is close. He is watching over us.'

Bloody good guardian he's turning out to be, Liz thought angrily, seeing how useless it was to try and reason with Kate. If I want to help the girls I must keep my thoughts to myself. Otherwise Kate and I will end up rowing and end our long friendship. The girls need me now more than ever. Hopefully in time, Kate will too.

Standing, putting the still full cup onto the bedside table, she said 'I must get back to the girls. I promised to bring a Chinese take-away for them.'

'You spoil them,' Kate said uninterestedly.

Pity the same can no longer be said of you, Liz thought wearily.

Sighing, she said 'I really must go. I'll come back first thing in the morning and drive you home. In the meantime, there are a few necessities in the bag beside the locker.'

'Thanks,' Kate replied flatly.

With nothing more to say, Liz turned and walked out.

In the corridor, hearing Kate drag the comfortable chair across the floor, she knew instinctively that she was placing it where she could look down the corridor and keep watch for Adam. Disheartened and depressed, Liz left the hospital.

Beth made a better recovery than expected and within a week she was back home. Kate's disappointment that Adam had not showed up at the hospital or made contact was hard to hide. Distracted, constantly on edge, expecting that at any moment she would hear from him, she found it near impossible to have a normal conversation with the girls, or Liz. When she spoke her voice was staccato and nervy. Her glance invariably directed towards the window, or telephone.

Annie, hostile, shopped and cooked. Endlessly arguing with Carla about who's turn it was to empty the dishwasher and the rubbish bin.

Absorbed in her own thoughts, Kate was oblivious to the rows. It touched her mind, but in a vague disinterested way, that she no longer had any love for the girls. They were strangers, noisy and unwelcome guests living in her space. Forcing her to pay attention, when all she wanted was think of Adam, to work out where he might be, and how she was to find him, and bring him back to her.

Beth, although physically recovered from the accident, was withdrawn and quiet. Her days spent on the sofa in the living room watching the television.

Annie, Carla and Liz paid attention to her. Liz bringing treats, colouring books and comics.

To Beth it seemed that her mother hardly noticed her at all, unless it was to talk about the day of the accident, forcing her to recall the moment before the car hit her. Asking time and time again, about seeing her father.

Now she dreamt of little else other than seeing her father standing on the pavement, waving. But she couldn't remember if he had really done that or if she had just dreamt that he waved cheerfully and smiled, holding aloft a brightly wrapped birthday gift.

The following Monday, Carla and Annie returned to school. Carla pleased to get out of the house and from under Annie's watchful eye, left the house early. Silently fuming, having been left to tidy up the kitchen, Annie followed at a slower pace.

Through the sitting room window, Kate watched Annie walk away.

Beth was still in bed.

As Annie had taken her toast and orange juice, Kate thought it reasonable that the child could be safely left for a little while.

Buoyed up with anticipation, a light spring in her step, Kate climbed the stairs quickly.

She had an hour to look for Adam. She was certain that he was nearby. At this moment he might be watching his daughters walk to school. Or perhaps waiting near the school gates, to get a glimpse of them.

Quietly, afraid she might disturb Beth and create a delay for herself, Kate slipped into her bedroom.

A few minutes later, leaving the house, careful not to let the latch on the door drop noisily, she walked away eagerly.

Conspicuously dressed in a scarlet red jacket, black skirt and red, flat shoes, if her husband was out here she wanted him to notice her; she walked the route the girls had taken.

Several people, neighbours, acknowledged her but her eyes were fixed intently on the road ahead. One or two gave her a strange look. Resolute, Kate walked on oblivious.

What if he's seen the girls, and then gone, she asked herself. The possibility was too awful. Dreadful enough to bring her to the utmost limit of panic and make her heart race at an alarming speed. Suddenly her hands grew clammy, she felt vaguely nauseous and her whole body began to tremble.

On reaching the school gates, it was necessary to make a mental effort to hold herself together. Afraid it would upset Adam to see her in such a state.

A late arrival, an untidy youngster, white ankle socks baggy and drooping over her unpolished black shoes, ambled through the open gates. The school bell rang out. The child shrugging her shoulders, walked on at the same slack pace, as though school hours and rules were of no concern.

The child held no interest for Kate. Continually looking at the doorways of the shops, opposite the school. Expecting that at any moment Adam would appear. Would he, she wondered, just beckon to her to follow him to his hideaway.

Searching, looking around, her eyes moving more than her head, expression desperate, Kate waited.

Nothing moved, save an old lady in a grey fleece and baggy trousers came out of the bakery and slouched off, making for the pelican crossing.

For Kate it was rather like being in the eye of a storm, this extraordinary stillness, eclipsing the mental turbulence she had suffered the past months.

Suddenly, miraculously, she saw him coming out of the chemist. Her heart soared. It was impossible not to grin like an imbecile.

That he hadn't seen her was certain. Otherwise he would not have walked away, head bent to the pavement, the collar of his dark brown jacket up. He was walking like a man with a purpose.

Careless of a passing car, Kate ran across the road to follow him.

Increasing pace, he disappeared around a corner. The road he'd taken would bring him to the main shopping precinct.

Kate ran to catch up. At the junction, there was no sign of him. For a moment it was all she could do not to wail in despair. Impetuously, she hollered his name.

Several pedestrians stared at her, maybe thinking her either mad or drunk, but she was too distraught to notice.

Running blindly on, bumping into people, hardly aware of the indignant remarks, or the heavy bag jolting against her hip, Kate made for the precinct, praying that Adam was heading there.

At the immense glass entrance, she paused for a moment to search the hordes of people thronging the walkways and the moving escalators. There were far too many heads to catch a glimpse of Adam's distinctive blonde hair. She felt marooned on the edge of the shifting swarm. Rooted to the ground, and paralysed by panic.

The crowd up ahead parted, and she caught sight of Adam's brown jacket. Mindless of the crush of people standing between them, she darted through, ignoring retaliatory shoves from elbows and bags. Moving as quickly as she could, checking the shop windows as she passed, she caught another glimpse of him making his way into Marks and Spencer.

Following him, she made a dash for the swing door, almost knocking a girl off her feet. Inside she scanned the Food Hall, and then made a dash for the escalator. As it crawled to the next floor, Kate ran up several moving treads. Afraid she may be going away from him, she checked the lower floor, searching heads, hardly able to breathe for the panic welling up.

There were fewer people on the first floor, and Kate ran from one department to another disregarding the sales staffs enquiring looks.

At the top of the next escalator two security men met her. Though she explained that she was looking for her husband, they escorted her to the manager's office.

Though suspicious, the manager relayed a call for Adam Fontaine. In an agony of suspense, Kate waited. When it was obvious that Adam wasn't coming, she made her way back to the entrance.

Standing on the pavement, her bag loosely held at her side, she looked to the left and right, and then across the street to the Bon Marche store.

She would not give up, she had seen Adam. Deciding to retrace her steps, reasoning that Adam had passed this way, there was a chance he would come back in order to reach the place he was staying.

Several times she went back to the High Street. Then beyond, to the area where Victorian houses had been converted into small flats, searching the windows for a glimpse of him.

One last look in the precinct, she told herself, and then she would make her way back home and try again tomorrow.

Shop assistants and manager were pulling down metal shutters as Kate walked under the vast glass dome of the shopping mall.

Suddenly, with awful clarity, she realised that the entire day had passed. Beth was alone in the house. Glancing at her wristwatch she saw that Carla and Annie would be home from school. A great sense of desolation washed over her. The whole day had gone.

Realising that she was being watched by two security men,

who were beginning to advance upon her, Kate turned, retreating to the entrance.

Annie was standing at the kitchen sink as Kate entered the house through the back door.

'You have been missing all day,' the girl screamed at her mother in anger. 'Beth, you may remember little Beth, your daughter, just out of hospital, and only nine-years-old, has been alone all day.' Rage flushed her cheeks. 'What sort of mother leaves a sick child alone all day? A bad mother, that's what, a bloody bad one.'

Kate groaned tiredly. 'Don't go on, Annie. I don't think I can take anymore.'

In anger, Annie slapped down the tea-towel she was holding. 'Why is it always about you?'

Kate fought to keep her temper. 'Right now, Annie, I'm having a real hard time. Will you please try to understand that?'

Annie's eyes flared. 'For a mother, you are bloody unbelievable. Why do you think it's only you having a bad time? Tell me that. If you can.'

'Please don't swear at me, Annie.'

'Oh, poor Mother-Dear, you're worried about me swearing. When you abandoned a sick child all day. Like I said, you're bloody unbelievable.'

Kate's calves burned with over exertion, and she slumped onto a kitchen chair. 'I just don't need this, right now.'

'What! Like you didn't need little Beth today. It's just as well someone cares. Liz came round, found Beth here all alone, and drove her home. Carla's gone there too.'

Kate's head shot up. 'Why's Carla gone there?'

Annie gave a fake laugh. 'Because she can't bear being at home, with you sulking all day. Not looking after us. How long is it since you even bothered to cook a meal? Or did the shopping? I have had to do it all. If it wasn't for me, we would have been sleeping in dirty sheets for months.'

Kate could no longer keep the news to herself, and she blurted out, 'I saw your father today.'

Annie's mouth drop open in surprise. Slowly, saying each word distinctly, she said 'You saw Dad?'

Pleased with the effect she was having on Annie, Kate nodded. 'Yes. I saw him.'

'Are you completely mad?' Annie whispered.

'No, of course not.' It was impossible for Kate to relinquish the smile. 'Like I said, I saw him.'

'You can't have.'

'But I tell you, I did. Now be a good girl, Annie, and open a bottle of wine.'

Annie's body went rigid, and her hands clenched at her side. 'You can't have seen him,' she bawled. 'He's dead. Dead. Do you hear me? He's dead.'

Kate felt the colour drain from her face. 'No. He isn't. You have got it wrong, Annie. I saw him today.'

Annie clutched the back of a chair for support. Tears streaming down her face.

'He's dead. I killed him the day you sent us back here together. Do you remember, Mum? You sent me away from Shore Cottage. To act as chaperone, you said.' Annie's face crumpled. 'Here, in this kitchen, I killed my father.'

Kate stared at her daughter. 'It's not true. Why are you saying these awful things, Annie? How can you be so cruel?'

'Because it is true. You must have known what was going on,' she said accusingly.

Kate's voice rose in panic. 'Known what, Annie?'

Hysterical, Annie shouted, 'My father was forcing me to

have sex with him.'

It was too awful to hear, and Kate covered her ears. Shaking her head from side to side, she cried 'Don't say anymore, Annie. These lies are too terrible.'

Grasping her mother's trembling hands, Annie drew them down, holding on firmly, she shouted, 'I was the other woman. The one you always suspected he had.'

Kate sobbed. 'No, Annie. It can't be true.'

'It is true and you have to believe it.'

In her mind's eye, Annie saw the bloody scene like a film on rerun. 'He followed me in here. I was standing by the sink. He said that as no one else was in the house, we could spend the night together.'

Kate gasped. Her eyes filling with tears.

'He started to fondle my breasts. I pushed him away. He laughed. Then he pulled me to him and put his hand between my legs. The carving knife was on the draining board. I grabbed hold of it and before he could go any further, I stabbed him hard.' Her eyes went to the floor where the dark red blood had pooled.

Kate took a threatening step towards her. 'You killed your father?'

Fearing her mother was going to strike, Annie moved and stood with her back to the wall, waiting for the blow to land.

Kate's eyes narrowed to slits. 'How long had it been going on?'

Annie wiped her eyes on the back of her hand. 'It started when I was seven.'

Kate was too shocked to speak.

Annie shouted, 'You must have known it was going on. How could you not? All that talk of the other woman was for my benefit, wasn't it? Because you were jealous and wanted him to stop.'

'Annie, how could you possibly think such a thing? I'm your mother.'

Shouting the hurtful words was like a balm and Annie wanted to inflict as much pain as she could. 'Oh yes, you're my mother, but you didn't protect me, did you?'

Kate looked at the floor where Adam had fallen. In the grouting between the tiles, she imagined she saw brown, dried blood. Adam's blood.

Annie screamed over Kate's thoughts. 'Well, why didn't you take care of me?'

The shock was robbing Kate of what little energy she had, and her voice came out flat and emotionless. 'How could I, when I knew nothing about it. Do you really think I would have allowed it to happen?'

Annie glanced at the floor tiles. 'He was lying here.' She physically moved as though stepping over his body. 'I went upstairs and got his sleeping bag and got him into it.'

Kate imagined Annie struggling with the dead weight of his body. Irrationally her mind flew back to the day when Annie had thrown her male teacher to the mat during a martial arts class. She and Adam clapped so furiously the other visitors began to stare.

Annie sniffed back tears. 'I dragged him into the garage and managed to haul him into the boot of the car. Then I got all his stuff together, to make it look like he'd left us, and put it in with him. I cleaned up the mess in here.' Again, her eyes went to the tiled floor. 'Then in the early hours of the morning, I drove the car to the old flooded quarry.'

The confession gave Kate a ray of hope that Annie was telling a pack of lies. 'You can't drive,' she said indignantly.

'Yes I can. Clark, Millie's brother, taught me ages ago.'

Parental habit made Kate want to scold her for behaving so stupidly.

Annie was no longer looking at her mother. Her attention was entirely focused on the scene at the quarry. Speaking slowly, almost to herself, she said 'I got out of the car, leaving the engine running and the gear in drive. Then I put dad's briefcase on the accelerator to hold it down. The car moved ever so slowly and when it got to the edge of the cliff it just tipped over. It hit the water and then slowly sank. It took ages for it to disappear completely.

Kate stood in stunned silence. All hope wrenched from her body and soul.

A false sense of calm descended on Annie. 'Are you going to call the police? Tell them that your daughter is a murderer?'

Pale as death, Kate crossed the room. Taking a bottle of brandy off the wine rack she poured two good measures into glasses. Her hand trembling, she handed one to Annie. 'Drink it,' she said.

As their cold fingers touched, Kate was transported back to the moment when she first discovered Adam was gone. Then it was Annie offering the brandy. They had sat on the bed together, staring at the empty space in the wardrobe where his clothes had once hung. What had been going through Annie's mind as she sat there? She appeared calm and in control. But only a couple of days before, she had killed her father. Driven to the quarry, and however competent she may think she is, the drive there must have been terrifying. For God sake, Kate thought with rising hysteria, her father's body was in the boot of the car. It was only a short time after she'd stabbed him, and cleaned up the mess on the floor.

Glancing up from the brandy glass, she looked to Annie's bent head. Was the girl insane? Or just demented at that moment? She might never know the truth of that.

Adam was dead, and whatever he had done, however terrible, it didn't stop her loving him. Grief would last her lifetime. Would she ever be able to forgive her daughter for being the reason for the pain and misery she was suffering? Probably not, she thought, looking towards Annie, raising the glass to her lips.

The last of the light was failing, the awful day coming to a close, as Kate drove up the track to the quarry.

Annie, stone-faced, was sitting beside her in the passenger seat.

Parking, climbing out, the long grass reaching half-way up her calves, Kate glanced at Annie. 'Can you remember exactly where the car went in?'

Silent, Annie started to walk ahead. Kate following her.

Abruptly, Annie came to a standstill beside a tall beech tree. 'It was here.'

Kate's ashen face was drawn to the still water. She imagined the silver BMW lying in the mud at the bottom of the deep lake with Adam in the boot. Of course he would no longer look like Adam. A terrible image of him, as he would now be, flashed into her mind, and the strained threads linking sanity and lunacy came close to snapping. With every grain of willpower left to her, Kate blocked the gruesome picture. Reinstating Adam as she would always think of him, physically perfect, handsome, with glinting golden hair. The only man she ever desired.

Although her hands were hanging limply at her side, in her imagination she ran her fingertips along the hard bone of his jaw, the bristles of his unshaven face, rasping against her skin. Had she ever made love with him, she wondered, and not traced the edge of his face. The masculinity and barb of his early morning beard an aphrodisiac, arousing her desire.

Tears filled her eyes. All hope of finding him was now gone. There was only the agony of bereavement left to her. A deep devastating grief that she could share with no one. Only Annie knew. How could a slayer and the grief stricken share the same sorrow?

She glanced at Annie's heartbroken face, now dry of tears. She wondered if she would ever forgive her for stealing Adam. Not once, but in two different ways, body and soul.

'I want to be alone for a moment, Annie. You go and wait in the car.'

Annie, kicking up small stones on the rough path, trailed back to the old saloon parked beneath a stubby tree. The door was unlocked. Climbing onto the front passenger seat, she sat hunched against the chill night, staring out of the dark windscreen.

Overhanging black branches moved eerily in the freshening breeze. Dry twigs tap-tap-tapping on the metal roof, like the bones of long dead fingers beckoning.

Annie shivering, pulling her coat closer, folding her arms across her midriff for extra warmth.

She managed to remain absolutely still for several moments, then her eyes were drawn to the quarry edge. In her mind she heard the rasp of the BMW's tyres on the summer dry grass as the car moved towards the cliff. The engine still running as the car drifted towards the dense black water, a hundred feet below. The purr of the motor only ceasing when the car tipped forward, the weight of the engine pulling it towards destruction. Gathering speed it plunged down. Then with a hollow splash, echoing off the cliff face, it hit the water. For long drawn out seconds the rear of the vehicle showed above the water line as the car filled slowly with water. Finally it disappeared, creating a small tsunami of expanding circles on the agitated water.

Rooted to the ground, she kept her eyes on the spot. Eventually the disturbed birds settled. There was no sound. Even her own breath was still. She had stopped breathing when the car moved slowly towards the cliff edge.

When the water was flat and calm, it had taken every ounce of her will to move, to take several backward steps away from the precipice. Once she was out of sight of the water, her limbs moved more easily. Cautiously, keeping to the shadows of the over-grown hedges and trees, she made her way back to the old quarry gates.

The night was still, glancing at her watch, she saw it was almost four o'clock. She had two miles to cover before she reached the house. Alert to shifting sounds, keeping to the hedges and walls, she made for home.

Hunched in the passenger seat, Annie shivered. It had been terrible, a terrible, terrifying night. So why did she feel divorced from it? As though it had happened to someone else, or in a former life. For God's sake, she had killed her father. So why did she feel numb? It was almost like being dead herself. If she pinched her skin, it hurt, but for some reason the pain didn't matter. Nothing did. 'Numb, numb, numb,' she muttered the words like a cant.

Kate standing at the edge of the precipice, staring down into the water, spoke quietly. 'So you never left me.'

She wanted to cry, but the sob in her throat was dry. We were so in love and so very happy. And now it's all over. Gone for ever.

Overhead, the branches of the beech tree moved, rustling the winter dry twigs.

Perhaps it's Adam's spirit, she thought. Clinging to the idea he may have drawn near, to comfort her.

'Oh Adam. Darling Adam.' Saying his name brought grief so raw it was a physical pain.

To die at the hand of a daughter, a person he had created, loved dearly, sheltered and cared for since her first day, was cruel beyond belief.

The white crescent moon came from behind sloe black clouds, silvering the water. In the inky darkness the tiny wavelets glinted phosphorescently.

Kate wondered at its depth. Vaguely, she remembered hearing or reading, that it was more than three-hundred feet. Poor Adam, and the beautiful car, with all that dark water above pressing down.

She closed her eyes and felt the tears leach out from beneath her eyelids.

Annie is responsible for this misery. Annie with her beautiful youthful body, glorious hair and smooth unblemished skin.

Anger was easier to bear than grief, and Kate directed her rage at Annie. Why had she not noticed that the girl was sexually attracted to her father? With feminine guile she had distracted him, hungry for his attention. Was it poor Adam's fault if he had responded to the temptation put under his nose?

Yes, she thought, becoming rational for a moment. It was his fault. He was her father. The man who should have loved and protected her. Instead, he took advantage. Fondled her, opened her mind to sex. Used and despoiled her and stole her childhood.

Angry with Adam and Annie, Kate turned away, unable to look at the watery grave a moment longer. It felt like she was walking out on Adam as her shoes swished through the winter bracken, as though they were half-way through a terrible row and she had the power to turn her back on him. Which in reality she had never had the courage to do. Adam was the partner in their marriage that did the walking away, leaving her desolate and insecure.

Opening the car door, she climbed in. Glancing coldly at Annie.

Redirecting her gaze to the ignition key, she turned it. The engine coughed into life. Easing off the stiff handbrake, Kate started the journey home.

It did not occur to Annie to ask what her mother was going to do. It didn't matter. Neither the police nor the possibility of prison touched her emotionally.

Kate's mind was in such turmoil she was hardly aware that she was driving. During the terrible months since Adam's disappearance, not once had she considered he might be dead.

Focusing on his return had been important. It was proof that she could remain positive, although Liz, Carla, little Beth, she could no longer include Annie in the roll call, were all positive he had gone forever.

From the corner of her eye she glanced at Annie, picturing her plunging the knife into Adam.

It was always a case of *when* not *if* he would return. And I was wrong. She sniffed tears from her reddened eyes. He would not come back, ever. For my daughter has slain him.

Anger turning to sorrow, she saw Adam in her mind's eye and the tears flowed again, as she pictured him lying in water in the boot of the car. His beautiful ice-blue eyes would never again glitter with amusement. Nor would the once warm lips touch hers.

It started to rain. Automatically she switched on the windscreen wipers. Listening to the stiff, swish, swish as the rubber blades scraped the glass almost clear.

Turning into the cul-de-sac she was sorry to see the house lights on. Carla and Beth had returned. Liz would be indoors too, as she would never dream of leaving the girls alone. As she herself had done, abandoning Beth this morning. And all because she wanted to rush off, to chase a false trail in her search for Adam. If she had not gone to the Mall and forgotten the time, today's events would not have unfolded. She would still be unaware that Adam lay at the bottom of the man-made lake. There would still be hope of his return, however false that hope was; it was still better than what she now had, which was nothing.

Pulling the car onto the driveway, she switched off the engine and climbed slowly out. Annie trailing her.

'Not a word from you,' Kate said opening the front door.

Fortunately, Liz only stayed a few moments after Kate and Annie's return. The girls were upstairs in Beth's bedroom, watching television.

In the kitchen, eyes drawn to the floor tiles, Kate wondered if she could ever enter this room and not imagine Adam's body lying near the sink. Walking on the spot, to get to the dishwasher, her skin prickled. Somehow, she would have to endure living with the horror of what had taken place. There was no way she could sell the house. Adam's name was on the deeds. Until he had been missing for seven years and presumed dead, she was stuck here. Trapped in poverty. Living with the humiliation of being abandoned by Adam. Subsisting on hand-outs and benefits.

Lifting a brandy bottle out of the wine rack, she brought it to the table. Pouring out two glasses, she handed one to Annie, no longer caring if the girl was too young to drink. If she was old enough to bed and kill her father, surely she was old enough to hold down a brandy, Kate thought cynically.

Taking a mouthful from the glass, Kate shuddered as the raw spirit hit her throat. Avoiding eye contact, steering clear of speaking of the hideousness, they stood leaning on the edge of the work surface, wrapped in their individual misery.

Unable to stand the silence, broken only by the tick of the kitchen clock and irritating drip of a tap, Kate walked out of the kitchen.

Drained to the core, Annie sat at the table, tapping a fingernail against the rim of the glass. Eventually she poured another brandy. Finishing it, she stood. Scraping the legs of the chair on the tiled floor.

Glancing at the spot where her father had fallen, she imagined him in the water-filled boot of the car, his eyes open, staring accusingly at her. The nightmare image had been with her almost every waking moment since the car had gone over the quarry edge. Unable to bear the dreadful look in his eyes, Annie dashed out of the kitchen and ran upstairs, searching for her mother.

Kate's bedroom door was open. She was searching in the dressing table drawer.

Standing in the doorway, Annie watched her for a moment.

Sensing the girl's presence, Kate looked up. 'What do you want?'

'Just to talk,' Annie said meekly.

Kate pulled a grey silk scarf out of the drawer, roughly. 'Talk about what? The sex or the murd…'

Annie face crumpled. Her lower lip trembling like a small child's. 'I didn't ask him to come into my room at night.'

'Don't you mean, into your bed?' Kate said nastily.

'It wasn't my fault,' Annie wailed plaintively.

'If you keep this up, Mum, I shall go to the police. Tell them everything. And I mean everything. The way it all started, when I was only seven.'

A look of fear flashed in Kate's eyes. The scandal, should it come out, would finish her entirely. People might think she knew about it. Or think her totally inadequate. Not woman enough for Adam.

'You'll say nothing,' she said, looking determinedly at Annie.

'You managed to say nothing about the other thing. You kept *that* secret.'

Tearfully, Annie shouted, 'I never wanted him to do that to me. I hated him for it. I was afraid.'

'Afraid?'

Verging on hysteria, Annie cried, 'Yes. Afraid of you. And what you'd do to me, if you found out what dad was doing.'

Kate slumped onto the bed. In her heart she knew that blaming Annie was wrong, even shameful. But she couldn't get passed the image of Annie and Adam lying together. Yes, she was jealous. As jealous as hell. But somehow, however difficult, she had to stop accusing Annie. It wasn't right. Wasn't socially acceptable to blame the child. She almost burst into frantic laughter, thinking of the social niceties of such a situation.

Emotionally and physically drained, Annie sat on the bed beside her mother. 'What are you going to do?'

Kate looked up in surprise. 'Do. I'm going to *do* nothing. What is there to do? I can't go to the police.'

She touched Annie's arm gently. 'I cannot tell anyone that your father was doing that to you. His reputation would be in tatters.'

It wasn't lost on Annie that her mother was still thinking of her husband first.

'And me. What about me?' Annie's eyes brimmed with

tears.

Kate rose. Picking up the scarf, she flung it in the direction of the dressing table top. 'Oh, you, Annie. You'll be fine. You'll get over it. Of that I have no doubt. After all, you're good at keeping secrets.'

Annie fled the room. Running to her bedroom, she slammed the door closed behind her. Sitting on the edge of the single bed, she started to cry like a small child.

Glancing in the mirror, seeing the tangle of her hair, Kate brushed it clumsily off her brow.

'I am a widow,' she said softly to the haunted reflection. 'I am a widow who can tell no one of my bitter sorrow.'

Chapter 13

Kate watched her three daughters walking to the end of the cul-de-sac. Turning the corner they disappeared from sight. She gave a sigh of relief. This was the first day in a month that she had been alone in the house.

The past four weeks had been excruciatingly difficult. She had been at Beth's beck-and-call from dawn till dusk. The child could be maddeningly demanding. And if that wasn't enough, Carla was acting sullen, not interested in doing anything. Annie had kept mainly to her room. When she did appear, she was silent, as though waiting for a hammer blow to fall.

Liz had called on several occasions. Kate wasn't sure which was worse, listening to Liz's idle chatter as she detailed what was going on at the restaurant, or trying hard not to spill the beans about Adam. Especially when Liz berated him as a husband and father. It would be so easy to shout out the truth. 'Annie killed Adam. He didn't forsake me for another. He's dead. His body is in the boot of the BMW, which is lying at the bottom of Sandman's Quarry.'

Telling no one of the hideousness, the despair, sorrow, and the bitterness she felt towards her eldest child was the hardest thing she had ever had to do. But the truth would bring everything crashing down. Adam's reputation would be sullied forever. God forbid, he could be branded a paedophile. Which she did not believe of him. Adam had been drawn to Annie's loveliness. Annie was a wilful child, always seeking attention, especially her father's. It had all been a terrible, terrible mistake. Now that he was dead, what was the point of going over and over the whys and wherefores?

Annie was responsible for his death. As her mother, she was protecting her. Keeping Adam's name clean. Which it most certainly wouldn't be if the truth was revealed.

When she was sure the girls would not return to collect something forgotten in the mad rush to leave the house, Kate turned from the window.

The house was quiet. Perhaps too quiet, she thought. Being solitary invited introspection and she was afraid to start down that road, for she would despair again. Shaking off the dark mood threatening to descend, she picked up the phone and dialled the number for the local collection and delivery service.

'A pity to throw this bed out, when there's nothing wrong with it,' the delivery man said dragging Annie's bed down the stairs.

If only that were true, Kate thought, as images of Adam and Annie came into her mind.

Once outside, the man took care to keep the bed unmarked.

Standing at the open front door, Kate watched him load it into the back of the white van. It was obvious that he either had a use for the bed, or he was going to sell it for a few pounds. Kate wondered what the new owners would think if they knew the history of it. They would probably burn it, she thought, as I would, if the garden was big enough to have a good bonfire.

Slamming the van doors closed, the man gave her a cheery wave. Adding a hoot of his horn as he drove away.

She was vacuuming the bedroom carpet, when the new single bed arrived for Annie's room.

Watching the man haul the bed upstairs, Kate was reminded of a video on rerun. For the first time in months, she wanted to giggle. Stifling the chuckle, she felt guilty that it had ever risen in her throat. What sort of person was she, to feel even the tiniest bit amused, when Adam lay dead and could no longer share such a moment?

She didn't bother to watch the man walk down the driveway to his van.

Going back upstairs, she eyed the new bed from the doorway. Yes, she thought, satisfied, the room already felt different. Since she had learned the truth about Annie and Adam it had been impossible for her to enter the bedroom. If by chance the door was left open, and she caught sight of the bed from the landing, she felt physically sick.

Mild sunlight, with no warmth to it, filtered through the black branches of the tree outside the window, glimmering primrose yellow on the beige carpet.

Entering the room, Kate began to strip off the polythene covering protecting the divan. It didn't take her very long to have the small wheels screwed into the base and the mattress hauled onto it. Slightly out of breath, she sat on the edge.

Now she would feel better about the bedroom and be free to come and go as she wished. With the old bed gone, she was sure she would stop thinking of Adam and Annie together.

Redecorating, changing the room entirely would help too, but she couldn't afford it.   She imagined it with a new carpet and curtains in brighter fresher colours. Picturing in her mind a blue carpet and blue and yellow patterned curtains. Predominantly beige, as it was now, wasn't right for a young girl's room. But beige was Adam's favourite colour for the house.

Adam came to the forefront of her mind. If she had thought she could banish him from this room by buying a new bed, she was wrong. His presence was tangible.   The sound of his laughter bouncing off the four walls.

She felt like crying.

The girls came home from school, arguing. Coming through the back door like a flock of angry magpies.

'For heaven's sake,' Kate sighed. 'Can't you come home, just for once, without creating a racket?'

Banging a bag of books onto the kitchen table, Carla slammed out of the room and up the stairs.

Sullen, Annie followed her.

Beth stood by the kitchen door, holding a large piece of paper, covered in poster paints, it was still damp. 'Mrs Such, the art teacher, said this is my best picture yet. Can I put it up in here?' Her eyes searched the kitchen walls, choosing the best position.

'You can, if you use blue tack.'

Placing the picture on the table, Beth said 'I don't think I have any left. I used it up when I put my new posters on my bedroom wall.'

'Well, you'll just have to find some more, because you can't use sticky tape.'

Pulling open a drawer, Beth started to hunt, noisily.

Carla's wardrobe door slammed shut.

Annie came running down the stairs. 'You didn't say I was getting a new bed.'

'Well, you have one,' Kate said filling the kettle, although her nerves were crying out for a glass of wine.

Annie looked incredulous. 'But how can we afford it?'

Kate sighed. 'I sold my gold watch.'

'But dad gave you that for your wedding anniversary,' Annie said innocently.

Kate's eyes narrowed spitefully. 'Do you think I do not remember it?'

'No, of course not, Mum.'

The reason for the new bed came to Annie's mind. That her

mother had got rid of hers, made her feel dirty. Not only had the bed been replaced, but the room was spring cleaned. Even the paintwork looked scoured. Turning, she went out of the room. With a sense of shame, she climbed the stairs. There was a bottle of vodka in the cupboard over the wardrobe, she would swig it neat.

Changing her mind about the cup of tea, Kate took the open bottle of Chardonnay out of the fridge and poured some into a glass.

'I can't find any blue tack,' Beth said, her head still buried in the open drawer. 'I'll go and ask Carla if she has any.'

'You do that,' Kate said hugging the glass to her midriff.

Looking out of the window, watching the parade of husbands returning home from work, she was no longer envious of their wives, as she had been, before she learned of Adam's death. Now it was resentment that filled her heart and soul. Resentment of everyone, but especially Annie. The daughter who brought such misery on the family and split it asunder. Spreading a dark cloud of suspicion, betrayal and ultimately death upon those that loved her. How she wished she had never given her life. For without Annie, Adam would still be beside her, loving and cherishing her, and her alone. Annie would never have come into the equation. There would be no doubts about his love. It was only Annie that had stood between them. The mistresses she so agonised over, hadn't existed. There was only Annie to tempt him, with her feminine wiles, pretty face, lithesome limbs and youth.

Oh, God. She wished she too was dead. Lying beside Adam in the cold watery boot of the car. With no more anger left inside her. No more pain stabbing at her nerves.

Annie came back downstairs. That she was resentful of the changes in her bedroom was obvious. Kate didn't care. Annie would just have to put up with it, she thought, eyeing the girl distrustfully.

The atmosphere between mother and daughter spilled over effecting Carla and Beth. Both girls becoming fractious and argumentative. They came close to fighting. Kate losing her temper, sent them both to their rooms. Their usual door slamming followed. Reluctant to let go of the argument, the two girls shouted at each other through the adjoining bedroom walls.

Exasperated, Kate came out of her chair. Going to the bottom of the stairs, she called up, telling then both to be quiet.

Coming back into the sitting room, her eyes went to Annie. Sitting hunched up on the settee. Her body tense. Face set in an expression of annoyance.

She had nothing she wanted to say to her. Conversation was impossible. How could they possibly talk about anything else but Adam's death? The act of killing him. The quarry grave. After all the terrible things that had happened, communicating wasn't an option. Resentment, anger and bitterness were the only emotions they had in common.

Glancing at her watch, Kate saw that it was still too early to escape to her room. For the next half-hour she endured the silence. Then unable to bear being close to Annie for another moment, she rose.

Without acknowledging Annie, she walked out of the room. Climbing the stairs, she wondered how she was to bear a lifetime of this agonising relationship.

As the door closed on her mother, Annie threw aside the book she had tried to concentrate on. Repeatedly she had reread a paragraph to get the gist but nothing made sense. She was too conscious of her mother sitting there, exuding angst. Every time she glanced up, and caught her mother's eyes, she saw the loathing there.

Getting up, Annie went out of the room.

Switching on her bedroom light, she looked at the new bed and the glistening furniture. Annie wasn't fooled. Her mother had scrubbed, cleaned and polished to erase not only her husband from the room but her daughter too.

Unable to look at the sterilised room, Annie switched off the light.

Climbing onto the single bed, leaning her back against the wall, she pulled the duvet over her shoulders like a cloak.

'I am not wanted here,' she mouthed to the darkness.

Remaining quite still, looking into the blackness, she listened to the house settling. Waiting for the click as her mother switched off the bedside light. After a long time, she heard the familiar *tick*. Without moving from her position, she waited again. Eventually, she moved, climbing off the bed as quietly as she could.

Going downstairs, avoiding the treads which creaked, she made it to the hallway. Taking a warm jacket off a coat peg, she slipped it on. With her bag over her shoulder, she opened the front door.

Pausing for a moment, she glanced towards the stairs, imagining little Beth and Carla asleep, peaceful beneath their duvets.

Stepping out, she closed the door quietly.

Kate was lying on her back, staring into the darkness. Sure she had heard a floorboard creak, she listened intently.

The front door opened.

A moment later it closed softly.

Annie's footfalls on the drive and then the pavement broke the silence of the night.

Kate listened until she could hear her child's tread no longer.